Past Echoes

A Jake Boulder Thriller

By

Graham Smith

Print ISBN: 978-1-912175-91-8

Also By Graham Smith
Jake Boulder Series
Watching The Bodies (Jake Boulder Book 1)
The Kindred Killers (Jake Boulder Book 2).

Praise For Watching The Bodies :

"Watching the Bodies is one of the best crime fiction thrillers I've ever read and a brilliant start to a new series."

Eva Merckx - Novel Deelights

"I love, love, LOVED this book! I've always been a fan of serial killer novels and this one absolutely nailed it."

Ellen Devonport - Guest Reviewer Bibliopihile Book Club

"'Watching the Bodies' is an exciting, fantastic start to a fab new series and I can't wait to join Boulder again on his next adventure."

Joseph Calleja - Relax And Read Book Reviews

"If you like a dark and twisty serial killer story then Watching the Bodies is a book you simply must read."

Gordon Mcghie - Grab This Book

"Fast paced, suspenseful, action packed and led by a stellar, brooding protagonist (Jake Boulder), I found myself unable to put this novel down."

Samantha Ellen - Clues And Reviews

Praise For The Kindred Killers :

"Smith is such a unique storyteller with a strong voice, I cannot wait to see what happens in book three!!"
Amy Sullivan - Novelgossip

"OMFG what an emotive, thrilling and utterly compelling read that has made me ever so excited!!!"
Noelle Holten - Crimebookjunkie

"This is a brilliant read. Brutally fast paced, socially relevant and full of gripping plot twists."
Joanne Robertson - My Chestnut Reading Tree

"This is only the second outing for Jake Boulder, but it has all the hallmarks of a great, long-running series."
Clair Boor - Have Books Will Read

"This is Graham Smith at his magnificent best...I absolutely love his Jake Boulder series.... Magnificent..."
Livia Sbarbaro - Goodreads Reviewer

To Daniel, for being the kind of son who makes a father proud to share his life.

'History rarely repeats itself, but its echoes never go away.'
– Tariq Ali

Chapter 1

The four guys who surround me are all holding weapons. The ones to the north and east have baseball bats, South holds a bike chain, and West a police baton. I could make a run for it, but I'd like to know who they are and why they think attacking me is a good way to spend their evening.

I don't dwell on the thought, but I'm happy their weapons have been chosen to inflict pain rather than end life. Had they held knives or guns, I'd be more worried. The problem is, I'd rather not feel any of their intended pain.

As they advance on me I assess the various threat levels. North and East are the biggest danger, followed by South. The police baton held by West could inflict a lot of pain in the right hands, but he's twirling it around as if he's leading a marching band, when he should have it grasped by the handle; ready to use in either attack or defence.

The streetlights are throwing orange glows into the night sky and weird shadows on the ground. There's the sound of late-night traffic in the distance, but there's nobody else in sight. That doesn't bother me as I've always fought my own battles, and there's no way these bozos are intimidating enough to see me run, or to shout for help.

I keep rotating so I can watch all four of them as they inch forward. It could be my reputation as a fighter that's making them cautious, or maybe they're just biding their time until their leader instigates the attack.

I don't think it's prudent to wait for them to strike first; I take a step towards the gap between North and East, spin, and run at West. He's too busy acting like a majorette to get any menace into the blow he flaps at me.

His baton thumps against my ribs. There's enough force behind it to cause me to grunt, but not so much that I feel or hear any bones breaking. This changes when my elbow slams against his jaw.

As he wheels away, clutching at his shattered mandible, I stoop to pick up the police baton and spin to face his buddies. When I see they are still a couple of paces away, I drive the baton's short point into West's right kidney.

He drops to one knee with an anguished howl. I'm confident he won't trouble me anymore tonight.

When I look behind me, North and South are fanning round to fill the gap left by West's departure. There's an extra level of caution in their eyes, but none of them have woken up to the fact they're about to get their asses kicked.

East looks familiar, but I can't place him. Now isn't the time to worry about who they are. That can be learned once this is over.

I now have the baton's handle gripped in my right hand with its shaft running along the outside of my forearm. So long as I can use the baton to protect my arm, I can offer a form of defence against the baseball bats.

The bike chain is another matter though. Should that wrap itself around my arm I'll be in trouble. Not only will it nullify my weapon, it could be used to imbalance me. If I hit the ground in front of these three guys, I'll be lucky to get to my feet before one of them lands a game-changing blow.

North is holding his bat over his left shoulder, which suggests he's left-handed. East has his bat in front of him like it's a sword.

I take three quick steps towards North.

He's slow to react and, when he does swing, I've got my right arm extended to deflect his blow. The bat only travels a couple of feet at most, but North's swing is powerful enough to send juddering vibrations throughout my right arm. Had I not held the baton at an oblique angle to deflect the impact, my arm would have been numbed to the point of uselessness.

The punch I throw at him with my left hand crashes against his cheek, but it does little more than turn his head.

Me driving the point of the baton into his solar plexus has a rather more impressive outcome. He falls to his knees gasping for air.

I'm about to reposition myself, so I can bury a foot in his groin, when I feel something slam across my shoulders that causes me to stagger forward.

I recover my balance and whirl round to confront whoever hit me. East's bearded face wears a nasty grin, topped by a confident expression.

His denim jacket is covered with various badges that have been sewn on in a haphazard fashion. Some represent liquor brands and others are the logos of rock groups. Right about now, I'd like to hit him in the Rolling Stones.

He comes forward, the baseball bat making whooshing noises as he puts his not inconsiderable muscle into swinging it time and again.

His aim changes as he swings at my body, head and knees.

I move back and wait for him to make a mistake. He doesn't make one.

I can see South circling round to East's right.

When my back touches metal, I realise they've been driving me into a corner formed by a pair of stationary pickup trucks.

South and East are too close to afford me time to clamber over the pickups; which means I'm trapped.

I keep going until I can retreat no further.

South pushes his buddy to one side. 'You're mine now.'

He swings the chain at my head. I duck below it, but it's close enough for me to feel the air move with its passing.

My lowered stance has given me an opportunity I can't refuse. I spin the baton around in my hand and sweep it up towards South's groin.

The half step he takes back means I miss his balls. The baton still collides with his bulging gut but it doesn't impact hard enough to elicit more than a slight "oof" from him.

He swings the chain at my head a second time, but he's gone from the horizontal to the vertical.

I throw my right hand up and yelp as the chain encircles my arm, trapping the baton.

In one move I yank the chain from South's hand as I whip round and launch a backhanded blow at his chin.

South ducks to avoid the blow and my chain-wrapped arm crashes into his temple.

The thudding footsteps of East running away can be heard before South has finished falling.

North is trying to get back to his feet but he's still gasping like a landed fish, so I revisit my earlier plan and bury the toe of my boot into his squishy bits.

I don't want to hurt him too much. South is unconscious and West's jaw isn't in what anyone would describe as a natural position. If I want to get answers, North is the only one who'll be able to speak to me.

A look up and down the street shows we're alone so I unwind the chain from my arm, and use the baton to prod North's shoulder.

'Want to tell me who you guys are and why you've attacked me?'

The answer he gives me isn't anatomically possible.

I put a different edge to my voice as I repeat my questions.

He gives me the same answer with a few extra curses thrown in for good measure.

It's a shame for him that he's more tough than he is smart.

The police baton catches him with enough force to stun him a little. If I have to persuade him to talk, I'd rather move him somewhere more private.

Chapter 2

Lunk scratches at his scouring pad beard and wipes his hands on oil-blackened overalls. He doesn't look happy about me turning up with a semi-conscious stranger and throwing him out of his workshop, but he has the good sense not to argue.

I lead North past the sedan with its engine in pieces, and steer him towards Lunk's anvil. As I pass a cluttered workbench I grab a length of electrical wire.

Two minutes later I've got North exactly where I want him and I'm looking around for some water to throw in his face.

It's late, I'm tired, and I want to get this over with as soon as possible. I've never tortured anyone before, and I can't say I'm terribly pleased about having to do it now.

I find a tap and pour a half gallon of water into a dirty bucket.

North lets out a string of profanities when he regains his senses.

I let him swear and writhe as he tries to pull his hand free.

He can't. I've fed some of the wire up through the square hole in the anvil that was designed to locate different sets of dies and moulds. The wire holds North's left forefinger tight against the oil-stained anvil. I've also tied his right hand to his left ankle to prevent him taking any more swings at me.

North realises he's not going to escape without my help, and looks up at me. 'You better let me go, Boulder. You don't know who you're messing with.'

'You're right, I don't.' I lay three hammers of varying sizes on the anvil. 'But I'm about to find out.'

Everything I know about torture comes from the thrillers I've read and the movies I've seen. I'm working on instinct, as plan A is nothing more than make-it-up-as-I-go-along.

One passage I read has particularly stuck with me. I'm sketchy on the exact details, but I'm three parts convinced that the story was written by an ex-CIA operative. He floated the idea that the most important tool to any torturer, is the mind. Once your victim fears the pain you're about to inflict, you can multiply their fear until they divulge what they know with relatively little physical torture.

It's this psychological effect that I'm gambling on, as I'm not sure I can bring myself to hurt someone beyond what can be classed as self-defence.

I pick up the smallest of the three hammers and touch it against the nail of North's trapped forefinger. It's not heavy in any way and is the kind of hammer that's used for fine, delicate work.

'This is what's going to happen to you if you don't tell me what I want to know.' I raise the hammer a half inch and let it drop on his fingernail. North flinches but stays silent. 'I will hit your finger hard enough to blacken your nail. If you haven't told me who you are, and why you were attacking me, by the time I get to ten, I will hit your nail again. If you still haven't told me by the time I've hit you three times, I'll move on to the next hammer.' I rest my hand on a two-pound lump hammer and caress the wooden handle of a twelve-pound sledge. 'Do I need to explain what happens if you don't tell me after three hits from the lump hammer?'

North's eyes widen in fear and his head shakes. I'm not surprised he's scared. If I were to bring the twelve-pound sledgehammer down on his finger, it would pulverise his flesh against the anvil.

There's also the fact that I've kept my tone conversational, and I'm doing everything I can to appear calm; as if torture and mutilation are a normal part of my day. In short, I'm making sure he fears me, and the hammers, more than the person he's protecting.

Another factor in my favour is that virtually every guy alive has hit a fingernail when using a hammer. Therefore, North will know how much it will hurt if I carry out my threat.

A sheen of sweat appears on North's face, and if it weren't for Lunk's all-pervading body odour, and a mixture of gasoline fumes and waste oil, I'm pretty sure I'd be able to smell his fear.

I lift the small hammer until its head is six inches above his nail. 'Who are you?'

He swallows and I can see him trying to decide between pain and betrayal.

I flick my wrist and land the head of the hammer square on the end of his fingernail.

He gives a loud yelp, and curses me out until he realises I'm counting. I've got to eight by the time he stops cursing and says, 'Okay. I'll tell you.'

Beneath his fingernail I can already see the colour of his flesh turning dark as the bruising begins to take effect. I know, from careless occasions in my own past, how much his nail will be throbbing.

'Who are you?'

'Donny. My name is Donny.'

I'm not bothered that he doesn't give me a surname; his Christian name isn't that important to me either. The real information I'm after, is why they ambushed me. Plus, there's the psychological effect: now he's broken his silence, each new morsel of information will be easier for him to release.

'So, Donny. Why did you and your buddies attack me?'

He swallows and looks from side to side as if expecting help to arrive.

I raise the hammer six inches, and an eyebrow one.

'We were paid.'

'Who by?'

He hesitates. Swallows again.

My wrist flicks and the hammer smashes into his nail for a second time.

I wait until he's finished cursing, and ask again who paid him.
'Benji.'

The name comes through gritted teeth. I'm not sure whether it's pain, or hatred for me that's gritting his teeth. I'm not bothered either way. I just want him to tell me what I need to know before I have to hit his finger a third time. The second blow has more than doubled the discolouration and there is a trickle of blood seeping out from under his nail. It must be throbbing like crazy, and I know from my own experiences there is very little that can be done to alleviate the pain.

I don't need to ask who Benji is. A couple of weeks back, I kicked Benji's ass when he was beating on a girl. The only issue I have with the memory is that I don't actually have it, due to being flat out drunk at the time.

A thought comes to me. 'Was Benji here with you tonight?'
'Yeah.'

'He the one who had the other baseball bat?'
'Yeah. What of it?'

'When I dropped you and your two buddies on your asses, Benji ran away. That's the kind of man he is. A coward who gets others to do his dirty work, then runs off like a scared kitten when things don't go his way.'

A look of disgust and anger overtakes Donny's face.

I lay the hammer down. There's no need for further hurt. 'How much did he pay you?'

'Three hundred bucks apiece.'

'How bad was the beating to be? Were you here to kill me or just put me in hospital?'

'Hospital, but Benji wanted your arms and legs busted.'

I lean against a workbench and look at Donny. He cuts a pathetic figure – strapped by the hand to an anvil. His demeanour is one of defeat, and fury at being set up and abandoned.

'What will you do if I let you go? Will you raise your hands to me, or will you go off plotting to come back and try again?'

'Ain't gonna take you on again. Might have me a few words with Benji though.'

Donny nurses his injured hand as I set him free and watch him leave Lunk's workshop. I've gotten the answers I want, and I suspect that Donny and his buddies will deal with Benji for me.

Now the threat is over, I turn my mind to the reality of the situation. A guy I'd once beaten up, with good cause, had decided to exact a spot of revenge. The price of this revenge, three lots of three hundred bucks, and maybe another hundred on gas to get them here.

I don't know the going rate for henchmen, but I'd like to think I deserve more than a thousand bucks' worth of mindless thugs.

Whatever the price, it says something that a guy whose ass I kicked has taken the trouble to hunt me down, and has shelled out his own money on accomplices.

That it's taken him almost three weeks to come looking is neither here nor there. It might have taken that long to track me down or to persuade his buddies. Perhaps he was saving up.

Chapter 3

The office is typical of small law firms the world over. There's a desk with overflowing in and out trays, a phone, and the obligatory picture depicting the lawyer's loved ones. A potted plant in one corner looks to be in rude health and there's a lavender smell coming from what I presume is a hidden air freshener.

Alfonse and I take the chairs we're waved towards and wait for the lawyer to take her seat.

Neither of us know why we're here, other than the fact that there has been a formal request for our presence. I can understand Alfonse being asked to come in: he's a private investigator, and in a small town like Casperton he picks up plenty of work. The local detective squad being worse than useless means there's always plenty of work coming his way.

The lawyer puts down the phone and smiles at us. She's the homely type, and I can picture her baking cakes or carrying out a huge pot roast.

The thought of food makes my stomach rumble. It took me a while to calm down after last night's events, meaning I didn't get to sleep until almost four, and didn't have time for anything more than a banana before making this nine o'clock appointment.

When she speaks, Pauline Allen's voice is stronger than expected, although there's a little edge, almost as if she's afraid of something. 'Thank you for coming in, gentlemen. I'm sure you're wondering why I've called this meeting.' Alfonse and I nod. 'I'll get straight to the point. I'm the executor of Ms Fifine Rosenberg's last will and testament. She made a codicil, which, I'm afraid, concerns the two of you.'

'What's the codicil?'

It's Alfonse who asks the question. I'm still trying to align the name Fifine with my memories of Ms Rosenberg. She was a diminutive woman with a huge personality. As the star reporter for the *Casperton Gazette*, her crusades kept corruption from the political offices. She had a fondness for cigarettes, scotch, and perfumes that could bring tears to a glass eye at twenty paces.

Ms Rosenberg may have had a viperous tongue and a complete lack of social graces, but she was always entertaining to be around – once your eyes had stopped watering.

Not being able to save her has kept me awake on more than one occasion. If she's left me any amount of money in her will, I'll never be able to accept it; there's no way my conscience will allow me to profit from a death I blame myself for.

It wasn't right that her funeral hadn't taken place until ten days after she'd died, but the FBI had insisted on having her body undergo three separate autopsies. I was told, off the record, by Chief Watson, that they had been done to counteract whatever moves the lawyer of the men who killed her may have made.

I get why they did it, and technically agree with their reasoning, but I do know that according to the Torah, Ms Rosenberg should have been buried within twenty-four hours of her death.

Her funeral was a lonely affair. The only mourners were myself, Alfonse, Chief Watson and a small handful of people from the *Casperton Gazette*. The paper's editor delivered a heartfelt eulogy and we all went our separate ways.

Alfonse's shoe bumps my ankle hard enough to bring my attention back to the room.

Pauline's voice now shows irritation. 'As I was saying, my client left instructions that, in the event of her death, I was to hire AD Investigations and hand this envelope to the two of you.' She passes an envelope to Alfonse. 'And that I am to instruct you to find her sole beneficiary.' She hands a folder to me.

I share a glance with Alfonse and open the folder. There are two sheets of paper. The first is a photocopy of an old picture.

It's black and white and shows a young couple holding hands and wearing the goofy grins that are shared by lovers the world over. By the look of their clothes and hairstyles, I'd say it was taken in the late sixties or early seventies. When I take a closer look, I can see the woman is a younger version of Ms Rosenberg.

The second sheet of paper holds some details about Ms Rosenberg's former beau. His name is Halvard Weil, and the address she's given for him is in Brooklyn, New York. I've never been to the city that never sleeps, but I'm guessing Brooklyn has its fair share of Jewish residents.

Halvard's date of birth shows him to be in his early sixties and there's a place of employment listed.

I shift my eyes from the page to the lawyer. 'Why do you need us to find this guy? All the information on here should be enough for you to track him down with no more than a few phone calls.'

'Read the footnote.'

I do as I'm bidden and realise why AD Investigations are required. The footnote admits that the information on the page was correct when Ms Rosenberg left New York forty years ago. Through online enquiries, Ms Rosenberg had learned that the apartment block where Halvard had lived, had been torn down. She'd also admitted that Halvard would change his job every few months as he didn't have any clear career goals other than making money.

From the corner of my eye I can see Alfonse stuffing his papers back in the envelope and looking at his watch. That he's impatient to be out of here means he wants to discuss the contents of the envelope with me when there isn't a lawyer present. I guess the pages he's read are self-explanatory as he's not bombarding Pauline with questions.

I have one or two for her though. 'This Halvard, do we know if he's still alive?'

Pauline's mouth tightens. 'I don't know. If you do find that he's no longer with us, the inheritance is to pass to any children he may have.'

'Fair enough.'

I say the words without thought as I'm trying to find a delicate way to ask the size of the inheritance. In the end, I abandon all subtlety and ask outright how much we're talking about.

'Nine hundred and fifty thousand dollars, and one letter. Once her house and its contents have been sold, those monies are to be forwarded to him as well.'

A whistle escapes my lips. I didn't expect a six figure sum, let alone one that's within spitting distance of a million bucks. Not for a reporter in a town as small as Casperton. She'd be well paid by the *Gazette,* but I can't see her earning enough to squirrel away that much money.

I feel Alfonse's gaze coming my way and glance at him before looking at Pauline. 'Where did she get that kind of money?'

'Not that it's important you know; she was an author as well as a journalist. I handled some of her affairs for that side of things as well. Mr Weil will also receive her book royalties.' Pauline's face takes on a gentle expression. 'I read one of her books. It was a beautifully haunting tale of a lost romance that was never rekindled.'

'Did she write under her own name?'

'No, absolutely not. She had a pseudonym and she refused to do any public appearances, or have her face on any of the books. She even paid a model, so she could use her picture for any online publicity that her publishers insisted on. One or two of her books even hit the bestseller lists.'

'What was her pseudonym?'

'Lorna Noone.'

The name isn't familiar to me but, if she wrote romantic fiction rather than crime or thrillers, it's unlikely our paths would have crossed in a literary environment.

Like Alfonse, I have a hankering to leave, but I have a final question for Pauline before we go. 'Assuming that you've passed on everything Ms Rosenberg asked you to, is there anything you should tell us that she hasn't already covered?'

She shakes her head. 'I've told you everything. And quite possibly more than Ms Rosenberg would have approved of, had she been alive.'

Pauline's final sentence is enough to embed a mental note never to hire her. Any lawyer who is as free and easy with their clients' information as she has been, can't be trusted. It's one thing to give a little more information when pressed for answers, it's another altogether to overshare without good reason. Ms Rosenberg may have died, but she should still be afforded the same respect as the living.

Chapter 4

I park outside the bank and turn to look at Alfonse. As we were travelling across town from the lawyer's office, we swapped information on the contents of the folder and the envelope given to us by Pauline Allen.

The point I can't get past, is Ms Rosenberg's second life as an author. That she'd trodden the well-worn path from journalism to novel writing didn't make her unique. The way she'd hidden behind a pseudonym didn't mean much on its own, lots of authors do that, but when you add in the fact that she had turned down all public appearances, and had gone to the length of paying a model for an image to pass off as herself for publicity material, you have a situation that doesn't add up.

My experiences of her may have been limited, but I'd learned she was more of a towering sunflower than a shrinking violet. The desire to remain unknown is one that many people have, but few of these people carve out a career where they are constantly in the public eye. It would be fair to say that Ms Rosenberg's journalistic skills hold a large amount of responsibility for the lack of corruption in local politics. Alongside the regular news articles that she contributed to the *Gazette*, she had a weekly column that carried her picture at the top of the page.

Try as I might, I can't connect the vivacious and often abrasive Ms Rosenberg I knew, with the reclusive Lorna Noone. It's like they were twins: identical in looks but poles apart in personality.

There's also the envelope Alfonse was given. It contains a sheet of paper, and a key for a safety deposit box. The sheet of paper holds instructions for Alfonse and me. It tells us that we are to open the corresponding box in the Grand Valley Bank, and use what we find to unleash justice.

It sounds melodramatic, on a bright sunny morning, so I pass her choice of words off as journalistic embellishment.

The bank is busy. The advent of online banking has meant there are three tellers working at a counter set out for eight.

When our turn comes, Alfonse shows the safety deposit key to the teller. She asks us to wait a moment and fetches the manager.

When the manager comes, he's tall, thin and wearing the kind of suspicious expression the public usually reserve for politicians.

'Gentlemen. If you'd follow me, please?'

The manager doesn't give his name, and I don't ask, as he leads us to a small consultation room. A whiff of expensive cologne emanates from him, but a look at the poor fit of his suit tells me he's not a preening showbird. I guess the cologne is a gift from a long-suffering wife or lover who are doing all they can to smarten him up.

The three of us sit down and the manager rests his hands on the table with his fingers interlocked. If I was a cynical person, I'd suspect he is using his body language to forewarn us of a refusal.

Alfonse must have had the same thought. Before a word can be said he passes across a letter of authority from Pauline Allen, which grants us access to Ms Rosenberg's box.

The manager reads the brief letter with furrows lining his brow. Once or twice his mouth opens and closes again, as if he's about to say something and thinks better of it.

He can act like a goldfish all he wants in his own time. We're here on business and the sooner that business gets done, the sooner we can get on with finding Halvard Weil, and inform him of his inheritance.

I'm happy to try being polite first, but have no issue escalating to rude, or even intimidating, if necessary. This guy is the type of pen-pushing jerk who makes me glad I toss drunks for a living. 'I think you'll find everything is in order. If you'd be so kind as to fetch us Ms Rosenberg's security box?'

The manager scowls at me and takes another look at the letter of authority. I presume he's trying to find a loophole that'll allow him to refuse our request. His next scowl is aimed at the paper, and he pushes back his chair as he rises.

'One moment, gentlemen.'

Something tells me he's going to keep us waiting as an act of defiance. I'm glad to be proven wrong when he returns within two minutes, carrying a flat oblong box – an inch or two bigger than a regular sheet of copy paper and four inches deep.

Alfonse uses the key to open it.

I find I'm holding my breath, but I don't quite know why.

Alfonse removes two standard envelopes from the box, takes a quick look at them, and hands them to me.

They both have my name on them, written in an old fashioned cursive script. They're also numbered 1 and 2.

The manager's face now has an inquisitive expression.

I'm tempted to open the envelopes straight away but something tells me that their contents shouldn't be advertised.

Before we leave, I have a question for the manager.

'When did Ms Rosenberg first take out this safety deposit box?'

He shrugs. 'I don't know. It's been open as long as I've worked here and that's coming up on twenty-five years.'

Judging by his age, I'd say he must have started here the day after he left school and worked his way up to manager.

There's no way those envelopes have been waiting for me for twenty-five plus years.

'When did she last come in and ask for this deposit box?'

The manager looks to the wall, in thought, before answering. 'I'm not sure exactly, but I'd say it was about a month ago.' He flaps a dismissive hand. 'We only have a dozen of these security boxes in use, and in all my time here I've only known Ms Rosenberg to access hers on a couple of occasions.'

What he says makes a certain amount of sense. Ms Rosenberg must have updated the information in it to correspond with the changes to her will that Pauline told us about.

My desire to open the envelopes is growing by the second, but I'm more convinced than ever that they should be opened somewhere where only Alfonse and I will see their contents.

Chapter 5

Cameron lifts his eyes from the paperwork strewn across his desk and rubs his nose. He hopes he's wrong in his suspicion that the tickle is the beginning of a cold.

Whether he's getting a cold or not, he has work to do. It's not the type of work he can boast about in the bars that he frequents on a nightly basis. Rather it's the sort of job you keep quiet about, say nothing to anybody, and hope like hell that the wrong people don't find out what you do for a living.

The house he lives in is functional with a lot of clean space and bare walls. To some people it would be empty and lifeless; to him it's just perfect. He has no need for clutter and no desire to burden himself with belongings that have no practical purpose.

Possessions are anchors to a free spirit, who drifts with the wind and makes occasional lurches upstream when he senses a better opportunity.

The thought of calling his work "a way to make a living" always raises a wry smile from Cameron, as he knows that his job may one day be the death of him. Not the industrial accident kind of death: the buried-in-a-shallow-grave-with-a-bullet-in-the-back-of-the-head kind.

He blows his nose on the pristine handkerchief that he keeps in his pocket, and returns his eyes to the rows of columns. To a lot of people, they're just rows of numbers, listing income and expenditure for a lot of different businesses, but to Cameron they're something else. To him they are evidence, confirmation and opportunity.

Evidence for his employer.

Confirmation of the suspicions he shares with his employer.

Opportunity for him, and him alone.

With his sixtieth birthday fast approaching, Cameron wants to settle down to a life that doesn't involve regret, fear and debt.

He's a smart man and he knows that, were it not for this opportunity, he wouldn't be able to dream of a future without fear and debt. The regrets he learned to cope with long ago.

Yet here it is. The possibility of enough money for him to see out the rest of his life in comfort has dropped into his lap with the softness of a falling feather.

There are risks attached to the opportunity, but he lives with risk daily and, if all goes to plan, there will be sufficient money available for him to start over with a new name, in a new location. He's good at doing that. He's done it twice so far, and he's already laid the groundwork in case he needs to move on at short notice.

His pen traces row after row as his brain seeks out weaknesses he will be able to exploit. The more he assesses, the more he formulates his plan to seize the opportunity that has been granted to him. His planning is in the early stages but, if he gets things right, he'll be able to make sure the finger of blame is pointed elsewhere.

Whatever happens he knows that, if he puts his plan into action, he'll either live a life of luxury, or die screaming.

Chapter 6

I t took all my self-control to not open the envelopes once we'd climbed back into my Mustang, but Alfonse made the excellent point that we'd be better waiting the five minutes it would take us to get to his apartment, so I could give the contents my full attention.

He switches his coffee machine on while I sit myself at the breakfast bar and tear open the first envelope, only to find a typed letter:

Boulder
If you're reading this, I'm dead.
Not that you would, but I don't want you to weep for me.
What I want, is for you to do something I had neither the skill nor the nerve to do.
In the second envelope there are clues for you to follow. They will explain why I left New York, fearing for my life, forty years ago.
I would like to have been less cryptic with my methods, but behind my brash exterior, I'm still the scared little girl who trembled listening to the tales her parents told of the pogroms, and of how entire families were snatched in the night and never seen again.
I cannot claim to know you well, but what I've seen of you tells me that you believe justice should be delivered to those who deserve it.
Many years ago, through fear for myself and my beloved Halvard, I failed to ensure that justice was delivered, by running away to Casperton.
I'm asking you to deliver this justice for me.

Please, Boulder. Show the courage inside you, follow my clues and find what I left. When you find it, raise all the hell you can behind a cloak of anonymity.

I implore you, if you do take on this task, not to expose yourself. You may think me melodramatic, but when you see what I have left for you, you'll understand that attaching your name to any of this, is akin to putting your head in a noose and insulting the hangman's wife. Your buddy, Devereaux, will be able to put this information in the right hands without anyone knowing where it came from.

Read the second letter now, and know that if you choose to have nothing to do with an old woman's regrets, I cannot blame you for fearing to do something I dared not.

Ms Rosenberg

P.S. I'm guessing that by now you've learned my Christian name. If you tell it to anyone I shall haunt you until the end of time.

I can't help but chuckle at the postscript she's left me. It shows the prickly, vivacious carapace that encased a soft heart, and, what I can only guess is a lifetime of regret and self-recrimination.

As the pieces of her life are being shown to me, I'm starting to form a picture of her that she didn't present to the world. Behind her bluster and putdowns, she was still pining for the man she'd left behind in another place and time.

I can imagine her torturing herself with questions about Halvard's happiness; whether he had found a new girlfriend and settled down to raise a family. She'd probably tried to imagine what he looked like as he'd aged.

I begin to wonder what she had done by way of tracking him. Had she scoured online obituaries – the print ones in major newspapers? Had she hired a private eye to track him down and update her on how Halvard's life had turned out?

Everything I think of paints a picture of a lonely old woman, filled with regret at a road never travelled.

My thoughts return to the real purpose of the letter. It's a clarion call to arms. She's given enough details to pique my interest but held back on the real story. The letter is also written in the way a psychologist would call coercive, as she invokes words like courage and justice to request my help. There is a get-out clause for me, but it's laden with reverse psychology.

Every part of me is intrigued by her big secret and, combined with the guilt I carry for her death, I feel compelled to open the second letter and follow her clues.

Except it is never quite that simple. I'm of a different generation, religion and mind-set to Ms Rosenberg. What she deems as a worthy and understandable clue, may well be indecipherable for me.

The chances of failure are high, and there is the certainty that if I do fail, I'll have let her down in death as well as in life.

'Jake.'

I look up at Alfonse. He's holding the first letter. 'What?'

'Stop beating yourself up for something you haven't done yet and open the other letter.'

I'd scowl at Alfonse but there's no point: he knows me too well and would know that the scowl was really aimed at myself.

There's no way I can, in good conscience, refuse Ms Rosenberg's request, and I'm aware that my delay in opening the second letter is nothing more than my psyche girding its loins for whatever may come next.

Alfonse and I know that as soon as I find the clues in the second letter I'll be hooked, and will follow them doggedly until I have solved them all.

I open the envelope and pull out a sheet of paper and another key for a safety deposit box.

I lay down the key and look at the paper; I see a list of names.

My coffee goes cold as I puzzle over the names.

Watson
Marshall
Evans

Devereaux
Clapperton
Devereaux
Boulder
Devereaux
Boulder
Clapperton

They don't make sense to me, not on any level. I'm on there, as are Alfonse and Chief Watson. I don't know who the Marshall or Evans are, but I'm guessing the Clapperton is her editor at the *Gazette*.

What's even more puzzling is the repetition of our names. I get two mentions, as does Clapperton, Alfonse gets three mentions, and the other names feature only once.

I pass the paper to Alfonse, and have a look at the key. It looks old and there are a series of numbers etched into both sides. One set of numbers has faded with age and the other looks as if it has been added recently.

1 7 7 3 6 7 6 2 2 4
I figure that the old ones denote the box number and the new ones are relative to the list of names. I can't see how yet, but I'm determined to figure it out.

Chapter 7

I can't help but pace back and forth across the waiting room. John, on the other hand, sits with his legs crossed at the ankles in a way that suggests he's calm and relaxed.

It should be the other way round. He's the one who needs bone marrow if he wants to see his children grow up. I'm nothing more than a possible donor. Well, perhaps a little more: I'm the half-brother he tracked down to hopefully save his life.

I want to ask what's keeping the doctor, but it would be a stupid question. As always, I've arrived early.

John has leukaemia and needs a bone marrow transplant. His sister, Sarah, is pregnant and he's flat out refused to ask her. Like me, he doesn't have any aunts, uncles or cousins. So, left with no other option, he travelled to Utah and, metaphorically speaking, knocked on my door.

If learning that my family tree has a whole other branch wasn't enough to sideswipe me, the reason he'd looked me up was an unexpected gut-punch.

We met up a couple of times for a coffee or a bite to eat. Our conversations were stilted at first, but after a while we found that we had a surprising amount of similarities. Our music and film tastes run along the same lines but, where I'm a reader, he's a devoted TV fan.

I've seen pictures of my nieces, and his sister's son. I know their names and their ages.

What I haven't been able to get past, so far as John and his sister are concerned, are their names.

I don't mean their surnames. I was a MacDonald myself until mother remarried and I became a Boulder.

It's my newfound siblings' Christian names that trouble me: they are John and Sarah.

I'm Jake, and my sister is Sharon.

My father and his new wife chose the same initials for their children as my father did with my mother. This kind of coincidence doesn't happen by accident – not when the initials are even gender matched. Had they been called Simon and Jenny I wouldn't have batted an eyelid; but John and Sarah? Those names had me thinking all manner of things about my father.

On the one hand I wondered if he was trying to replace the children he'd lost, but on the other hand I hated him for supplanting us. I don't know which version is right and it's not like I'll ever find out. It's nigh on thirty years since my father left our home, and just over twenty since he walked out on John's mother.

It's unkind of me to even think it, but I can't help speculating if there is perhaps a James and Susan out there, or a Jason and Samantha.

Whether there is or isn't, it doesn't matter. Right now, my every thought is on whether or not I'll be a match. If I am, I'll be able to save my half-brother's life and, in some karmic way, atone for the fact that I couldn't save Ms Rosenberg's.

A buzzer sounds and a tinny voice announces my name.

I toss a "here goes" look towards John, and lead him down the corridor.

Dr Becker has been the family doctor since we moved here. As the years have passed I've seen his waist expand in perfect synchronicity with the receding of his hairline. He's a kindly man who genuinely cares for his patients.

His face is grave but I don't read anything into it. Grave is his natural expression.

'Come in, Jake, take a seat.' He glances at my half-brother. 'I'm guessing you're John?'

I make sure John takes a seat before I do.

There's a folder on Dr Becker's desk and I can see my name on the label.

Dr Becker doesn't miss much, and he picks up on where my eyes are. 'I'm not going to beat about the bush here, Jake, John. I'm afraid the results are negative.'

I'm at a loss for anything to say.

John isn't. He looks at Dr Becker with a forlorn expression, thanks him, and stands to leave.

I grab John's arm and look at the doctor. 'Are you sure?'

'I'm afraid so.' Dr Becker's expression softens. 'You're aware of the Human Leukocyte Antigen markers we test to see if you're a match?' I nod. 'We got a match on five out of eight, but you need six HLA markers to match before any hospital will even consider it.'

I want to swear and rage at the world in general, but I don't. If John is taking this news in a respectful way, I must too.

With me being out of the running for a transplant, our – or should I say John's – options are slim to zero. Sharon's results came back yesterday, and they too proved negative.

Like blood, many people donate their bone marrow to be used by strangers. Because John's blood is the rare AB negative – as is mine and Sharon's – the odds of him finding a match from an unknown donor are much slimmer than usual.

John is stoic and silent as we clamber into my car.

I don't know what he's thinking but, if I had to guess from his expression, I'd say he's trying to find a way of breaking the news to his wife.

It's a train of thought I'm determined to derail.

'There's only one thing for it: we'll have to find our father.'

I can't use the word "dad". Dads are loving and caring. They teach their kids things; nurture and support them. They build toys on Christmas Eve and go out searching for batteries on Christmas Day. Dads get kites down from trees and defend you when your mother complains that you've come home covered in mud.

Nor can I use our father's given name. To do so would afford him a respect he doesn't deserve.

I think of him as Father. Not as "a father", just "Father". Like the stern Victorian patriarchs who only saw their kids once or twice a week and expected children to be on their best behaviour at all times.

'How?'

'I have no idea how to find him.' I toss John a smile. 'But I know a man who will.'

Alfonse already has one old man to find: Halvard Weil. What's another?

Chapter 8

As usual when he's working at his computer, Alfonse is oblivious to the world around him. I've let myself into his apartment, made us a coffee, and sat puzzling over the twin problems of finding a father and making sense of Ms Rosenberg's clues, without him even looking up.

His hand releases the mouse long enough to reach for the cup I've placed on his Simpsons coaster.

Whichever way I look at it, the trail to find my father will start with my grandparents. I haven't seen them since I visited Glasgow a decade back and they were pushing towards frail then – Granny told us the same things numerous times, while Grandad sat with rheumy eyes and his typically proud expression.

The Christmas letter they send each year is increasingly hard to read as Granny's handwriting worsens.

It goes against my instincts to try to find my father. Many years ago, Sharon and I resolved together that we would forget about the man who'd walked out on us without a goodbye. We told each other we were better off without a father, that we didn't want the return of one who didn't have the guts to be honest with his kids. Together we welcomed Neill Boulder into Mother's life, as it was obvious that he put a song in her heart and the smile back on her lips.

Neill possessed enough tact not to try and replace our father. Instead he assumed the role of a favoured uncle. He would offer advice when it was requested and silence on matters we didn't share with him.

He is a good man who chose to take on a sullen girl, and a boy who couldn't help but get into one scrape after another. I was never the kind of teen who stole, or got involved with drugs, but I did more than my fair share of fighting and there were several incidents when I was caught in compromising situations with different girls.

Now I've decided to look up my birth father, Neill's feelings must be considered – along with those of my sister and mother.

Sharon has a good heart and I know she'll understand. Mother, on the other hand, will use it as a stick to beat me. Mother is a narcissist who's never encountered a topic she couldn't make about herself. I know she'll rant about how I'm being insensitive and inconsiderate – for a few hours – before she concedes that I'm doing the right thing.

Alfonse pushes his keyboard forward and gets to his feet. 'How'd you get on?'

I shake my head.

'I'm sorry, man.' He nods. I know he'll leave my feelings alone unless I tell him how the news has affected me. 'How did John take it?'

'Like he didn't expect good news. There is another option though.'

Alfonse studies me and wipes an imaginary crumb from his polo shirt. 'Your father?'

'Yeah.'

There's not a lot else to say. Alfonse is the one person in the world, other than Sharon, who I've shared my real feelings about my father with.

'I thought it might come to this if you weren't a match.' He looks me in the eye and holds my gaze. 'Whatever you need, buddy, I'm here.'

I don't need to thank him any more than he needs to hear the words. He and I are tight. We've had each other's backs since the days when a bookish nerd helped a lazy Scot pass exams, and a lazy Scot stopped a bookish nerd getting his ass kicked.

'Let's recap the case first, then we can discuss what needs to be done to find Father.'

'Fair enough.' Alfonse lifts a sheet of paper from his printer and hands it to me.

He knows I absorb things better if I read, rather than hear, them.

His report is as brief and blunt as ever.

Alfonse has checked the usual sources and come up blank. For the last five years, Halvard Weil has been living at no fixed abode. His last address is a few hundred yards from the one Ms Rosenberg gave us.

His social security number showed him as being employed by a small pawn shop in Brooklyn, but when Alfonse called them, they said he'd quit some years ago.

It's possible he's slipped through the cracks in the system, but not probable. I don't know what to make of it, and judging by his defeated expression neither does Alfonse.

All along we've thought it would be a simple case of tracking down Halvard, and either calling him or sending him a letter to request that he contacts Pauline. Now that he can't be easily found, we'll have to take other measures. The first of which, will be a visit to the pawn shop.

It will be me who'll travel to New York. Alfonse's skills are with a computer, whereas I'm better at questioning people and getting information from them.

'What about the clues Ms Rosenberg left us? Where have you got with them?'

'Nowhere. I looked at them all ways, and have as much idea now as I did when I started.'

I'm not considering the clues she's left us as a priority, and I'm only asking as I know that Alfonse will have tried to crack them.

When I think about them a little more, I realise they maybe should be higher up our list of priorities. Alfonse and I agreed that the safety deposit box key she'd left in envelope 2, was most likely for a box held in a New York bank. The clues would tell us which bank.

If I am going to New York to track Halvard, it would make sense to locate the bank, and claim the box's contents, when I am in town.

'I'll take a look at them. See if I get anywhere.'

'Cool. I'll get you booked on a flight to New York tomorrow morning.'

'Don't book it just yet.' I swallow before continuing. 'Taylor's going to a wedding in New York in a couple of days. I wasn't going to go, but if I'm going to be in New York …'

He chuckles at my discomfort. Taylor is my girlfriend, and all the signs are there that she's going to be around longer than the usual three months my relationships last. For the first time in my life I've done the whole meet-the-parents thing. Both ways.

Within ten minutes of meeting Taylor, Mother had produced my baby pictures and started discussing possible names for the grandchildren she wanted Taylor and me to supply her with.

My cheeks had burned for the whole evening, and I only managed to refrain from drinking myself into a stupor by focussing on the fact that I should never share the same space as hard liquor.

Always a step ahead, Alfonse hands me a notepad, pen, and the phone from his desk. Letting Taylor know I can join her in New York will be easy; asking Grandad about Father, not so much.

Chapter 9

I t's good to hear Grandad's voice. He's the one who taught me how to look after myself. Not in a metaphorical way, more physically.

Before Mother, Sharon and I left Glasgow, when Neill's new job relocated him to Casperton, Grandad took me into the back garden and spent an afternoon teaching me the fighting skills he'd learned in the Clyde shipyards.

None of the methods he showed me could be considered fair, moral or anything other than dirty, but he taught me that fair fighters are rarely victorious fighters.

I explain to him about John and hear his breath catch. It catches again when I tell him that neither Sharon nor I are matches.

'That's not a good thing to hear, son.'

Despite all the miles between us, I can picture him sitting in his chair with his back ramrod straight and his eyes fixed on a point in the distance. It's how he reacts to bad news. Grandad isn't a man who shows his emotions. Like all Glasgow's sons, he frowns upon lavish praise. If Grandad tells you that you look "no' too bad", or that you "didnae dae ower bad efter a'", you're getting his equivalent of a ticker tape parade.

The counterbalance to this is a conversation I once overheard him having with a neighbour. He was praising Sharon and me to the rooftops, with one endorsement after another. While he'd never give compliments to your face, he was your biggest champion when you weren't there to hear the pride in his voice.

'I can only think of one other person who might be a match.'

The line is silent for so long I think he's hung up on me. 'Yer faither?'

'Aye.' As always, when speaking to Grandad or Granny, I've slipped into Scottish terms and slang. 'Or possibly his other children, if he has more I don't know about.'

'Naw. There's jist the four of you.' I can hear his breath rasp down the phone as he composes his next sentence. 'I expect you'll be wanting to ken where he is?'

'Aye.'

One word seems to be all I can manage. This is a conversation I'd promised myself I'd never have. Yet here I am, having it.

The fight with the compass points last night was a doddle compared with this. Physical pain is something I can handle and am used to. Emotional hurt is something else altogether.

What's making it worse is that I know it's not just me who's suffering. Grandad will be too. He never liked the way my father had walked out on us, and would have liked it even less when he did it to John and Sarah's mother.

My call will bring it all to the surface. Worse than that is the news I've given him about John. People don't expect to outlive their children, let alone their grandchildren. It's the natural order of things, and here I am upsetting the balance of his life.

I hear a hearty sniff and remember Grandad's misshapen nose. What makes my heart ache is that there's no trace of a cold in Grandad's voice.

'I'm sorry, son. I dinnae ken where he is. He calls when it's oor birthdays and at Christmas, but he never gies me a number I can call him on.'

'Thanks. I'll be honest, Grandad, I expected as much. Did he say where he is living?'

'I asked him last Christmas. He said he was in the States and wouldnae be more specific.'

'I'm sorry I can't remember, but when are your birthdays?'

'They're past for this year, son. Next call will be Christmas.'

Christmas is three months away. Three months is a long time when you're dying from blood cancer. John can't wait three months for someone who may only be a possible donor.

'What dates are your birthdays, Grandad?' He tells me and I write them down. The more information I can give Alfonse, the better he'll know where to start looking. 'Can I speak to Granny?'

'Of course you can, son. Jist dinnae say oot aboot your brother. There's nae point worrying her aboot things she cannae dae onything aboot.'

I spend a pleasant few minutes letting Granny tell me all about what's happening in her neighbours' lives, and promise to call her more often.

We both know the promise is made with the best of intentions and the worst of odds.

It's not that I don't enjoy speaking to them, it's that every time I plan to call them something gets in the way, and by the time I clear the obstruction another week or month has passed.

Chapter 10

I stretch my legs as much as the seat in front allows and focus on the sheet of paper in my hand for what seems like the thousandth time.

No matter which way I look at it, I can't make sense of Ms Rosenberg's clues. The names and numbers do not speak to me in any way.

Alfonse has managed to book me on the same flight as Taylor, but we aren't sitting together, and all the seats around us are occupied by families so we are unable to swap.

It's not too much of a bad thing. I need to solve Ms Rosenberg's puzzle and Taylor has the ability to distract me with nothing more than a flick of her hair.

I've thought long and hard about Ms Rosenberg's chosen pseudonym and the way she hid behind it. I now know she was scared that she might be tracked down by whoever forced her out of New York, but another thought about her pseudonym has stayed with me.

It's the surname Noone. When someone tries to hide, they become faceless and blend in. They choose a place where nobody knows them, and they do their best not to draw attention to themselves. They don't fulfil their potential, nor do they strive to become famous. Rather, they try to be no one. Or, in Ms Rosenberg's case, Noone.

While Ms Rosenberg was well known in Casperton, nobody living fifty or more miles away would be aware of her. Rather than pursue any dreams of journalistic stardom and Pulitzer prizes, she'd hidden herself away in a backwater town and settled for being a mid-sized fish in a small pond.

I'm sure the choice of pseudonym has something to do with a professional writer's love of words. Maybe it was her extending a middle finger to those who'd driven her out of New York. She was still successful, she'd just been unable to publicly accept the acclaim that came her way.

The other thing that's distracting me is the conversation I'd had with Mother. She'd pursed her lips, scowled, and proceeded to insult my intelligence when I'd told her that I was going to find Father. When she'd finally stopped railing on me, I'd asked her if she thought I was doing it for any reason beyond a desperate attempt to save John's life.

She hadn't known how to answer, and had sat staring at me, making no effort to hide the tears in her eyes.

I'd tried to reassure her that once Father had agreed to help John, I would leave them to it and have no further contact with him. She'd shaken her head with a vehemence I had never seen before, and told me that if my father wanted to reconnect with me, he'd find a way of persuading me to do it.

In the end, it had been Neill who'd settled Mother, and got her to see what I was doing was for John's benefit, rather than my own.

Mother had insulted me a little more before telling me she couldn't add to what I already knew.

I had relayed her answers to Alfonse who, with his typical grace, had told me to worry about tracking down Halvard Weil and to leave finding Father to him.

Now I'm sitting on a plane with time to think, I wonder about the searches he'll run. Alfonse is a master hacker who can penetrate anything he wants. He's got my father's full name and date of birth. From those he'll be able to look in all the government databases, such as social security, immigration, and police files. If Father has been picked up for anything he's done in the USA, Alfonse will be able to find out.

The sheet of paper in my hand mocks me with its silent tease. Each word or number is mute against my thought processes.

Alfonse has tried using the numbers as map references, but there should be six numbers for each reference. Having ten, meant the references were five by five. Regardless of the numbers, without knowing which map to use, the numbers were useless.

I turn over my sheet of paper and try something else.

Watson – 1
Marshall – 7
Evans – 7
Devereaux – 3
Clapperton – 6
Devereaux – 7
Boulder – 6
Devereaux – 2
Boulder – 2
Clapperton – 4

Assigning each name with a number from the sequence, I take the corresponding letters and write down what they spell – the first letter of Watson, the seventh letter of Marshall, and so on, until I get to Evans – not enough letters in the name Evans – W L ? V E A E E O P.

I spend a while trying to rearrange the letters into a word, but I can't form one that makes sense to me.

My heart isn't really in it as I'm not sure I'm on the right track – Evans contains five letters and its corresponding number is seven.

I try reversing the order of the numbers against the names: C R A U E R E V A S are the letters offered up to me, and as there are ten of them, I'm more confident they will tell me the location of the safety deposit box.

A flight attendant brings the trolley up the aisle. There's no grace to her movements and she's using the trolley as a battering ram against the elbows and feet, which overhang the narrow seats, protruding into the aisle.

I raise a hand to halt her stampede, and buy a few pieces of over-priced fruit rather than subject myself to the airline's sorry attempt at a meal.

While I usually enjoy puzzles, to keep my brain active, I can feel my frustration growing at my failure to assemble the random letters into words or names I recognise.

The crying toddler two rows in front doesn't help my mood; neither does the gangly teen surfer-type behind me who keeps bumping the back of my seat.

There's nothing I can do about the crying toddler, so I rise from my seat, turn to the teen behind me and lean in close to his ear. When I speak, my Scots accent is thickened to a growl. 'The next time you bump my seat I may well give in to my growing desire to shorten your nose. Do you understand me?'

He nods.

I pat his ridiculous hairstyle and tell him he's a clever boy.

By the time I reach the toilets I'm starting to feel the first prickles of guilt for acting like a bully. They disappear when I consider the fact that the teen is old enough to know better than to be an inconsiderate nuisance to other travellers.

My mood lifts further when I see Taylor walking towards me with a salacious twinkle in her eye.

Chapter 11

A solitary phone call is all it takes for Cameron to break down the barrier between a possible opportunity and a life changing decision.

The call is made from a public booth at the other side of town. It could have been made from his home phone or his cell, but that would have left a trail. When you're running off with seven figures of someone else's money, not leaving a trail is a good idea.

With a new identity being prepared for him, he is one step closer to having his escape route in place.

Next on his to-do list is opening a new bank account. The money he plans to appropriate – he doesn't think of himself as a thief, therefore he won't be *stealing* the money – needs a new home. A home that can't be traced.

Swiss bank accounts, and those in offshore banks, are very good at refusing the authorities information on their customers. Where they have problems, is in the protection of their employees and their employees' families. The people he's appropriating the money from won't hesitate to threaten a bank manager's family to get the information they need.

This means he needs to be clever with where the money will end up. There's no point exchanging it for cash or gold. There would be too much to move around without a van.

Cameron has an idea though. It's a good one that he knows just how to execute. His employer has shown him a different world and he intends to utilise his knowledge of it to enact his plan.

The best part is, he's known to the people who'll facilitate his deception. He has traded with them on his employer's behalf in the past and all the correct protocols have already been established. All he needs to do is lie convincingly and all will go well for him.

It won't be easy, but earning millions of dollars in a day was never likely to be. His plan to make the money untraceable is a simple one that needs no real brilliance.

All it needs is a fair amount of organisation, the establishing of some credentials, and a few forged documents.

These will all be established before he goes to the bar on the corner, for his usual steak dinner washed down with beers and a few whisky chasers.

Once that part is in place, there will be no way that either he or the money can be traced. He's even prepared to write off a few hundred thousand as expenses if necessary.

Chapter 12

The pawnbroker's shop is nothing like my expectations. In my head I had a vision of an over-filled room, crammed floor to ceiling with random objects in a style that was haphazard and precarious. I'd imagined the sign above the door to be faded and that the proprietor would be a bespectacled man with grey hair and a shabby cardigan.

What I encounter instead is a slick, modern building with glass cabinets, ample lighting and a collection of styled youths behind the counter. There's music playing through a hidden speaker and, while I don't recognise the tune, I know it's not a song that's likely to achieve classic status before another decade has passed.

It's only when I look at the store's merchandise and its clientele that I realise why my expectations were wrong. My thinking was of hard-up homeowners, pawning beloved items until they'd saved enough money to pay off the loan from the pawnbroker.

I'm decades out with my assumptions. Today's pawn shops are more like a trading post. Teens with pasty complexions are buying video games by the handful, couples are examining the cabinet filled with jewellery, and there is a group, of what I can only assume are traders, scouring the cabinets containing cell phones, iPads and other digital equipment.

As I look for a member of staff who may be classed as a manager, or has at least started shaving, a pre-teen boy leads his father in and heads straight to the exchange counter. I watch idly as the father empties various video game boxes out of the backpack he carried in.

I pay attention to the boy and his father. The official buyers in a place like this must have a certain amount of seniority. I take

Taylor's hand and lead her across the room until we're standing in line behind the boy and his father.

The words I whisper in Taylor's ear get me a stern look, but she does as I ask and removes her necklace and places it into my hand.

My plan is a simple one. While there will be some known information about a video game's value, jewellery is a different matter altogether. That requires someone with a certain amount of proper training and years of experience.

Taylor's necklace is a good one. She told me it was a gift from her father on her twenty-first birthday. Having been invited to her parents' home to meet them over dinner, I know for a fact they're not worrying about where their next buck will come from. Everything about them spoke of quality, without crossing the line into ostentation. I could tell from the one meeting that they dote on their only daughter, and I'd be happy to bet that Taylor's necklace, while not overly fancy, will have a recognised hallmark and a price tag that'd equate to several months of my salary.

The boy's father tries to haggle a better price than he's offered, but the server is resolute and doesn't budge. The father huffs and puffs a little but, after a minute of trying to wangle a more favourable deal, he gives up and takes the handful of dead presidents the server has laid on the counter.

I smile at the server and lay the necklace on the counter. 'I'm told this is valuable. How much are you willing to offer me?'

The server runs a hand through the mop of un-styled blonde hair on his head, lifts Taylor's necklace and squints at it.

'I'll give you a hundred bucks.'

'Try again. I've heard it's worth a lot more than that.' I fix him with a stare. 'You've just looked at it. Closely. You'll have seen the hallmark. If a hundred bucks is all you're offering, I'll take it elsewhere.'

'I ... I'll need to speak to my boss. He may be able to offer you more.'

Now we're getting somewhere. The server was chancing his arm. I half expected as much. He's played safe after seeing the hallmark. Perhaps he thought he'd get a promotion if he managed to buy cheap and sell dear. On the other hand, there may be a Miss Blonde Server he wants to impress; a necklace like Taylor's would go a long way towards impressing whichever girl he had his eye on.

He goes into a back room and I hear him call out to a Mr Weil. I share a look of excitement with Taylor. This has been too easy. If it's Halvard who comes through the door, we're home and dry. If it's not, I'll lay a cent to a dollar they'll be a close relative of his.

The man who appears isn't Halvard. Not unless he's been drinking an elixir of youth. Our man is in his late twenties, or early thirties.

He smiles at us and glances at the necklace. He takes another look at Taylor and me. It's a scenario that's familiar to me. With her elevated cheekbones and flawless complexion, Taylor has a timeless beauty; whereas I'm average. Average height, average looks, average build.

I'm punching above my weight with her and I know it. Fortunately, I'm good at punching. In fact, I almost consider it to be a hobby.

Weil pulls a jeweller's loupe from his pocket and examines the necklace. When he lays it on the counter it's with a delicate, almost reverent, care. The loupe is returned to his pocket.

When he speaks his tone is respectful. 'I am prepared to pay you five thousand dollars for this exquisite necklace.'

'I'm sorry, but it's not actually for sale.' I keep my voice low to remove any offence from my words.

Weil sighs, takes another look at the necklace, and another look at Taylor. 'Six thousand and that is my final offer.'

I pull a sheet of paper from my pocket, unfold it and lay it on the counter so it's the right way up for him to read.

'The necklace isn't for sale. I'm sorry to have jerked you around, but I needed a way to get to the person in charge.'

Weil's eyes are fixed on the paper; I'm guessing he's fighting back surprise. The paper holds the image of Halvard Weil, which Ms Rosenberg had so treasured. Alfonse has cropped her from the picture to maintain her anonymity.

I figure Weil is experiencing a gamut of emotions as he looks at an old picture of a younger version of himself. There is no doubt in my mind that he's a close relative of Halvard. The hook of their noses is the same, as are the shape of their eyes and their chins. My guess is that he's Halvard's son or, at the very least, his nephew.

He looks up from the picture and into my eyes. His pupils are full of questions but his face is otherwise implacable.

I realise he's not saying anything for a reason. He's waiting for me to speak. Like all experienced negotiators, and that's a lot of what pawnbrokers do, he knows when to ask questions and when to wait for someone else to speak.

'I'm not going to insult you by asking if you know who's in that picture. I'm going to tell you that I've been hired to find Halvard Weil by an attorney. The attorney is the executor of a will that Mr Weil is the main beneficiary of.'

'I see.'

His words may not be a lie, but there are still questions in his eyes. He doesn't see, not really. If I'm right about him being Halvard's son, he'll be busy trying to work out who's died and why he hasn't heard about it.

Maybe he's too polite to ask, or he's keeping his cards close to his chest like all good negotiators, but again he waits for me to speak.

I'm happy to oblige. The sooner we get this sorted, the sooner I can spend a little time exploring New York with Taylor. I've heard plenty about the Big Apple, but this is my first visit and I want to see as much as I can while I'm here.

'Would I be right in saying your father is the man in this picture? That you're Halvard Weil's son?'

He nods.

'I hope you'll forgive my bluntness, but I take it your father is still with us?'

Another nod.

'Would you be prepared to give me his address?'

A baleful look is followed by a shake of his head.

I begin to wonder if Halvard is fit and well. He may be in poor health and living in a care home somewhere; either waiting to die or being tormented by the imaginings of his mind.

It's my turn to wait Halvard's son out.

He's stubborn and resolute.

So am I.

He cracks first.

'I cannot give you his address as I do not know who you are, who you represent, or if my father will welcome a stranger coming to his door talking of an inheritance when nobody likely to leave him money has died.'

Now it's me who nods at him. I understand where he's coming from. His very presence indicates the existence of a Mrs Weil, which is why I've not used Ms Rosenberg's name. The last thing I want to achieve is disharmony. I'm here to deliver a message of newfound wealth, that's all. Causing trouble isn't part of my agenda.

'In that case, can you arrange for me to meet him?' I spread my hands wide. 'I can meet him at any time over the next three days.' Taylor's elbow connects with my ribs. 'With the exception of tomorrow afternoon and evening.'

I write my cell on the reverse of Halvard's picture and tell him there are several hundred thousand reasons why he should get his father to call me.

Other than a slight widening of his eyes, he doesn't react to the hint I've dropped about the size of his father's windfall. Either the sum isn't that significant to him, or he doesn't believe me.

Chapter 13

I shift from foot to foot and try not to look as uncomfortable as I feel. The suit I bought off-the-peg after visiting the pawn shop yesterday had seemed a better fit at the time. Now it is bunching where it shouldn't and hanging loose in all the wrong places. To compound matters, every other guy in the room is attired in expensive, fitted tuxedos.

The wedding dinner is a meal comprised of several courses of foods I couldn't easily identify. My tastes are simple when it comes to food. Give me a hunk of red meat and a heap of fries and I'm more than content. I'm not yet at the point where I need to eat again, but I'm not far off. With luck there will be a decent buffet that will allow a spot of light gorging before my stomach starts to protest its emptiness.

Taylor is never far from my side but I've long given up trying to remember the names of all the people she's introduced me to. There have been lots of polite handshakes, some hearty backslaps and enough air kisses to make a Hollywood actor feel at home.

It's the backslaps that bother me the most. Every one of them seems to land on the same part of my back that East's baseball bat has left bruised and tender.

There's a hum of conversation in the air and, as befits the occasion and plush venue, it's polite and reverent. The people are nice enough, but there's so many of them I know nothing about. They are all talking about past experiences I haven't shared and people I don't know.

For Taylor's sake I keep my smile fixed and my tone polite. This is her family occasion and I've come along as a last-minute addition. It's also her Fifth Avenue hotel room I'm sharing, so the whole trip to New York does have its upsides.

While I may have been raised in a city, Glasgow never had the same metropolitan feel that New York exudes. This is a busy city, peopled by people who are important. Or at least to themselves they are. Glaswegian streets were busy, but not so busy that you couldn't make progress round a slow walker. The Glasgow I grew up in was one where I knew, and was known by, every neighbour within two streets. It was a community within a city.

New York is different. It's all hustle and bustle as its inhabitants strive to get from one important place to another. The importance of their journey is set on their faces but, to an outsider like me, the relative merit of any individual's perspective is subjective.

I didn't help myself when I was walking the streets – I'm sure my constant stopping, to look up at one landmark or another, was a nuisance to other sidewalk users. Sometimes I would just stand by a crosswalk and gaze along the streets, or look up at the towering skyscrapers that dominate the skyline.

The subway has been the worst part of my time in New York. I've never been properly underground before, and my first experience being one that included huge crowds, a lost sense of direction and the impersonality of city life, didn't endear me to subterranean travel.

Had Taylor not been with me, I would no doubt have gotten myself thoroughly lost. It's not that I can't find my way about; I'm spending so much time working out where I am, and where I need to get to, my progress is that of a geriatric sloth compared to the rest of the thronging crowd. This in turn made me feel rushed, which led to me making snap decisions about which direction to take.

Along with the sights, come the sounds and the smells of the city. In one block you can catch a whiff of coffee, burritos, hotdogs and a dozen other foodstuffs from around the globe. There is a constant pick-pocking of heels on concrete, car horns, and the murmur of a crowd as they grumble, cajole or shout into their cell phones.

Like many others before me, I've found New York to be an exciting and vibrant living beast that can turn intimidating at a moment's notice.

The high point of my morning was a text I received from Halvard's son. He suggested a meeting place from where he could take me to meet his father. I agreed to his terms at once to hopefully show integrity, but looking back I maybe should have been a little less eager.

Yet another member of the waiting staff offers me a flute of champagne, which I refuse. I'm quite happy with soda, and when I'm unhappy with a soft drink I'll make damn sure I'm nowhere near Taylor or any member of her family.

Alcohol and I have an understanding. I don't consume it and it doesn't make me do stupid things like start fights, or wake up in a motel room, hundreds of miles from home, with no memory, wallet or clothes. Once in a while I'll take a drink, but only after making sure I'm not in a place where I could hurt those I care about.

'Hey there, gorgeous. You're looking as good as you always have.'

The speaker is someone I don't know. His whole demeanour is that of Ivy League entitlement. He's got an arm draped over Taylor's shoulders and his eyes halfway down her dress. I fight every one of my instincts that are telling me to punch him as hard as the garlic on his breath is hitting me.

I toss my gaze at Taylor's face. Her expression is one of infuriated tolerance.

Behind Ivy League, trails a young woman who's pulling at his sleeve. Her face bears a pleasant smile, but her white knuckles on Ivy League's sleeve tell me she's every bit as angry as Taylor is. When she speaks, her voice has the whiny tone of the long-sufferer.

'C'mon, Jason. I want you to meet someone.'

'Goodbye, beautiful.'

Jason goes to plant a kiss on Taylor, but she turns her head at the last minute so he connects with her ear.

'Who the hell does that guy think he is?'

'The groom's brother. He's got a trust fund big enough to give him a life of luxury, even if he lives to be a thousand.' She shakes her head. 'Sadly though, he can't buy class.'

I chink my soda against her champagne flute. 'Very true. You, on the other hand, don't need to. Me? I can't afford it. Just say the word and I'll follow him to the bathroom and recalibrate his sensibilities.'

Taylor's melodic giggle draws a few smiling glances. 'Every woman in this room under the age of forty would love to say the word. It's not going to happen though.'

One of the things I appreciate most about Taylor is that she recognises me for what I am and doesn't try to change me. My being in a lower social class than her isn't an issue, but then again, class distinction is much more a British thing than a US one. Nor has she shown much concern about my tendency to use violence as a first option.

The only fear I have about our relationship, is that one day she'll tire of her "bit of rough". It's not a scenario I enjoy thinking about, so I only give it brain space in my darker moments.

I see Jason coming back so I suggest Taylor makes herself scarce.

'Hi, buddy. Great place this, isn't it?' Jason goes to walk past me, after Taylor, but it's what I'm expecting and I sidestep so I'm in his way. Sometimes you have to take one for the team. 'That meal was delicious, wasn't it?'

'Yeah, very good.'

His eyes focus on me, which gives me hope that Taylor has escaped his gaze. His head turns and he locates a member of the waiting staff. His fingers click and he waves her over.

'About time, girl. Damn near died of thirst.' His tone is full of entitlement as he grabs two glasses from the girl's tray.

I have to give the server credit. She doesn't rise to his rudeness and gives a polite smile as she turns away.

He thrusts a glass towards me. 'Here, it's a wedding. You should be drinking champagne, not soda.'

'Not for me thanks.' I keep both of my hands on my soda glass, and try not to picture what he'd look like after a few well aimed punches. The temptation to find out if my imaginings are accurate may just get too much for my self-control.

'You're Scottish right? Thought you Scots were big drinkers?'

'We can be.'

The glass is pushed forward a second time. 'Then have a drink and don't be such a pussy.'

There is nothing but challenge in him. He's used to being the Alpha, and someone refusing him isn't something he's familiar with.

'Thank you, but no.' I keep my tone polite but I can hear anger at the edge of it.

'I said … take a drink.' He holds the glass in front of my face. His voice is cool enough to freeze the drink solid. 'It's my brother's wedding and I think you should be celebrating it with a glass of champagne.'

'Thanks, but alcohol doesn't sit well with me.'

'What are you? A man or a mouse?'

I toss a devil-may-care grin at him. Perhaps it's the fact I've gone from picturing him bruised and bloody, to imagining what he'd look like on fire, but I'm calm and relaxed enough to let my smile be natural, as I lean forward and whisper into his ear. 'I'm man enough to turn down a drink I don't want. I'm man enough to refuse to conform to another person's wishes when I know doing so is a bad idea. I'm man enough to stand up to bullies.' I know I shouldn't say what comes next but I've held temptation in check long enough. 'I'm also man enough to kick your ass up and down Broadway, if the notion takes me.'

For a moment I think he's about to do something stupid like curse me out, or even throw a punch. If he hits me, I'll have to let him land a few before I subdue him. Any other course of action will see me labelled as the bad guy. That's not what I want at an occasion where I am trying to put my best foot forward with Taylor's family.

He throws his head back and guffaws loud enough for heads to turn. He's the centre of attention again, which is just how he likes it.

I slink away, hoping those who matter notice how unimpressed I am by him.

Chapter 14

Halvard Weil's son opens the door of the Brooklyn coffee shop a few seconds after I knock. He'd told me the coffee shop was one that closed due to a lack of business. It doesn't surprise me that it failed. It's down at heel, and a bright new Starbucks sits gleaming across the street.

Consumers are fickle beasts who'll decry corporate monsters while shovelling money into their coffers, while mom-and-pop businesses are closing their doors on a daily basis.

The coffee shop is empty, save for a couple of tables laden with upturned chairs and a thick layer of dust.

'Is your father here?'

'Not yet, Mr …?'

'Boulder. But most people call me Jake.' I hold out a hand. 'And you are?'

He hesitates for a moment until his manners get the better of him. 'Gavriel.'

I turn as I hear footsteps. Two men emerge from a back room and they're both so large they need to duck as they pass through the doorway.

'I'm sorry, Mr Boulder … Jake, but for reasons that will become apparent when you meet my father, I'm going to have to ask you to allow my cousins here to search you for weapons.'

This is a surprise I wasn't expecting, but it doesn't bother me. I hang my jacket on a skyward-pointing chair leg, and lift my hands to my head. 'Feel free. I have no weapons on me. My jacket has my wallet and cell in the inside pocket, and I have my car keys in the front right pocket of my jeans.'

As Gavriel's two hulking cousins pat me down, I assess their actions from a different point of view. The need to assume this level of security tells me a few things.

First off is the fact that Halvard, his family, or both, do not trust me. Second, they are not going through these measures because they're jumping at shadows. There must be some kind of clear threat to Halvard. Third, the level of threat is a significant one – the presence of guys as large as Gavriel's cousins is a serious deterrent.

I can handle myself, yet I don't fancy my chances against guys this big. To compound matters, they move with economy and grace rather than the lumbering bovine movements usually associated with huge men. It's quite probable that they are trained in a martial art. Krav Maga, as developed by Israeli Special Forces and Mossad, would be my guess.

Two shaken heads receive a short nod from Gavriel. If his cousins are the brawn, he must be the brain, or the son of the brain, as the power in the room lies with him despite him being the smallest of the four of us.

My jacket is checked for hidden weapons and handed back to me.

'Now you've established I'm unarmed, do you trust me?'

Gavriel's smile is the wrong side of patronising. 'Jake, I'm a New York pawnbroker. I've learned not to trust anyone.'

I return his smile and wait for him to tell me what's next. This situation is one I don't care for, but I'm here to deliver a message of good news. Once it's delivered, I'll say my goodbyes and walk away leaving their distrust behind.

'Follow me.'

Gavriel leads me through the back of the coffee shop and into a narrow alleyway. I'm flanked by the cousins as I follow him, through a mesh of dirty stinking alleys with overflowing garbage bins and high brick walls, until he comes to a door.

Should I decide I don't want to be here, my only hope of extricating myself from this situation is to be fleet of foot. It's not a theory I want to try out. The cousins are close enough to assume the role of jailers as well as bodyguards.

Gavriel gives a complicated knock, and the door is opened by someone who looks as if he's the cousins' big brother.

I'm crowded through the door and led up a stairwell, which has a threadbare carpet, peeling wallpaper and the strong ammonia stench of cat urine.

Gavriel leads me along a corridor and into what was once someone's lounge. He gestures for me to sit on the sofa and, when I do, I find myself wedged between the cousins. Gavriel leaves and Big Brother takes up station in front of the door.

I could try and make conversation but not one of the three has spoken to me since I met them. Besides, I don't want them to hear any catch of fear that may feature in my voice.

I'm not so much scared as unnerved. The dramatic way of bringing me to this room, when I would have happily met Halvard Weil in a public place, is nothing more than a display of power and control. They want me to feel intimidated and at their mercy. The three giants add to the menace with their indifferent silence. The only thing I'm pleased about, is that Taylor isn't here with me.

To pass the time I try to spot some doorframe behind Big Brother. I fail.

In their own way they're testing me: seeing what I'm made of and how far I'll go to speak with Halvard Weil.

Their test isn't one I plan to flunk, so I sit quietly and look out of the grimy window at the bricks of the neighbouring building.

The door opens and Gavriel enters with a man who can only be his father.

Halvard Weil has aged, compared to Ms Rosenberg's picture of him, but there is no mistaking that he's the same man. He sits in the single chair opposite me and looks me over, from head to toe.

'You say you're here because I am the beneficiary of a will. None of my friends or family have died, so I'm sure you must understand my caution at meeting you.'

The look he gives me is part suspicious and part apprehensive. I get why he's cautious, but I don't say that I think he's overcompensating. Instead, I ask myself why he's so cautious, and what he has to be fearful of. Once I have an answer to my question, I'll be able to understand his point of view.

'Your benefactor is someone I believe you haven't seen for nigh on forty years.'

His eyes close and his head droops forward. When he speaks, his voice is little more than a pained whisper. 'Boys. Leave us please. I need to talk alone with Mr Boulder.'

Chapter 15

When his son and nephews have padded their way out of the lounge, Halvard lifts his chin from his chest and looks at me with tear-filled eyes.

'Are you talking about who I think you are?'

'If you're thinking Fifine Rosenberg, then yes, I am.'

His face somehow manages to convey pain and love at the same time. 'My Fifi still thought of me?'

I'm reeling at the thought of the formidable Ms Rosenberg being called Fifi, so I give him a shrug and a nod. The unspoken truth is that she must have thought of him every day. That she'd left him her fortune was a red flag regarding her feelings.

Another sure indicator were the books she'd written. I looked them up online and saw they all dealt with lost love. The reviews they'd garnered were positive, but many of them mentioned a melancholy feel. Lots of the reviewers said the books "perfectly encapsulated their feelings about a love that had never blossomed into fullness".

His chin returns to his chest and rises again so he can look me in the eye. 'I can't take her money. I can't accept it. Not after the way I failed her.'

Pauline had hinted that Ms Rosenberg had anticipated this reaction, and that I was not to take no for an answer.

I like to think I have principles, but I'm not sure I'd be able to turn down the kind of money he's been left.

'I think you'd be failing her again if you refuse to accept her last request.' I let my words have a moment to register, and point out that he hasn't asked how much the inheritance is.

'It doesn't matter if it's one dollar or a billion. My feelings on the matter are the same either way.'

This isn't the reaction I was expecting, but I have to admire him for his principles. 'You should know that Ms Rosenberg was insistent that her money be handed to you. Should you not have been alive, it was to be passed to your descendants.'

'Tell me, Mr Boulder. If you had let a good woman go, and had regretted it every day for forty years, would you take her money when she died? Would you take her money when you had been too selfish to accompany her when she'd fled town in fear of her life? Would you take her money knowing you'd broken her heart?'

'No, I guess not.' The admission is out of me before I realise it's damaging my side of the argument. I pick my next words with greater care. 'But I'd also want to respect her last wishes. She chose you as her sole beneficiary for a reason.'

His chin saws against his chest as his head shakes from side to side. 'Perhaps.'

'Don't think of it as profiting from her death.' I recognise that he's starting to waver, so I press home my slight advantage. 'Think of it as enduring proof of her love for you. If not for yourself, accept her gift for your family. Use it to give them a better life.'

I know better than to mention numbers at this point. It's principle we're discussing, not dollar signs.

'I didn't give my Fifi a better life. I made hers worse by not having the courage to go with her.'

'Do you think she saw it that way? Do you think she blamed you? That she hated you for not going with her? She loved you. From the day she left New York, until the day she died.' I make sure I have eye contact with him. 'I talked to her editor at the *Casperton Gazette*. She never dated anyone since you and she said goodbye. She didn't sleep around or join the dating pool. Your Fifi didn't want anyone but you, and if you ask me, the reason she left you her money is because she had forgiven you. To refuse her last request would be to refuse her forgiveness. You've lived with the thought of failing her for forty years. Can you live the rest of your life knowing you'd spurned her forgiveness?'

'You, Mr Boulder, are a very persuasive gentleman who knows how to press the buttons of an emotional old man.' He pauses to lick his lips and wipe a tear from his cheek. 'If I took the money and put it into a trust for my grandchildren, do you think she would consider that I had accepted her forgiveness?'

It's a compromise for all concerned, but I'm sure Ms Rosenberg – she'll never be Fifi to me – would agree to his terms were she here to speak for herself.

Halvard calls out, something I don't catch, and Gavriel walks in with a bottle of malt whisky and two glasses.

'Now then, Mr Boulder. Will you join an old man in toasting a remarkable lady? I have a lot of questions to ask you about my Fifi.'

Chapter 16

Halvard pours me a generous slug of whisky for the third time, and raises his glass in a silent toast.

I've told him everything I can about Ms Rosenberg, and he listened with teary eyes as I praised her determination to get to the heart of the stories she'd covered.

When I told him of her secret life as an author, and the pen name she'd adopted, he twisted his lips into a tight grin and told me she'd loved the novel *Lorna Doone*.

Now that I've answered all his questions, I have a few of my own I want to put forward.

'Ms Rosenberg left New York in what I gather was rather a hurry.' I pull the paper that has the list of names and numbers on it from my pocket. 'She left me this and told me to raise hell with what I find. I can't crack her puzzle, nor can I begin to guess what I'll find that will raise hell. Can you help me at all?'

He falls silent as he looks at the sheet of paper.

I nurse my whisky and wait him out. The whisky is a good one, but I'm doing my best not to drink too much of it. One more glass will tip me past the point where I can stop. After that it'll be a race to the bottom of this, and any other bottles I can find. No doubt I'll wake up somewhere I shouldn't and there may or may not be a fight involved.

'I'm sorry, I can't help you with this.' He pauses, looks out of the window and then at his shoes. 'But I can tell you a little of why my Fifi left New York.'

The whisky I've consumed makes me want to giggle at his insistence on referring to Ms Rosenberg as Fifi, but I manage to control myself as I gesture for him to continue.

'You told me she was determined to get to the heart of a story; she was the same all those years ago. Dogged and persistent. The problem was, she'd uncovered the wrong story. She had it all written up and, when it went to her editor, it got deep-sixed.' He takes a gulp of his whisky. 'Naturally she had demanded to know why, but he'd told her to leave it and said no more on the matter. The next day I got a visit. The person who visited me was what they called a "made man". If you know what that means, I don't have to spell things out to you.'

I nod to show that I know what a made man is. The term is a mafia one for those who've been formally accepted as a member. This puts a whole different slant on things, but my thought processes will have to wait until I've finished speaking with Halvard.

'The visitor told me to tell Fifi that she had twelve hours to forget everything she knew about her story and leave New York.' He grimaces. 'It took me three frantic hours to find her, and another two for me to persuade her that her life was in danger. Two hours after that, I was at Grand Central Station waving at a train.' His voice falls to a whisper. 'Don't say anything to Gavriel, but I've spent the last forty years of my life regretting not being on that train with her.'

I'm desperate to ask what the story was about, but recognise he needs a moment to salve painful memories. I go to take a sip of my whisky, only to find my glass has become empty.

Halvard notices and splashes another three fingers of amber liquid into the glass.

I take the tiniest of sips and put the glass on the floor. If that glass gets emptied a fourth time, there's no guessing the trouble I'm likely to find myself in.

'You probably want to know what the story was?'

'Hell yeah.' As soon as the words are out, I regret the flippancy the whisky has brought to me.

Halvard doesn't pay my rudeness any attention. 'So would I.' His head gives a sad shake. 'She refused to tell me. Said it would be safer for me not to know.'

I fall silent and think of the old man in front of me. He's spent forty years regretting actions he didn't take. To make matters worse, he never knew the reason why his girlfriend had to leave town, and him.

Whichever way up you stand it, their situation is nothing less than heartrendingly tragic.

Chapter 17

Cameron exits his car and takes a look at his surroundings. Around him are the trappings of wealth. Not the comfortable lifestyle, kind of wealth: more the serious kind of wealth where a top-of-the-range Ferrari will be one of several cars in the garage.

The man he's here to see has dealt with him before. Granted, Cameron was acting as an intermediary for his employer, but the relationship was established all the same.

More important than any other part of Cameron's plans, is the fact that a protocol has been established. He isn't some chump walking in off the street with a bag full of empty promises. He is a recognised employee of a customer you don't say no to.

As is befitting of his employer's status, Cameron deals with the owner of the dealership, rather than one of his sales team.

'I trust you can accommodate me with something suitable?'

'Of course.' The salesman's smile is far wider than it is sincere. 'What will your budget be?'

Cameron sees the dealer's head bob when he tells him how much he is willing to pay. The guy is probably working out how best to flannel him with a line of sales bull. He needs to make sure he gets the right end of the bargain.

'We've traded before. There's every likelihood we'll trade again. I'm trusting you to discount one of your better ones to fit our budget rather than mark up a lesser priced one. Do I have to remind you whose trust I represent?'

'No, no, of course you don't.' The dealer makes a dismissive gesture, as if the idea he would cheat Cameron is ridiculous. 'I have several options available that would suit your needs. If you'll give me a moment I'll get some brochures and, if you like any of them, we can go and take a look.'

Cameron looks at his watch and takes a moment to admire the view from the dealer's window. The sun is glinting off the water and there is a beauty to the scenery that reminds him of another country. He still pines for the land he left all those years ago. Not the weather or the grimness of life in Glasgow, more the people. Glaswegians are a garrulous bunch who are welcoming, loud and, when the occasion calls for it, hard. They'll feed and water you with a smile on their face, but should you step out of line they'll think nothing of dressing you down.

As well as the people, he misses other staples of Glasgow life as well. The greasy mutton pies, the roar from Hampden when Scotland score, the banter between Celtic and Rangers fans and the walk home from the pub with a bag of chips and a deep-fried haggis in crispy batter.

He knows he should miss his family and feels bad that he doesn't. Not bad for them, bad for himself, as he recognises he must have something missing in his psychological DNA.

Life in America has been good to him and, as far as he's concerned, it's about to get a hell of a lot better.

The dealer returns with the brochures.

As he leafs through the various options, Cameron is recalling the research he did online before making this visit. He dismisses three of the seven options as being marked up to match his budget, and concentrates his attention on one he's seen advertised elsewhere for a million dollars above his proposed expenditure.

'This one looks very nice. I trust you'd still make a profit if you sold it to me for the agreed figure?'

Cameron is pleased to see the dealer squirm a little. He's caught him trying one of the oldest tricks in sales: learn your customer's budget and persuade them to exceed it.

'I'll be honest, Cameron, I'd need another five hundred thousand for this one.'

'That's such a shame. It's by far the nicest option, but you're not exactly showing me, or the man I represent, much respect by trying to upsell, are you?'

The dealer's hands rise in a surrender gesture. 'Please, Cameron, I don't mean any disrespect. I guess I've been a salesman for so long, upselling has become a habit.'

Cameron waits before answering. All the power is with him and he's drawing out his response to make sure the dealer will do what he wants. He may have trained as an accountant, but his real skill is in negotiating purchases.

Cameron is the official buyer for his employer's many legitimate businesses. He is also tasked with getting the best deal when it comes to vehicles, properties, and any fripperies he decides he wants. In the last month he's closed deals for a work of art, two bars, one vintage sports car, and a whole range of smaller items.

'I think if you were to agree to waive the extra half mil, I could find a way to forget the disrespect you've shown me.' Cameron smiles. 'Subject to a viewing, and my approval of course.'

Cameron can tell from the look in his eyes that the dealer will lose money on the sale, but he doesn't care about that. His concern is with himself and the purchase he's making. This is his way of laundering the money he's planning to appropriate from his employer. Once the money trail becomes evident, the dealer will have other issues to think about.

The dealer's hand trembles as he offers it to Cameron. 'Subject to your approval after viewing, I can let you have it for your budgeted amount.'

Cameron has the grace to keep his smile the right side of smug. He'd always expected to get a good deal, just not this good.

As for the dealer, Cameron expects him to fold and tell everything at the first sign of trouble. His employer's men won't ask polite questions, they'll threaten, intimidate and use violence as a matter of course. He knows that the dealer's betrayal won't be personal, and that the man's instincts will concern his own survival.

Chapter 18

I don't like the way the bartender is looking at me. It's a look I'm more than familiar with. Hell, I've used it myself on many occasions when door-minding at the Tree. It's telling me I've had as much drink as he's going to give me.

His judgemental attitude can take a hike. I don't need some snooty bartender in a fancy hotel deciding when I've had enough. If he won't get me another whisky, I'll get it someplace else.

From the corner of my eye I can see a pair of managerial types. Their heads are close together but, from the glances they're flicking my way, I can tell it's me they're discussing.

This little tableau is typical of a high-class hotel. The staff aren't used to tossing drunks, and as such, they're nervous about how I'll react when they try to manage me. Were this to take place in a less genteel establishment, there would be either security at the door or a weapon under the bar.

I pick up my glass and wobble my way to a cream leather sofa, where I collapse in a heap of whisky fumes and troubled thoughts.

The last thing Halvard told me was that, when Ms Rosenberg's murder had made the news, he'd received a visitor who'd requested that he pass on information about anyone who came to see him regarding her.

That means the mafia are still fearful of the story she wrote all those years ago.

Halvard assured me that he wouldn't tell them about my turning up, but their contact with him highlights the seriousness of the task that Alfonse and I have been given by Ms Rosenberg.

Never once have I considered that I would be going up against the mafia; that the secret I have been tasked to find would damage them. I can think of other ways of putting my head in a noose, but none of them seem as foolhardy.

Yet, I'm a believer in justice. My moral code tells me that the good guys should defeat the bad guys; that heinous crimes should never go unpunished.

In my drunken state, I've decided to carry on searching, and make a judgement call when I uncover whatever Ms Rosenberg has stashed in the safety deposit box.

'Excuse me, sir.' It's the female managerial type. She's holding a tray bearing a large coffee pot and a cup, along with a plate of cookies. The tray is placed on the table I'm slouched beside. 'Compliments of the hotel, sir.'

Her smile is bright, although I can tell she's nervous. She has no need to be.

The coffee is what the hotel will class as a masterstroke. It will give me something other than alcohol to drink, and the cookies will be intended to soak up some of the whisky swilling around inside me.

It's a shame she doesn't know much about alcohol and its effects on the human body. Coffee is a stimulant, which will make me more active. The cookies are a nice touch, but the alcohol they're intended to soak up will be absorbed into my bloodstream by now. Sure, they'll help with any future intake, but neither they nor the coffee will do anything to sober me up.

All the same, the hotel management have managed me with dignity, so I decide that my next whisky should be drunk in a place that will serve me as many as I care to order.

Even though I'm three parts drunk, my brain hasn't stopped chewing over the puzzle left by Ms Rosenberg. An idea comes to me, so I lurch my way to the bar and ask for a pen and some paper.

I slide a ten across the bar and ask the bartender to list all the New York banks he can think of.

Ten minutes later I have his list and I'm scribbling away. My thought patterns aren't brilliant, but there's no way I'm going to stop what I'm doing.

Except I do stop, or rather, pause. The papers and pen are stuffed in a pocket and I'm on my feet heading for the exit as fast as my unsteady legs will carry me.

There's neither a crisis nor an emergency – other than the empty whisky glass that I'm sure won't be refilled here.

The street is packed but I don't care that I'm unsteady on my feet or bumping into random pedestrians as I go looking for my next drink.

Chapter 19

The call from Alfonse has given me more to think about. It was a brief call; his tone had changed as soon as he heard the slur in my voice.

I know I should go back to the hotel and sleep off the drink I've already had so I can deal with everything with a clear head. Had Alfonse not suggested I do so, there's a good chance it's what I would have done.

He did suggest it though. This means the contrary asshole in me must to do the opposite.

I order another bottle of beer and a whisky. I'm not sure how many I've had, but it doesn't feel like enough. It never does.

Alfonse has managed to locate my father. I have a vague understanding that he tracked the calls that Father had made to Granny and Grandad and worked back from there.

That doesn't matter right now. What matters is that Father lives in a place called Clifton, which is one of the towns surrounding New York.

This means I could be knocking on his door in a couple of hours. Introducing myself to the man who walked out of my life without so much as a goodbye.

I realise that a selfish part of me had been hoping Alfonse wouldn't be able to find Father. That way I wouldn't have to confront the man I least want to meet.

A slug of whisky doesn't wash the sour taste of self-loathing from my mouth. My brother needs me to find my father. It couldn't be simpler. It's a matter of life or death, yet I don't want to do it.

Of course, I will do it. But every moment I spend with him, I'll be expecting to once again feel the pain of his rejection.

The door of the bar opens and a vision of beauty walks in. At least, she's beautiful when she first walks in. As soon as she sees the shape of me, some of her beauty is tarnished by the scowl that covers her gorgeous face.

Taylor sits opposite me and lets her expression and body language do the talking for her. They speak of disappointment and exasperation.

She glances at her watch and I remember we're supposed to be having dinner with her parents before they fly back to Casperton.

'I'm sorry. Halvard wanted to toast Ms Rosenberg and I kinda got the taste for it.'

Her nose wrinkles and she pulls away when I reach for her hand.

'I trust you are aware that I'll have to lie to my parents about your absence from the dinner table.' Her top lip curls into a breaking wave. 'I *hate* lying to my parents.'

'I'm sorry.'

Her face tells me that words aren't going to be enough to sort this; I'll have to prove myself to her all over again.

The strange thing is, I want to prove myself. Letting her down doesn't make me feel good.

I stand up and wobble for a moment until my muscles hold me more or less upright.

'Hey, sugar. Don't you be after wasting none of your time on that bum. You come over and talk to Old Fred here and he'll make sure you're looked after real good.'

I refocus a bloodshot eye on Old Fred. He's about my age, a couple of inches taller than me, and a damn sight nearer sober. Because Taylor is with me, I choose to ignore the urge to see what he looks like with a broken nose.

'Thanks for the offer, but I'm quite happy with Young Jake.'

Taylor's words are a joy to behold as they show loyalty and commitment. They're also the type of putdown that generally sees egos deflated.

Graham Smith

Old Fred's ego doesn't like being punctured. It compels him to cross the room and square up against me. 'Let's see how much you like Young Jake once Old Fred has kicked his ass.'

Taylor goes to step between him and me but he shoves her aside.

So far as I'm concerned that's all the provocation I need, so I thrust my forehead towards his nose.

He's ready for me and recoils, causing me to miss. I haven't just missed, I'm off balance.

The punch he throws collides with my ribs. This is a good thing. Had he landed the blow to my stomach, there's every chance I'd be splashing his boots with beer and whisky.

I grab his shirt with both hands and throw another head-butt at him.

This one lands on target and busts his nose. I follow it up with a hard uppercut that drops him to his knees.

The kick I deliver to his balls leaves him lying on the ground in the foetal position; a mixture of moans and curses spill from his lips. Old Fred may talk in the third person, but he's less than half the man he thinks he is.

I don't have time to celebrate my win as I'm grabbed from behind by what I assume is one of Old Fred's buddies. A man wearing anger like an overcoat steps in front of me.

He's a big guy and I'm guessing the bulging muscles he has on display are forged through hard work rather than gym training and steroid abuse.

His first punch splits my lip and loosens a tooth or two.

I don't intend him to land a second.

To free myself from the guy holding me, I bend at the knees and throw my head back as I straighten them.

I wriggle my left arm from his grasp, whirl to the side, and use his right arm to throw him towards his buddy.

Lady Luck has decided to favour me, as Mr Angry's next punch lands square on his buddy's chin, knocking him out.

That just leaves Mr Angry to deal with.

The problem he's got is, I'm angrier than him. It's one thing some bozo chancing his arm with my girl; when said bozo gets his ass kicked for pushing her, his buddies should have the decency to recognise he had it coming.

My retaliation is neither pretty, nor filled with technique. I launch myself forward, intent on throwing punches until Mr Angry joins his buddies on the floor.

I catch a few punches as I move forward, but Mr Angry is too busy defending himself against my onslaught to mount a decent counterattack.

A pair of right crosses, and a straight left followed by a gut punch, see him double over and sink to the ground.

I'm about to follow him to the floor so I can deliver a memorable life lesson, when I feel a hand on my arm and hear Taylor's voice.

'Jake. That's enough!'

Chapter 20

I wake to discover someone is using the inside of my head as a squash court. At least, that's what it feels like.

The dryness of my mouth is Saharan in its intensity, and I think my stomach may have been replaced by a decrepit cement mixer.

I try and recall what happened last night until I'm brave enough to open my eyes. Vague recollections of a fight explain the tenderness of my face and I have no trouble remembering Taylor railing on me.

As I run my hands down my body, I find that I'm still wearing my jeans although my shirt has been removed. There's what feels like a decent sheet covering me, so I surmise that I made it back to the hotel.

I open an eye to confirm my whereabouts but there's nothing but dark shadows. For a moment I fear the fight has caused damage to my eyes.

The fear is dispelled when I see the luminous hands on my watch. It's just after three, which I'm guessing is a.m., therefore it'll be dark outside.

I slide a hand slowly across the bed and touch silky hair. A sniff gives me the familiar aroma of Taylor's perfume.

So far, so good. I'm in the right bed with the right girl. Yeah, she might be pissed at me, but I'm confident I can change that state of affairs.

Truth be told, I'm pissed at myself. There was no need for me to continue drinking once Ms Rosenberg had been toasted. It was an indulgence that I'm going to spend the rest of the day paying for.

What's more, it was stupid of me to go on one of my benders when there are so many things that need my full attention. I've completed one of two tasks for Ms Rosenberg and I still have to face my father. If he's anything like the man I think he is, he may need to be persuaded to help John.

My bladder reminds me why I woke up so, taking care not to wake Taylor, or distress any of my aches, I slip from the bed and pad my way to the bathroom.

The face I see in the mirror doesn't look good, but I've seen it look worse.

As I'm finishing in the bathroom, I remember that I'd been trying to crack Ms Rosenberg's code, and recall stuffing the notes I'd made into my jacket pocket.

I don't feel like sleep, so I retrieve my shirt, jacket and boots, and return to the bathroom to dress before going downstairs in search of coffee.

The doe-eyed receptionist greets me with suspicion, but arranges to get me the coffee I request.

I take a seat in the empty bar and unfold the crumpled pages of notes. Each has the names and numbers listed along with the words they spell out. In my drunken state, I'd rotated the numbers against the names looking for a solution.

It's the sixth page that holds my interest.

In a scrawl I hardly recognise as my own, I have written:

Watson – 6	*N*
Marshall – 2	*A*
Evans – 2	*V*
Devereaux – 4	*E*
Clapperton – 1	*C*
Devereaux – 7	*A*
Boulder – 7	*R*
Devereaux – 3	*V*
Boulder – 6	*E*
Clapperton – 7	*R*

It might not look like much, but the list of banks someone has written down for me includes one called Carver. This must mean N A V E is an address for the specific branch of the bank to go to.

I work on the assumption that A V E is short for avenue, which means I need to find a street beginning with the letter N and ending in avenue.

Google gives me the answer in thirty seconds. There is a branch of the Carver bank located on Nostrand Avenue.

I'm tempted to go and check it out, but it's not the best idea for me to go wandering around Brooklyn in the middle of the night with a bad hangover and very few city smarts. The fact I'm battered and bruised from a bar fight will attract trouble like flies to dung.

Instead of action, I opt for coffee and thoughts.

The coffee is good and the thoughts are bitter.

Chapter 21

The Carver Federal Savings Bank is nothing like I was expecting. I had pictured a grand, old building which would dominate the space around it, with an imposing frontage and an air of respectability.

Instead I'm faced with a wall of glass and a single-storey building. It doesn't match any of my pre-conceived ideas, but then nothing about Ms Rosenberg has. I spent several hours this morning thinking about her life, as well as the secret she has charged me and Alfonse with not just finding, but sharing too.

My best guess is that she had uncovered a crime and was hounded out of town because of it.

The anonymity Ms Rosenberg enjoyed in life, wasn't afforded to her in death. As the final victim of a bunch of twisted racists and bigots, her death had hit the headlines at a national level alongside the other victims.

That Halvard was visited so soon after Ms Rosenberg's murder, shows that the person implicated in the story is still very much alive.

I also chewed on the fact that blowing her secret open, may present a level of danger should the implicated person or persons find out who is behind the unveiling. I have to trust that Alfonse will find a way to inform the necessary people without leaving a trail to us.

'Do you want to stop standing there, looking at the bank, and go in?'

It's not like Taylor to be so caustic, but considering how she was when she woke up, she's come a long way. She's decent enough to have accepted my heartfelt apologies, but she's not beyond putting me through the mill a little to make sure I'm reminded of her displeasure.

I give her a nod and stride into the bank. It's just like any other: there are a number of tellers dealing with business people, depositing the weekend's takings; a young mother with a kid in a stroller is speaking loud enough for everyone to hear her displeasure at the bank's refusal to raise her credit limit; and there are a dozen or so people waiting their turn with bored expressions.

Taylor and I join the queue and wait. I should probably try and make small talk to show contrition, but I'm not sure she's ready for it yet. Besides, my focus is on what we might discover in Ms Rosenberg's safety deposit box.

It takes fifteen minutes for us to get to speak to a teller. The one we get is a guy in his early twenties, and I can tell by the lack of emotion in his greeting that he's less than ecstatic to be here. Teller Boy wears enough hair product to pollute the Pacific Ocean and his beard may well thicken out in a decade. Or two.

'I'd like access to my safety deposit box please.' I hold up the key in case he's too dumb or disinterested to understand my words.

The lie that the box is mine isn't the worst one I've ever told and I'm not sorry for it. The last thing I want to do is draw the bank staff's attention to me, and whatever Ms Rosenberg may have left.

'Take a seat. I'll have to get Mr Nolan.'

He levers himself off his padded stool and approaches a door. He knocks, opens it, and walks through it, without waiting for an answer.

Taylor and I take seats as instructed. Now that we're this close to finding out what's in the box, I start to doubt myself. It's not that I think I'm wrong; more that I begin to wonder if I'm going to be left looking stupid when the key doesn't open the box.

Another part of my brain imagines a different scenario. One that has me and Taylor bundled into the back of a panel van by a bunch of gun-wielding hoods. Ms Rosenberg's secret will be taken from us, and Taylor and I will be sent to sleep with the fishes.

I know I'm jumping at clichéd shadows but, after hearing Halvard's story, I can't stop thinking that every person looking our way is a mafia spy watching us.

I'm aware of how ridiculous it sounds. If the mafia were watching this bank they'd know more than just the branch details.

None of this does anything for my jitters though. I can fight, I'm good at it, and on primal levels, I enjoy it, but there is a world of difference between tossing drunks and fitting people with concrete overcoats. Sometimes in life, you have to recognise your limits.

I see a man emerge from behind the counter. He's dressed the way a bank manager is expected to dress. His shoes are buffed to a glossy finish and his suit is sharper than anything that's ever been in my cutlery drawer, let alone my wardrobe.

It's his head that lets the side down. He probably imagines that the stubble makes him look cool; instead it makes him look uncouth. Coupled with the horseshoe of hair that hangs to his shoulders, it destroys everything his clothes set out to create.

'I'm Nolan, the manager.' He proffers his hand for a shake. 'If you'd like to follow me, sir, ma'am.'

Nolan's hand is rough and his grip strong. I now have a mental image of him dressed in denim and leather, sitting astride a Harley. In the pillion seat is a wrinkled woman with more tattoos than teeth.

Nolan leads us through a side door, taking care to make sure we don't see the number he keys in. We're in a short corridor with four closed doors. He takes us to the door at the end of the corridor and repeats his secretive number pressing.

When Nolan opens the next door he reveals a staircase. The cloying smell of decay and age wafts up at us, making me think that the door hasn't been opened in a long time.

He sets off down the stairs and I gesture for Taylor to go after him. When we get to the bottom, we are confronted by the kind of huge door I've seen in a thousand heist movies.

Nolan spins the dial on the front of the door through a series of clockwise and counter-clockwise turns, until there's a faint clunk. Next he grips what looks like a ship's wheel and spins it. The whine that accompanies his exertions makes me think this door is rarely opened.

The door doesn't creak when he hauls it open, but I can see beads of sweat covering his forehead as he battles against unoiled hinges.

'Which box number is it, sir?'

I read the number on the key and watch as his eyebrows rise. 'Interesting.'

He doesn't elaborate, and I don't make anything of his comment. Instead, I wait for him to take me to the actual box.

His interest is intriguing to me though. I'm guessing he and his staff have wondered about this box many times. The fact it's lain untouched for forty years will probably have puzzled them and led to wild speculation. It's not beyond the bounds of possibility that he, or a previous manager, has had a peek at the box's contents out of curiosity. I know it's unfair of me to malign bank managers this way, but they are a section of society I've never felt able to fully trust. To my mind they are money-grubbers, whose main aim in life is the collection of other people's assets.

Nolan leads us into the vault and I see a range of different sized safety deposit boxes. Some are like drawers in a dressing table and others are large enough to be used as football lockers. If Ms Rosenberg has one of the larger boxes and it's full, there's no way the backpack I'm carrying will suffice.

Nolan stops before a column of the smaller boxes, points at the third from the bottom, and steps aside. 'This is the one.'

I could blame the dusty air and the confined space for my dry mouth and shortness of breath, but it would be a lie. This is the moment of truth. I'm about to find out what's in the box.

I look at Taylor and get a nod as confirmation that I should open the box. Nolan, to his credit, has retreated to the door and turned his back.

The key doesn't slide into the lock with ease; I push it a little. Not hard enough to jam it, but with sufficient power to force it through decades worth of dried oil.

It's the same when I try to turn it. The key goes a fraction clockwise then stops dead.

I press a little harder, fearful that the key will snap in the lock.

It doesn't budge, so I turn it counter-clockwise until it is back to its locked position. I draw the key out and use my fingers to remove the fragments of dried oil.

The key slides in easier the second time, but it still won't turn past that first fraction.

A touch on my arm alerts me to Taylor. She's holding the miniature bottle of perfume that she keeps in her purse.

I get her meaning at once and remove the key, clean it with my fingers again, and give it a liberal spray of perfume. I scoosh a few squirts in the lock and try inserting the key again.

This time, after a few gentle twists in either direction, it rotates through ninety degrees.

I pull on the box's handle and the drawer slides open with a tortured screech.

The lid lifts with ease. All I can see is a large brown envelope and, while it doesn't look full, there are enough papers inside to give it a bulge.

I lift the envelope from the box and slide it in my backpack. Whatever it contains has waited forty years for discovery. Rather than open it in front of Nolan, I decide that its secrets can wait another few minutes until we're somewhere private.

When the safety deposit box clangs shut, I realise I've been holding my breath. I draw in some air and leave the dusty vault, which now has a hint of summer flowers from Taylor's perfume.

As we leave, I hand the key to Nolan and tell him that we have no further need for the safety deposit box.

Chapter 22

Taylor sends me to the bathroom while she orders coffee. I don't need the bathroom; we both agree I should open the envelope somewhere private. The coffee shop was her idea.

I also think she's making sure I have plenty of fluids, although I'm already energised by coffee after spending half the night either drinking or thinking. I still haven't told her that Alfonse has given me an address for my father.

I tried to assess my feelings about meeting him, as an adult, but didn't get very far. The whisky that was still in my system had me oscillating between wanting to punch his lights out, and hoping he would break down in tears, proclaiming that leaving Mother, Sharon and me was the biggest mistake of his life.

Now I'm sober again, I know that hitting him isn't the best idea when I need his help, or should I say, my half-brother needs his help. Nor do I believe he'll show any degree of repentance. If he had wanted to connect with me or Sharon, it would have taken one call to my grandparents to find out where we were. That call may have happened, but whether it did or not, he never turned up on my doorstep with a hangdog expression and a mouthful of apologies.

When I spoke to Grandad on the phone, I was on the point of asking him if he'd kept my father updated on my life, when something stopped me. Looking back, I think it was the fear of Grandad telling me that Father had never asked about us. Whatever else happens when I confront him, I know I'll be guarding myself against the pain of further rejection.

A cubicle becomes free so I enter and concentrate on not breathing through my nose.

When I pull Ms Rosenberg's envelope from my backpack, I see a signature has been scrawled across the sealing flap.

I take a close look at the signature and see the envelope has remained unopened. Either Nolan and his predecessors are unworthy of my distrust, or they've been deterred by the signature.

I'm not. I tear the sealing strip back and fish out the contents.

There are some pages that have been torn from ring-bound notebooks, two typed pages, six black and white photographs, and a small envelope.

The envelope can wait. I look at the loose notebook pages first, but see nothing except a series of indecipherable squiggles. My best guess is that it's shorthand. With luck, Taylor will be able to translate it for me.

Next, I look at the typed statements. After reading them, the reason I'm holding my breath has nothing to do with the cubicle's previous occupant. What's on these pages is huge. Not quite earth-shattering or world-changing, but still huge. I now know why Ms Rosenberg had feared for her life. In her place I'd fear for mine.

Except, I am now in her place. I'm the one who holds damning proof.

I tear open the small envelope and find a key to a post office box. There's no mystery to this one. Just a scrap of paper with an address.

I don't know what it contains, but if it's as incendiary as this envelope, the country will be rocked by the level of corruption.

The people in the pictures aren't anyone I recognise, but I'm sure they were recognisable when they were taken.

Taylor's face is expectant when I join her at the small round table in the centre of the room. Nobody is paying us any attention – other than a pair of city workers who're probably entranced by Taylor's beauty.

Regardless of our anonymity, I'm nervous about bringing Taylor up to speed in a place where so many people could overhear us. I lean towards her and whisper that I'll tell her everything as soon as we're alone.

We take a walk after finishing our coffees. Half a block along from the bank we find a children's playground. We sit on a bench with graffiti scratched into its paintwork and I let Taylor see the contents of the envelope.

When she's finished reading she looks at me and gives a grimace. 'It's a long time since I learned shorthand, but I can make out most of what Ms Rosenberg has written. We can pick up a notebook on the way to that PO box.'

I'm so pleased by her willingness to help, that I could kiss her. So I do.

She breaks after the kiss. 'Maybe we'll get some mints for Mr Whisky Breath before you get your usual ideas.'

This tells me I'm forgiven for last night's mistake. Sex hasn't been on my mind this morning, but it is now. With luck, we'll get to the PO box, retrieve its contents, and be back at our hotel soon.

It's then that I remember my father's address. It's within striking distance of New York. Any romantic thoughts will have to be shelved until I've met the last person I want to introduce myself to.

Chapter 23

Taylor brings me a coffee, takes a seat and sips at her water, leaving a smear of fuchsia lipstick on the glass. On the table in front of us is a great sheaf of envelopes that we've retrieved from the PO box. Some are yellowed with age, whereas others are crisp and bear postal stampings with recent dates.

We've kept them in the order they were put into the PO box, and we start with the first. It's a newspaper cutting with notes about the people mentioned, and their involvement in the crime Ms Rosenberg had uncovered.

I've known the secret for over an hour now and I still can't get my head round it. I've read the evidence Ms Rosenberg had compiled, more than once, but I'm still struggling to take it all in.

Taylor's expression tells me she's going through the same thought processes I am. Neither of us follow politics with any great attention to detail, but we're both aware of the major issues.

'This is amazing, isn't it?'

Taylor's voice is low, but she needn't worry. The dive bar we're in isn't the kind of place where people care about the conversations of others. There's two guys sitting at opposite ends of the bar, drinking themselves stupider, and what I presume is a hooker, numbing herself ahead of her working day.

'That's one way of putting it.'

She looks at me, all hazel eyes and prominent cheekbones. 'To think he's built his campaign on exposing his opponent's links to organised crime, and this ...' – she waves a hand at the envelope-strewn table – '... this just proves that he's worse than they are. We have to expose him, Jake. There's no way he can be allowed to become Mayor of New York.'

'You're right. The thing is, the minute we put our names to exposing this, we'll be painting huge targets on our backs.'

Taylor looks scared. She should; it's not some random bunch of thugs or bad guys who're involved in the mayor-elect's corruption. It's the mafia.

The mafia cannot ever be allowed to identify us as whistle-blowers. If that happens, Taylor, Alfonse and I will die. Their numbers and contacts are too great for us to believe that exposing their links to the mayor-elect will lead to their incarceration – and that of anyone who may exact revenge on their behalf.

Every envelope we open is filled with details of the mayoral candidate's career, first as a lawyer, then a judge. Specific cases are highlighted with examples of links between the defendants and organised crime.

Three of his rulings as a judge, favoured what Ms Rosenberg had revealed as shell corporations, owned by known mafia individuals.

This case may have cost Ms Rosenberg her job and a life with Halvard, but it was quite obviously never been one she could stop building. Her dedication to compiling evidence crosses the line into obsession.

It's going to take a while for Taylor and me to collate all the evidence, then we must find a way of duplicating it all, so it can be shared with as many news outlets and law enforcement agencies as possible.

I'm not sure if this should go to Homeland Security, the FBI, the police, the NSA, or some other three-letter organisation. Although I am sure that it should go to as many as possible to ensure it gets into the right hands.

For someone to get into office as the mayor of New York with such a corrupt background is unthinkable.

I need to speak to Alfonse. He needs to know what we've got, and I'm hoping he'll come up with the best way to distribute it without putting a noose round our necks.

Chapter 24

Cameron has everything in place. All he needs to do is transfer the money, wait until it's been verified as received, and he'll be able to start his new life. Or as he likes to think of it: his final new life.

He logs on to the site and keys in all the necessary passwords. A minute later, he's ready to make the transfer.

Seven million dollars are moved from his employer's account and into the account of the dealer.

He reckons that by the time he turns up at the dealership, the money transfer will have gone through and he'll be able to escape with his purchase.

He only needs an hour or two head start and he'll be home and dry.

Everything he needs is in his car apart from one bag, which is sitting by the door ready for collection.

The only way his plan can go wrong, is if his employer checks his bank account before he gets to the dealership. Cameron knows the odds of this are small, as it's his job to manage the accounts for them.

He throws the bag over his shoulder and opens the door.

There's a man standing on the porch, with his hand raised as if he's about to knock. The man looks uncomfortable, as if he'd rather be anywhere but here.

None of that matters to Cameron.

All that matters is that he recognises the face.

It's the face he used to see in the mirror many years ago. This version has a cut lip and scrapes synonymous with received punches, but it's still the same face.

'John? Is that you, John?'

'I'm Jake. Your *first*born son.'

Cameron doesn't know what to say. All of a sudden, his legs are weak and he's aware of his breath shortening.

Despite the fact he's kept moving around, and has changed his name on several occasions, he's always feared the day that one of his children would turn up unannounced.

He finds his voice, but still isn't sure what to say.

Jake is looking at him in a way he can't fathom. Cameron isn't sure whether his son is getting ready to punch or hug him.

To say something, and break the silence, he looks at the woman with Jake. 'Sharon, my little girl, you've grown up to be a beautiful woman.'

'This isn't Sharon. This is my girlfriend. She's called Taylor.'

Even when Jake speaks, Cameron struggles to gauge his mood. Right about now, Cameron could use a stiff drink. And if his son hadn't picked the worst moment in the last twenty years to show up, he'd damn well have one.

He knows he needs to get this unwelcome reunion over and done with so he can make his escape. Every minute spent playing happy families, is a minute stolen from his getaway.

'I'm sorry, but this isn't the best of times for me. Perhaps we can arrange to meet somewhere later?'

Cameron knows he should feel guilty about arranging a meeting he'll never attend, but he feels nothing except a burning desire to get to the dealership.

'You haven't once asked how I am, how my sister is, or if our mother is still alive.'

Jake's tone holds a ferocity that rocks Cameron. He takes a look at his son's hands and sees the white-knuckled fists; he knows what happens when the MacDonald blood gets heated.

'I'm sorry, it's just such a shock seeing you here.' An idea comes into Cameron's mind. Another pair of hands may be useful, and having the boy's girlfriend around will certainly improve the scenery. 'Why don't you come with me? I can drop you at the station as I pass it.' He hands Jake the keys to his car and the bag from his shoulder. 'Jump in. I'll just be a second.'

Cameron goes back into the house and into the kitchen. He turns on the gas stove, but doesn't spark the igniter, and lays a can of gasoline on its side after removing the top. Standing behind the front door, he sparks his lighter and touches the flame to the wick of a candle. By the time the gas fumes reach the candle that one of his lady-friends brought over, he'll be at least a mile away.

Chapter 25

Now that I've met my birth father, all the years I've spent hating him seem justified. I can't think of him as my father anymore; he may be, biologically speaking, but having experienced the offhand way he greeted me, his long-lost son, I'm beginning to think that him walking out on us was a good thing.

The moment I've both dreaded and rehearsed for many years has come and gone, and none of it happened how I'd imagined. Sometimes I've thought he'd welcome me with open arms, other times I've imagined him spurning me.

Disinterest wasn't a reaction I'd anticipated, not even once.

It's like my visit is a nuisance to him and he'll be happy to be rid of us.

He's asking me questions, but since I had to give him prompts, I don't believe he's asking out of genuine interest. Rather, I believe he's controlling the conversation so I don't ask him for any answers.

Finally, he asks the question I've been waiting for.

'The reason I looked you up, is because my half-brother John came looking for me.'

Cameron nods. I can't even call him Father in my head anymore. Mr MacDonald would be another option, but that term would afford him a respect he doesn't deserve. I could call him a derogatory name, but that would indicate I care enough about him to get angry. There's no way I'm going to give him the satisfaction of knowing I'm still hurting. As far as I'm concerned, he's Cameron.

'It's nice that he found you. I've always thought boys should have a brother.'

It takes all my self-control not to ask why he didn't stick around to give me a brother. Instead of snarling abuse at him, I decide to use bad news as a sucker punch. 'John needs a bone marrow transplant, otherwise he'll die of leukaemia. He looked me up hoping I'd be a match.'

'For his sake, I hope you are.'

'I'm not. I was close, but not close enough.'

I fall silent and let him join the dots by himself.

His eyes close for a moment and then he swallows.

'So, you looked me up to tell me your brother is dead?'

'No. I looked you up to tell you my brother needs you to save his life.'

It's Cameron's turn to fall silent.

I let him have some thinking time. My own moral compass would never require time to consider a request such as this but, while we may have similar genetic codes, I have morals that were instilled by a strong woman with bags of determination and a good heart. Mother may be a narcissist but, regardless of how much she complains, she would always put Sharon and me first.

His behaviour promotes a different set of values that centre around the sole needs of Cameron MacDonald.

As I look out of the window at the streets of Clifton, I try and guess what brought him to live in New York's commuter belt. Sure, there will be anonymity, but he could find that wherever he went. His house, if it is his house, looked like a good one. I've no idea what house prices run to around these parts, but I'm guessing it'll be worth at least three times what I paid for my apartment.

Part of me is willing him to make the right decision; to save the life of a son he abandoned. Not just because it means my brother will get to live, but because it means that whatever relationship I have, or don't have with Cameron in the future, I'll know that for once in his life, he has stepped up and done the right thing for one of his children. I never had a proper father I could look up to – although Neill Boulder was everything a stepfather should be – so I would like my one association with Cameron MacDonald to be one I could think about with something akin to pride.

When he speaks, his voice wavers. 'How urgent is it that he gets the bone marrow?'

'He's got another three weeks. After that, he'll be flying back to Scotland so he can die with his wife and daughters at his bedside.'

Some people might consider mentioning John's wife and daughters to be a low blow. They can go screw themselves. I'm trying to persuade a selfish prick to save his son's life. I'll hit as low as I need to.

'You mean he's here? In the States?'

Cameron hasn't asked about John's daughters, which doesn't go unnoticed by me, but it's hardly a surprise. If he can abandon his own four children, he's not going to suddenly care about grandchildren he's never met.

'Yeah. When his rare blood type prevented any donors being found in the UK, he came looking for me and Sharon. With neither of us being a match, you're his last chance.'

'Jake, I want to help. Please believe me, I want to help.'

His tone is plaintive, almost pleading, I get what he's saying. More important, I get what he's not *asking*. Namely: how he can help and where he should go to give bone marrow or at least get tested.

The problem is, there's a but coming. I decide to wait him out; give him chance to ask how he can help.

'I'm sorry to have to say this, Jake.'

I feel Taylor's knee press against the back of my seat. She's probably warning me to proceed with caution. Warnings never did go down well with me.

'Say what? That you can't help him? Or that you'd rather your son died, than inconvenience yourself for a couple of days?'

'Dammit, boy. Don't you give me any of your snash. You make out like I should just drop everything and ride to his rescue. Things aren't that simple you know.'

The anger in his tone takes me aback for a moment, but I use the time to gather my wits and fire back at him in a low growl. 'Growing up without a father wasn't simple. Neither was trying not to expect him to come home at any minute. Listening to your mother cry herself to sleep every night, because your father had abandoned her, wasn't simple. Trying to work out if you had left because you hated us, wasn't simple.' I rest my hand on his leg and squeeze until he bats it away. 'My life hasn't been simple, but I got by. Tell me, what's so complicated that you're prepared to let your son die?'

Cameron begins to speak. His words sound foreign to my ears. What he's telling me, doesn't happen to people from Glasgow. Certainly not to people like him.

The sad thing is, what he's telling me is too far-fetched to be made up.

I turn and look at Taylor. I'm hoping for advice from her, but she stays silent. Her point is clear: the decision is mine. It's one I'll live and quite possibly die by.

It's not a choice I should have to make, yet there's no escaping the fact it is one I have been presented with.

To save my brother I have to help my father commit a crime. Not a small crime against a faceless corporation; a personal one against his employer. That there will be repercussions is a given.

The only saving grace is that his plan seems as if it will work, and it should allow him to drop off the radar.

'I'm in.'

A warm hand caresses my shoulder and I feel a brief squeeze of support.

I hide my sigh of relief. Apart from everything else I'm risking by agreeing to help Cameron, my relationship with Taylor may not have survived my decision.

Chapter 26

I want to cross-examine Cameron about the crime he wants me to help him commit, but instead I stay quiet. Sometimes knowing everything isn't a good idea. He's given me the broad strokes and that's enough.

That he is working as a double agent for two warring businessmen is all I need to know. The heist he's been tasked with seems simple enough on the surface. While nothing ever runs according to plan, I can't see any massive danger in what we're about to do.

In a lot of ways this heist is quite ingenious and, while I'd be the first to confess that my only experience of crime is in the novels I read, I believe we can get away with it. Once the job is done we'll be able to hop on a plane back to Casperton.

I want to send John a message, telling him we'll be there in a couple of days, but something makes me hold back. If I'm honest with myself, I think it's because I don't trust Cameron.

It's an odd sensation not trusting the person who sired you. I guess it's akin to having a spouse be unfaithful, or a sibling con you out of money. It's not a feeling I'm comfortable with, and part of me wants to point the finger of blame at myself for having unfounded suspicions.

Yes, he's let us all down in the past, but it's one thing walking out of your children's lives, and another thing condemning them to death. I guess, because I share his blood, I don't want him to be callous to the point of being uncaring.

When he opened the door, and I saw him for the first time since childhood, I got a glimpse of my future. I've no doubt the surprise in his eyes was reflected in mine.

On the rare occasions I've imagined what I'll look like in my sixties, the images I've conjured have been more or less what Cameron looks like now. Perhaps a little less stressed and with more of a twinkle in my eye, but still very much like him.

All I can hope is that the only things I've inherited from him are the MacDonald temper and his looks. The last thing I want to be, is as selfish as he is.

There have been times in my past when Mother's narcissistic ways have made his leaving understandable. What hasn't been easy to comprehend, is how he could leave two children who idolised him. I guess at some point over the next few days I'll sit down with him and pick at those scabs, but I'm determined to wait until he's saved John, before I start asking the kind of questions that could see Cameron walk out of my life for a second time.

I turn my mind away from thoughts I'm not yet ready to give voice to, and start paying more attention to where we're going. Or rather, where Cameron is taking us. So far as I can tell, we've travelled south, past the western edge of New York, and swung east. I see a sign for Staten Island, but Cameron has pulled into a lane that, according to the road markings, will take us to a place called Perth Amboy.

Cameron seems assured with his driving. He's not bothered to set the GPS and he's always in the right lane at the right time. It's a sure indicator that he's come this way on more than one occasion. This wouldn't concern me, were it not for the constant looks at his watch.

He's worried about the time, which means he's worried about how long it'll take until he can get on with his plan.

I get that a heist has to run to plan, and that timings will be a crucial part of said plan; I don't get why he's not driving a little faster. The traffic is light enough for us to add another five to ten mph to our speed without any trouble. He doesn't though, which rings alarm bells. I just need to listen to those bells and interpret their tune.

Chapter 27

The dealer is all smiles for Cameron as he rounds his art-deco desk. The rest of his office is styled the same way and, just like the dealer, it lacks any real personality beyond that necessary to make the sale.

'You have the deeds?'

'But of course. Can I get you anything: a coffee, something stronger?'

'Just the deeds, thank you.'

The dealer lifts a folder from his desk, opens it and hands the papers inside it to Cameron.

An old hand at legal documents, Cameron only takes a moment to pick out the salient points.

Number one: the deeds are in the name of the shell corporation he'd told the dealer to register his ownership in.

Number two: neither his real name nor the one he's been using in the US are on the documents.

Number three: the documents are a perfect match for the uncompleted ones in the briefcase resting in the trunk of his car.

'Very good.' Cameron gives a curt nod and makes for the door. 'Shall we?'

When he emerges, he sees Jake and the girl standing by his car. Jake looks pensive while the girl has a red tinge to her cheeks that he puts down to excitement. He guesses she's never so much as jaywalked before, so this experience will be a new one for her.

He might not know his son, but he's always been a good judge of character. What's more, Cameron is self-aware enough to see his own faults being reflected at him. He figures the girl may well be trying life with a bad boy.

If he can avoid Jake's notice for a while, maybe he'll see if the girl would like to try upgrading to a bad man.

Cameron resists the urge to keep checking his watch, as the dealer insists on showing them around the motorised yacht.

The two crew members he's hired are busy loading the yacht with the provisions from the trunk of his car.

His crew aren't the professional sailors you would normally find on a seven million dollar yacht, but they'll do for the short time he needs their services.

Cameron manages to get the dealer off the yacht, and is on the harbour wall helping to cast off the mooring ropes, when he hears a name he was planning to leave behind. His head snaps up and he sees three of his employer's enforcers.

They're not the top enforcers, but they are still vicious thugs who're surrounding him. Once upon a time, he'd have been confident against any two of them. Now, he's too old, too slow and too out of practice to make more than a token gesture of defence.

Chapter 28

I see the three men surrounding Cameron and know at once that something is wrong. It's not like I wasn't expecting trouble; instinct made sure the first thing I did when I got on the yacht was to find a vantage point where I could keep an eye on Cameron.

I dash towards the gangplank and run across it, trying not to picture myself falling into the water.

There's a definite menace about the men, so I slow to a brisk walk as I approach the nearest of them. He's got slicked-back hair, tied in a ponytail, and looks as if he should be directing bad porn movies. When he turns, he suggests I go away and multiply with myself.

He's trying to keep things private, but I see one of his buddies reaching into his suit jacket.

I decide to err on the side of caution and presume he's not going to pull out a pen and ask for my autograph.

He sees me halt, and draws his hand back a couple of inches. It's all the advantage I need.

By the time I've dashed the six paces between us, his hand has just got inside his jacket. To keep his gun away from me, I thrust my shoulder against his arm and barge him towards the water.

I drop to my knees at the last second and let him topple the twelve feet into the harbour.

As I spring to my feet, I hear the thud of knuckles on flesh behind me.

The wannabe porn director has a broken nose, but the other guy is raining blows towards Cameron. As he's the biggest threat, I go for him first.

I use the distraction of him beating on Cameron, to get behind him where I can bury a fist into each of his kidneys. First right, then left.

He drops to one knee and gasps in pain. Long term, repeated blows to the kidneys can cause damage but, after a few days of pissing blood, this guy will recover.

His buddy pulls a knife and uses the back of his free hand to wipe away the blood that's dripping from his chin.

I step between him and Cameron.

'Get the yacht ready; now!' I push Cameron towards the gangplank while keeping my eyes on the guy with the knife.

He's twisting his arm at the wrist as he waves the knife around. His grip is assured and his eyes are filled with confidence.

'Leave now, buddy, and you won't get hurt.'

I shake my head. 'That's not gonna happen. Why don't *you* leave? I've already taken care of your friends. That knife isn't going to stop me taking care of you.'

He lunges forward. Fast.

The knife flashes across where my stomach had been a second earlier, then he follows up the move with a backhand slash towards my head.

His eyes gave away his intentions, but it's still too close for comfort. I don't even have time to counterpunch.

He smiles at me and reveals a missing tooth. He's confident that he's got the better of me.

I feint a step forward and dance back as he repeats his earlier move.

When his knife arm passes me on his backhand stroke, I pounce.

My left hand grabs his right wrist, preventing him from using the knife on me, as I use my right hand to grab his collar and drag his face towards my thrusting forehead. If his nose wasn't already broken by Cameron's punch, it will be now.

I lift a knee to his groin and give a vicious twist on his knife arm. In his beat-up state he drops the knife.

A blow to the temple drops him.

Five seconds later his knife plops into the dark harbour water, and I'm yelling at Cameron to set sail.

Chapter 29

Cameron watches as Jake bounds up the gangplank. As soon as his son's feet hit the deck, he barges the crew member away from the controls and rams the throttle against its stops.

The motor yacht gives a deep roar as its engine reaches maximum output. The stern settles lower in the water, and after a minute they're speeding through the harbour at a gathering pace.

What happened on the dock is way too close a call for his liking. His employer must have been watching their bank account. That spoke of distrust.

It's now imperative that they put as much distance as possible between themselves and New York. There will be a pursuit, that's for sure. So long as he can get out of their sight for a few hours, his plan will still work.

A small sailing boat is crossing the harbour, and its path means a collision, but Cameron is in too much of a hurry to slow down. Instead, he waits until the last moment and spins the wheel over, so his yacht rockets between the stern of the sailboat and the side of a pleasure cruiser that is taking tourists on a sightseeing trip. The wash from his yacht rocks the sailboat, and threatens to swamp or capsize the small vessel, but Cameron doesn't care. All that's on his mind, is getting the yacht out of the harbour and over the horizon.

Jake appears at his elbow. He's wrestling with a life preserver, but Cameron knows that the struggle he's having with the straps, isn't responsible for the anger in his eyes. If his assessment about his son is right, he'll be demanding better answers than the lies he's been told so far.

The lie he'd spun Jake earlier hadn't been one of his best, but Cameron put it down to being in a state of shock. He was used to having his life planned out in great detail. Surprises don't happen when you anticipate everything, and he'd long given up expecting one of his children to track him down. That one had found him, and brought news of another's dire need, had been unforeseeable.

Still, it had rocked him, stolen his usual composure and delayed him long enough for his employer's men to arrive at the dock before he'd set sail. He knew his employer must have been either suspicious or contacted by the dealer. He guesses the former. Had the dealer contacted his employer, the enforcers would have shown up at his home or would have been waiting for him on the yacht.

Once he's passed the north part of Sandy Hook, Cameron allows the crew member to take back the controls. The guy looks pissed about being shoved out of the way, but Cameron knows he won't press the issue. His crew are being well paid for a couple of days' work and will tolerate whatever he decides to throw at them.

Cameron turns and sees that Jake has got the life preserver fastened, and is watching him with a look that's part anger, part bewilderment, and part assessment. He knows his son is re-evaluating him and is keen to learn the truth.

'Not now, Jake. We can talk once we get clear, but now isn't the time.'

He catches the nod his son throws his way; knows that if Jake is as smart as he thinks he is, it would be wise to speak to him before he works out for himself what's going on.

Cameron turns and scans the sea in front of them. The waves are kicking up now and, free of the calm waters of the harbour and the bay, the yacht is beginning to pitch and yaw as it crests waves at an oblique angle. So far, it's nothing the yacht can't handle, but it was designed to be a rich man's plaything rather than an oceangoing racer. If the swells get larger, they'll have to slow to a more sensible pace.

He casts a look back at the bay, squints, and lets out a low curse. The motor boat coming out of the bay is sleek and nimble, and travelling like the person at its helm is trying to beat a world record.

There's no doubt in his mind that it's being piloted by one of the enforcers.

Chapter 30

I watch as the motorboat powers alongside us. Since its arrival from the bay, Cameron has been hidden below decks. So far as I am concerned, it's the best place for him.

The breakneck race from the harbour and out through the bay would have been exhilarating, had it not been for the whirl of nasty ideas forming in my head. Most of these ideas involve me falling from the boat and being swallowed up by the murky depths of the water. Sometimes, to add a neat twist to the horrors of drowning, I'd imagine a many-toothed sea creature eating me, as the water forced its way into my lungs.

The worst ideas though, are the ones about my father; they're all about betrayal, double-crossing and manipulation. The stealing of this yacht is no more to do with settling a debt than his lies which brought Taylor and me with him.

Guys with guns don't attack you on a harbour wall over a dispute between rival companies; unless those companies are the non-legitimate kind.

This is the second time in as many days that I've gotten myself mixed up in something that concerns organised crime. I'm big enough to look after myself and make my own decisions; it's Taylor who worries me. She's been stoic and has kept a brave face, but I can tell she's scared witless by the events at the harbour.

If I thought it would be safer for her, I'd insist she be dropped off at the nearest port or harbour, but there's every likelihood she would be picked up by their accomplices.

The motorboat coming after us is another worry. It may be some rich guy playing with his toy, or it may be the coast guard coming to reprimand Cameron for his mad dash through the bay, but deep inside I know that both of these ideas are nothing more than wishful thinking.

Even as the motor yacht rolls its way through the swells, the motorboat is barrelling forward, cresting waves and slamming down into troughs. The roiling of my stomach is a mixture of the boat's gyrations and the sense of impending doom as the motorboat narrows the gap.

It catches up and rolls alongside us, fifty or so yards away, close enough for its crew to communicate that they want us to stop.

Of the four men aboard the motorboat, I recognise two from the harbour wall. They don't look like there's much fight left in them, but the other two are fresh.

In this situation, freshness doesn't matter. There's four of them and, counting my father and the two crewmen, there's four of us on this yacht.

This wouldn't be a problem, as I'm confident I could soon get the odds firmly in our favour, were it not for one little fact.

Each of the four men have guns.

Granted, the guns are pistols, which means they are all but useless at fifty yards. Doubly so when they are shooting at a moving target from an unstable platform.

They don't need to shoot us though. All they have to do is force us to stop, or follow us until we do.

I have no idea how far the fuel in our tanks will carry us, but it's a moot point. If they are representing organised crime they will have the resources to summon help. They'll be able to get another boat to take over from them when their tanks threaten to run dry.

That's not something we can do. We have to keep moving and somehow evade them at a dock or harbour somewhere.

The sound of the engine throttling back makes me look towards the bridge. The crewman at the yacht's controls has raised his hands above his head and is making sure the four gunmen know he's being compliant.

I can't blame him for his actions. To the best of my knowledge, he owes Cameron no loyalty other than a fair day's work for a fair day's pay.

It's not the crewman's place to risk his life.

Me, on the other hand; I've beaten up two of them and dumped their buddy in the harbour. If they get on the yacht, I don't think they'll be asking my name so I can be added to their Christmas card list. It's much more likely I'll receive a severe beating, or a bullet in the brain.

With nothing to lose, I dash towards the bridge as the motorboat closes the gap between us.

I'm four paces from the yacht's controls when I hear a shout.

What I see when I look back is the last thing I'm expecting.

Chapter 31

Cameron has a submachine gun in his hands. There's a yell from the other boat that is drowned out by the deafening chatter as Cameron opens fire.

All four men dive for cover but there aren't many places for them to hide.

Splinters of wood and fibreglass fly from the motorboat, as Cameron empties the entire clip at them. I don't see any of the rounds strike flesh, but that doesn't mean much. The sea breeze carries wisps of smoke past me and I get the unfamiliar smell of cordite.

There's another short burst of noise from the submachine gun as Cameron empties a second clip at the motorboat and its occupants, although as far as I can judge, he still hasn't managed to hit any of the men. There's no attempt to return the gunfire, perhaps they know they're out-gunned. Or maybe, just maybe, they have no intention of pulling their triggers.

The person trying to control the motorboat is spinning the wheel – as am I, on the yacht – and within a few seconds we've pointed our sterns at each other. I push the throttles as far forward as they'll go.

Another option is that they have orders to deliver Cameron to his employer, so he can either witness or carry out whatever punishment he deems appropriate for Cameron's deceit.

After a minute or so, the motorboat turns and hangs a couple of hundred yards behind us.

I count four men standing at the back of the motorboat, and reason that Cameron's ability to surprise is far superior to his aim.

The guys in the motorboat have wisely decided that surveillance is the most prudent course for them.

Cameron producing the submachine gun has raised more questions in my mind. On the one hand he repelled the boarders and possibly saved all our lives; on the other, the father I've known for less than four hours has turned out to be a gun-toting thief who's mixed up in organised crime.

It does, however, explain why he didn't break any speed limits on our way to the harbour. Had he been stopped, and the submachine gun found in the trunk of his car, his plan would have surely failed.

'Here, you take the wheel.' I wave the nearest crewman forward. He looks nervous, but I smile at him. 'Don't worry. They won't come back anytime soon.'

He swallows the bull I'm feeding him and takes control of the boat. 'Where are we going?'

'South,' Cameron's voice booms from the rear of the bridge. 'Stay far enough out to sea to keep the coast out of sight. Our fuel tanks are full. They'll run out long before we do.'

I'd marvel at his confidence were I not dumbfounded by his behaviour.

I walk over to him. 'It's time we talked, you and me. I'd like to know what's really going on, where we're headed and why a sixty-year-old man is auditioning for the next Rambo movie.'

Chapter 32

Cameron is sitting on a chair in the rear deck area. His legs are crossed and there is a relaxed quality to his posture.

Like so many things about him, it's a lie. There's a tremor in his hands and the submachine gun rests on the table beside two spare clips.

'Well?' I glare at him for a moment and continue speaking. 'Are you going to tell me what's going on, or will I just turn the wheel and head for shore?'

He gives a knowing smile that doesn't so much as threaten to touch his eyes. He's faker than a five-buck Rolex and can't be trusted on any level.

I decline the bottle of beer he tries to hand me. 'Talk.'

'What do you want me to say?' There's a smugness to his voice. He holds all the cards and he knows it. I need him way more than he needs me, and it's obvious he's going to milk the situation like it's a prize cow.

'This yacht. Who does it belong to?'

'A company I own. It's all legal and above board.' He shrugs. 'I just got someone else to pay for it, that's all.'

'Who?'

He shakes his head. 'That doesn't concern you. All you need to know, is the bozos in that boat,' he uses the submachine gun to point at the motorboat, 'represent the person whose money bought this boat.'

'Would I be right in saying that the person whose money bought this boat may be a tad displeased with you using their money?'

'I think it's fair to say that he'd be displeased to death.' A nonchalant shrug. 'My death of course.' Another shrug. 'And the death of anyone who's with me.'

His lack of concern is pissing me off, and intriguing me. Like a grandmaster playing chess against an amateur, he's many steps ahead of me.

I need to fight him at his level, not mine. I lean against the rail and stare at the motorboat while I think things over.

When I turn to face Cameron, he's looking at me with curiosity, trying to assess what I've figured out.

I gesture at the motorboat. 'You're not worried about those guys, which tells me you have a plan. The fact you had a gun indicates forward planning. Your gun being bigger and better than theirs, means you had foreknowledge of your opponents.'

He gives a nod to validate what I'm saying, and rolls his hand for me to continue.

I watch the motorboat for a minute, but I don't really see it, as I'm composing my thoughts.

'The boat that's following us doesn't worry you. I'll credit you with enough brains to know they'll be calling for reinforcements. That could be anything from a boat with a sniper on board to a helicopter. Yet you're still looking calm. This tells me you have a plan to deal with whatever, or whoever comes our way.'

Another nod. 'What time is it, Jake?'

I take a look at my watch. 'Twenty after seven.'

Cameron doesn't speak. He just raises an eyebrow and waits for me to work things out for myself.

I give my watch another glance and cast my gaze around. When I notice there is less light on three sides of us, I realise his plan. He intends to wait until dark and use its cover to escape from our pursuers.

I look at the sky and see a thick cloud cover; the kind of clouds that threaten rain and hide moonlight. Both welcome qualities.

'So, once we've gotten away from these guys, what's your plan?'

A smug look appears on his face. 'I sell the boat. We do what needs to be done for your brother, and we go our separate ways.'

'You make it sound simple.' I tap my toes on the deck. 'I've no idea what this yacht is worth, but I'll be surprised if it's less than a few million. Who has the money to buy such a thing with cash?'

'Everything in life is simple provided you do the necessary planning. I know of twenty boat dealers who would be able to buy this boat without having to check that their account has the necessary funds. Especially if I make the price appealing. I paid seven for it; I'll take five and a half.'

Something about Cameron has changed. He's stopped showing his usual signs of deceit. I figure he's now trying to impress me with his cleverness, and his newfound wealth.

Money has never held much sway for me and, while I appreciate intelligence, unless Cameron can find a cure for cancer, end worldwide famine, and put an end to all wars, he's never going to be my favourite person.

'It's time.' Cameron stands and heads for the stairway towards the bridge.

It's his way of telling me our conversation is over and, in a way, I'm glad – despite still having unanswered questions. I have some thinking to do, and I want to find Taylor and make sure she's okay.

Chapter 33

For the first time since boarding the yacht, I notice its plushness. Every surface is polished to a glimmering sheen and there is little that doesn't suggest extravagant opulence. Cameron said he had paid seven million bucks for it second-hand, but it's a fair bet it was worth twice that brand new.

When I find Taylor, she's huddled between two cream leather sofas. She hears my voice and lifts her head.

'God, Jake. I heard the gunfire and I was so scared. I thought you'd get shot and the man with the gun would come for me.'

I bite down on a flippant remark before it passes my lips. The rush of adrenaline I felt when it kicked off has left me keyed up, but I can tell Taylor needs reassurance rather than wisecracks.

'Don't worry. Cameron has a plan and it's a good one.'

While my words may be factually correct, I can't help feeling that Cameron has overlooked something, or will be caught out by a counter to one of his strategies.

Taylor hugs me and nestles her head against my chest. The gesture is for reassurance, not romance, so I keep my breathing level and hope that if she can feel or hear my heartbeat, it's now back to somewhere near its usual rhythm.

I've left the cabin door open ready to react should I need to. When nothing happens but the disappearing of the coast, Taylor and I watch as dusk turns to night and the sky darkens towards black.

There are a few slow drops of rain that become heavier and thicker until they form a proper downpour.

Despite knowing I'll get a soaking, I venture outside for a quick look around. Cameron is hunched beside the guy by the wheel and he's urging him to go faster.

I'm not sure this is the best idea: not only are the waves increasing in size, we're also running without any lights in near zero visibility. This has disaster written all over it.

I keep my reservations to myself. It may not be the safest way to travel but the Atlantic Ocean is a big place, and the odds of us colliding with another vessel are slim.

The presence of what looks like some kind of radar on the yacht's bridge is reassuring; as is the fact that, no matter how hard I peer into the rain-drenched gloom behind the stern, I cannot see even the merest sign of the motorboat.

My fears subsiding, I retreat to the cabin and re-join Taylor. Her face is more relaxed although I can tell she's still walking the tightrope between composure and emotional collapse.

'Jake?'

'Yes?' I return the serious look she's giving me.

'Did you mean what you said last night? I know they say a drunk man speaks the truth, but I also know that you need to come to things in your own time.'

I rack my brains and try to recall the conversations we had. I remember her railing on me for getting drunk and for fighting; I also have memories of us sitting side-by-side on the bed, me talking to her as I clasped her hands in mine.

It's no good. I can't remember what she's talking about, which leaves me with two options. Number one is to lie, and number two is to admit that I was so out of it I can't remember what I said.

I try to think of a third option but I strike a blank. Option one has to be out as I am not a liar and I don't know what I said to her. In my befuddled state I could have said anything from "we're finished" to "will you marry me". Telling Taylor I meant what I said isn't something I can do until I *know* what I said.

She gives one of her gentle smiles. 'You don't remember, do you?'

I shake my head.

Her smile broadens and lights her eyes. This is why I love her: she's so forgiving, wonderful, and most of all, she gets who I am and allows me to be me.

This realisation brings a memory with it. Last night, for the first time in my life, I looked into a girl's eyes and told her that I love her.

Granted, the moment should have come after a romantic moonlit walk, over dessert in a swish restaurant, or perhaps when we're goofing around enjoying each other's company. Not when I'm only halfway coherent and stinking of whisky.

My eyes fall to the floor in shame, but Taylor is better than that. She lifts my chin. 'I can see you remember now.' She smiles. 'For the record, I love you too.'

'I'm sorry, Taylor.' I look into her eyes. 'You deserved for me to say it sober, but it's true. I do love you.'

The kiss she gives me is long and deep; it suggests more than forgiveness to me. I feel a stirring in my loins as Taylor presses her body against mine. I've heard about the effect that exposure to danger can have on some women, but this is the first time I've experienced it.

She pushes me onto a couch, walks to the door and locks it, a hungry expression in her eyes.

Chapter 34

Banging on the cabin door wakes me. After a quick check to make sure Taylor's decent, I unlock the door to be confronted by Cameron. If the set to his jaw is anything to go by, he's not in the best of moods.

His eyes flicker around the cabin and he gives a snort. 'So, while we spend all night out there, you're in here getting laid.'

I square up to him and meet his gaze with enough ferocity to see his anger and raise him a psychotic rage.

'You are the one who decided to rip off a criminal gang. You are the one who stands to walk away with more than five million dollars. You are also the one who's lied to, manipulated and used every other person on board this yacht. Forgive me if I don't work myself to death on your behalf.'

Cameron moves forward until our noses are less than an inch apart. There's no way I'm going to back away, but there aren't many people I'd allow to invade my personal space like this. If I didn't need him to save my brother's life, and if I didn't respect the fact he is my father, despite not respecting him as a man, I'd make him bloody and horizontal.

'I don't give a rat's ass what you have to say. I need you topside. There's work to be done and the sooner it's done, the sooner we can get back to dry land. You'd like that, wouldn't you?'

I hate the fact that he's not only making sense, but that he's cottoned on to my biggest fear: drowning.

I can swim, but it's not what anyone would call graceful or balletic. Like a kid in water-wings, I make a lot of effort, and splash a great deal of water, without making any significant forward motion. Only once in my life have I been out of my depth in water and I still have nightmares about it.

I pull on my life preserver and head out to see what he wants done. A look at the morning sun tells me we're now heading north rather than south. It's a simple deception that might or might not work.

Both crewmen are on deck, along with an array of packages and a selection of tools, and the sun has burned away last night's rainclouds.

Cameron passes me a cordless drill with a screwdriver bit, and a few of the packages. 'Go and change these. Toss the old ones overboard.'

Each of the brown paper-wrapped packages bears a shipboard location, handwritten in thick black ink.

I go to the bridge and unwrap the first one. It's a nameplate, the same size as the one screwed to the central console.

Less than five minutes later, Lady Ursula has become Dunsettlin. Well, on the bridge at least.

As I work my way around the boat, replacing nameplates, I have to fight not to smile at Cameron's choice of name. Dunsettlin is the kitsch name that people give to houses back in Scotland. Dunroamin was a popular one for those who'd tired of frequent relocating.

It also shows his inner humour. In his own way, he's flipping the bird at the people he's ripping off. Socking it to them with a dry joke at how he's no longer prepared to settle for the scraps they toss his way.

I'd let myself smile were it not for the fact I share his humour and, therefore, I recognise that I'm more like him than I want to be.

As I make my way around the yacht, I see that Cameron is directing the crewmen as they complete another task.

Both crewmen are in a life-raft and they're working at the stern of the yacht as it bobs on the waves.

Cameron passes the men a couple of spray paint canisters, and I hear the hiss of escaping paint a moment later. A large cardboard tube is wedged between Cameron's feet, and I presume it's a premade sticker to replace the now painted-over Lady Ursula.

The people Cameron has stolen from will be on the lookout for Lady Ursula being sold. By changing the name, Cameron has at least bought some time to get away from anyone who may be pursuing him. Who knows, he may never be traced.

It takes me an hour to locate and replace all the nameplates. When I'm finished, I join Taylor on the rear deck and watch as the crewmen complete their task at the yacht's stern.

Chapter 35

It's early afternoon when we sight land. I have no idea where we are until one of the crewmen shows me a map and points to our destination.

Cameron's plan appears to be working as there is no sign of any pursuit. He looks more relaxed after grabbing a few hours' sleep in the stateroom. His demeanour is one of confidence and there's a certain smugness about his face.

His phone has been pressed to his ear throughout the day and, although I've never heard what he's said, his expression has always suggested that the calls were important.

He joins Taylor and me on the rear deck and offers us a bottle of beer. I refuse mine, but Taylor takes one and rolls it across her forehead before taking a sip.

'I've got someone meeting us at a marina. He's interested in buying the boat.'

I don't answer him. I'll be glad to get my feet back on terra firma, but something is nagging me; there's something going on and I can't yet identify what it is or who's behind it. All I know is that I'm not happy with the setup.

For me, Osterville, on the peninsula that forms Cape Cod, is too near New York for comfort. Had we travelled down the coast to Florida, I would have been more confident that our docking would be a safe affair.

To my mind, trying to sell the boat only a few hours' drive from NYC is foolish. Yes, there's a lot to be said for double bluffs, and doing what your opponent least expects, but there's also the fact that he used to work for the people he's stolen from, therefore they'll know what a tricky, contrary person he is. They'll expect him to do the unexpected and will ensure that his unpredictability plays into their hands.

The yacht putters its way through an opening between two headlands and into a calm bay. We continue past various yachts, sailboats and other boats, before a stilling of the engine signals that the yacht is preparing to dock.

There's a marina, and the crewman manoeuvres the yacht until its bow is swinging away from the floating pontoons that comprise the dock. The deck vibrates beneath my feet as the crewman puts the boat into reverse and starts edging the yacht towards the pontoons.

Taylor touches my arm. 'You're quiet. What are you thinking?'

I don't answer. My eyes are scanning everywhere and there's a sense of foreboding that is dominating my thoughts. Something is wrong here.

I look around the marina. The car park is empty; there isn't a single person working on a boat, ferrying supplies back and forth, or doing any of the other things you'd expect. Other than the seagulls, I can't see another living creature.

I look at the bar and restaurant building next. With so many yachts and pleasure craft moored here, the bar and restaurant should be booming. It looks closed.

Something moves on the roof of the building. It's a human shape and is holding a long, thin item. It could be a worker hiding on the roof with a mop, but I don't think so.

'Ambush.' My yell startles everyone on the yacht, but I'm not worried about hurt feelings. I point at the man piloting it. 'Get us out of here. Fast!'

He leans on the throttle lever but the yacht is a pleasure craft, not a racer, and despite getting full power, it reacts with the kind of sluggishness you'd expect from a vehicle this size.

There's a crack, and a hole appears in the bridge's windshield. Cameron and Taylor are on the exposed rear deck, while the two crewmen show their loyalty to Cameron and jump overboard.

I'd do the same myself were it not for the girl I love and the brother I'm trying to save.

With nobody at the helm, the yacht will crash into another boat before it has gone two hundred yards. I give myself a mental crossing and dive for the helm. I'm trying to make myself as small a target as possible, when I hear another crack of rifle fire.

Not feeling any pain, or being aware of the bullet striking anywhere near me, I turn and look to the others. Cameron is backing away towards the cabin but, like the coward he is, he's using Taylor as a shield.

His arm circles her chest and he's keeping his body behind hers.

I forget all about steering the craft and leap over the rail so I can separate them and get her into the safety of the cabin.

My feet land with a thud and I roll towards them but, as I'm straightening my legs, I hear another crack.

This one is followed a millisecond later by a dull *thunk* that snaps Taylor's head back, over Cameron's shoulder.

A mess of red and grey splatters the side of his face and the bulkhead.

Cameron drops Taylor at his feet and dives into the cabin.

As much as I want to follow him, and punch him until my hands are raw and broken and his head is a squashed pulp, I know what my priority is.

The man with the rifle will just train his gun on the cabin door, and wait for us to emerge while his buddies close in on us.

I scramble up the stairs and take control of the yacht as another bullet smacks into the windshield.

I keep myself as low as I can as I twist the wheel left and right to make sure the gunman's opportunities to score another kill are as limited as possible.

Once we're away from danger, I'll deal with Cameron.

Chapter 36

There are three more cracks and three slaps, as bullets crash through the windshield or into the timber deck.

I chance a look back, see the sniper on the roof has raised his rifle, and surmise that he's given up. From nowhere, a bunch of shapes are running towards the pontoons. I figure they mean to steal another boat and follow us.

That won't do them a whole lot of good. Not with what I have in mind.

Cameron's actions have turned my veins into glaciers. To say I feel murderous is an understatement.

Despite my anger, and the urge to go down into the cabin and beat my father to death, I have a cold, dispassionate part of my brain, and this is controlling my actions and working out ways to survive.

As furious as I am with Cameron, I know that killing him will sentence John to death. Even in my fury, I still have enough control not to submit to base emotions. There will come a time of reckoning between me and Cameron, but it cannot happen until John's transfusion has gone ahead.

With the yacht on a course that'll keep it free from any possible collisions, I clatter down the stairs and go to the cabin. The door is locked but I'm long past the point of caring about the yacht's resale value.

My foot crashes against the lock side and it splinters inwards. A second kick sees it swing open.

'You.' I point a finger at Cameron. 'Get to the bridge now. Things have changed. I'm in charge now.' My tone doesn't leave room for argument, and he's wise enough to do as he's told.

I grab my backpack and return to the bridge.

I cannot bear to look at Taylor.

It's bad enough seeing bits of her smeared across Cameron's face, without looking at her ruined beauty for a second time.

When Cameron joins me on the bridge, I hold out my hand. 'Cell.'

He hesitates, so I double him over with a powerful gut punch and pluck it from his pocket. It's sailing over the rail before he's finished his second gasp. The punch felt good to me. Too good in fact. It is all I can do not to give in to the desire to throw a few more. Say, a million or two; that might be enough to sate my need for revenge.

I put my own phone to my ear and connect with Alfonse. I give him Cameron's cell number and tell him to do a trace on anyone who's been tracking it. He goes quiet when I ask him to make sure he can't be tracked himself. I want to tell him about what has happened to Taylor, but I can't bring myself to say the words. Acknowledging her death will make it real and definite.

Deep inside, I know she really is dead, it's just I can't yet bring myself to believe it.

I cut the call and turn to Cameron. 'You have one minute to get anything you think we may need, and then we're leaving this boat.'

His face goes ashen as he realises that I'm serious. He's not going to get the windfall he was hoping for.

Cameron nods as he faces up to his new reality. There are now finger trails running through the remnants of Taylor on his face. It's obvious he's disgusted by the gore and has tried to scrape it from his cheek. The sight offends me as much as him, so I toss him a rag. 'Clean your face. I don't want you touching her ever again.'

He ducks away. The sniper attack has shaken him. He's been outclassed and his plans have turned to crap. I'm his best chance of survival and, as much as I'm furious with him, he knows that, for John's sake, I won't kill him.

As I plan a way to get us off the boat without getting shot, I'm thinking ahead: analysing the ways our pursuers can track us, and how to evade any traps they might set.

I'm not just thinking about the next few hours, I'm thinking about tomorrow and the days after that.

John needs Cameron to be in Casperton. As soon as I can find a way to lose our tail, I can then begin to consider how to get Cameron to the hospital.

The only thing I'm certain of is that Cameron cannot be trusted not to disappear the second I stop watching his every move.

A second thought dominates my mind. One of vengeance and violence; retribution and revenge.

Once I get Cameron to Casperton I will act upon my second thought.

My fingers grip the yacht's wheel until they turn white, as I imagine myself killing the man responsible for Taylor's death.

I make a vow to myself that Taylor will be avenged, or I will die in the attempt.

'Cameron?' His head snaps towards me. 'Hold on. Things are about to get bumpy.'

Chapter 37

Cameron sees what Jake is planning and grips the rail surrounding the rear deck with both hands. What his son is doing will cost him millions of dollars, but right now he doesn't care. With his plan ruined, the only thing on his agenda is staying alive.

It's a shame the girl died. That wasn't part of his calculations. He hadn't expected the sniper to fire at him when he was shielded by an innocent. Still, better her than him.

Cameron knows that Jake will blame him for the girl's death, due to the way he'd used her, rather than the man who had pulled the trigger. The look in his eyes had been murderous, but the fact that Cameron's bone marrow is needed for John was enough to save his life.

That will continue to save him until he can slip away from Jake and start a new life again. Money will be tight to begin with, but he'll find a way. He always does.

Cameron knows he should feel guilty about abandoning John to his fate, but really, he thinks it's a bit rich – only looking him up when they need something from him.

He left both of his families behind for a reason. The same reason each time: they suffocated him; made demands on his time that he wasn't prepared to give. Sure, reading a story to a pyjama-clad child is endearing. But only if you do it once in a while. To do it twice and thrice a day is monotonous and stultifying. Doubly so when it's the same story, night after night.

His ex-wives were no better, with their nagging about the lawns that needed cutting, or the shelves they wanted erecting.

On and on they'd droned until he'd lost sight of the thing that had attracted him to them in the first place.

The yacht falls silent as Jake cuts the engines and lets momentum carry them into the shore.

Cameron braces himself and only just manages to stop himself from being thrown forward, as the bow digs into the soft sand, ten yards from shore.

The yacht's momentum carries it a few yards further before it grinds to a complete halt and then slowly, it lists twenty degrees onto its starboard side.

Cameron goes to the front of the boat and looks down. It's ten feet from the rail to the waves lapping on the beach. The water is perhaps a foot or two deep, which means a five foot drop if he hangs from the deck.

It's doable. The water and sand will cushion his blow and prevent him from breaking any bones.

He looks at Jake.

His son has gone to the rear deck and is kneeling by the girl's body. It's the perfect chance for him to get away.

Cameron slides his body over the lip of the deck and hangs by his fingertips for the briefest of moments before letting go.

Chapter 38

I crouch beside Taylor's body and take a last look at her. Were it not for the hole that has shattered her right cheek, she could be mistaken for being asleep.

As I bend forward to kiss her lips, I reaffirm my earlier vow to seek out the person who ended her life. Not just the person who pulled the trigger, but the man who put the gun in his hands and money in his pocket.

I hear a splash and turn my head.

There's no sign of Cameron so I give Taylor's forehead a kiss, and dash to the bow as best I can on the tilted deck.

I see Cameron; he's forging his way up the beach towards the many trees that shield rich men's houses from prying eyes.

He's not looking back, or even making a pretence of waiting for me.

I'm neither surprised nor disappointed. All his escape attempt has done is confirm my fears that he will dump me at the first opportunity.

I grab my backpack, stride back from the rail, take three quick steps and throw myself forward, hurdling the rail before gravity takes hold of me.

I land in a foot of water and manage to stagger forward until I stumble into an ungainly roll at the edge of the water.

In less than a second I'm back on my feet and chasing after Cameron.

When I reach him, he's trying to pull himself over a six-foot wall. I'd throw a punch or two as retribution, but I need him to be both compliant and fit to move without being carried. Laying him out will only add to my problems. Plus, there's the issue of him turning up at the hospital with obvious signs of a beating. Should I give him a black eye or two, the doctors may well decide he's being coerced into donating the bone marrow, and refuse to do the transfusion.

As much as it galls me to keep my hands off him, I know that I must, for John's sake.

Cameron sees me and jerks his head. 'Good. You've caught up.'

Had I not seen him use my girlfriend as a shield, I might have bought his comment, but I let it wash over me rather than waste time and energy challenging him on it. We need to get out of here before the guys with guns either storm up the beach, or circle round and get to us from the land side.

There's a guy cleaning a pool. He's engrossed in his task and has the ubiquitous leads trailing from his ears. It's the first bit of luck we've had since getting on that damned yacht.

I lead Cameron through the heavy bushes and skirt behind the pool guy. The house is large and expensive, and there's little doubt that the pool guy's truck will be sitting out front.

Rather than take the home owner's car, and risk it being fitted with a tracker, I plan to steal the pool guy's truck. I don't need it for long and don't plan to damage it in any way. I'll even leave him a few bucks for gas if we travel far.

As I anticipated, he's been kind enough to leave his keys in the ignition.

What little luck we've had, runs out when I see there are huge wrought iron gates barring our exit from the house's grounds. As I stop in front of them, they open with a subdued whine.

I glance to my side and see what must be a sensor, disguised as one of the rocks lining the driveway.

Two minutes later I'm powering along the road as fast as I dare go without attracting too much attention.

Cameron is silent in the passenger seat, but he can do as he pleases as far as I'm concerned. I've no doubt that he's plotting his next move. I know I'm planning mine.

'Did you bring your gun from the yacht?'

'Of course.'

'Next time we go over a bridge, toss it into the water.'

'No way. I'm keeping it.' His jaw sets in determination. 'It's saved us once and may save us again.'

'Agreed. But it may well condemn us.'

'How?'

I can't believe he hasn't figured this out himself. He's obviously good with pre-planned situations, but is unable to react, or think on his feet when the need arises. I'm the opposite; I don't ever plan too far ahead and tend to go with what seems right in the moment.

'If we get pulled by the police and they find that gun, we're done for.'

I choose not to mention the papers in my backpack. They are nothing more than another complication, should we find ourselves talking to the police.

Another thing I don't mention is how I don't trust him not to pull the gun on me.

'I have a permit for it.'

'Maybe you do.' I take my eyes off the road for a second to look at him. 'What do you think the police will want to talk about when they find that gun on you? When they get our fingerprints from the yacht we've just left? You know, the one with my girlfriend on it; you must remember her? She's the one who caught the bullet intended for you.' I make no effort to hide the resentment and anger in my voice.

He scowls at me, but even as he's scowling he's nodding his head.

There are still a lot of points to consider. The first being that the people we're up against have resources, enough manpower to scramble a team to be ready for us when we docked, and no fear of killing.

As soon as we were free of the ambush, I realised that the only way they could have tracked us was Cameron's phone. The same thing will be true for his credit and debit cards.

For the time being I reckon I'm clean, but it's only a matter of time before they find out who I am. This gives me a window of opportunity.

I hand Cameron my cell and tell him to bring up our location on the maps app. I need to know where we are, so I can plan our next move.

We need to draw as much money from our banks as possible. My account is pretty much empty and I'm against using our cards as they'll leave a trail.

Cameron shows me the screen and I see the nearest town in the direction we're travelling is East Falmouth.

It will have a bank and so far, that's all we need.

When we have some money we can hole up in a motel, while I try to figure out a way of getting us back to Casperton.

Chapter 39

As we're driving through Mashpee on our way to East Falmouth, Cameron points at a building I've missed due to a suburban that was threatening to cut me up.

I glance at where he's pointing and see a bank. There's an ATM beside it.

I swing the wheel over and park fifty yards from the bank. Cameron has the door open and is about to climb out when I grab his arm. 'Not so fast. I'll get money here. As soon as your card goes into one of those machines, it's at risk of being traced.'

Alfonse answers my call on the first ring. He tries to speak but I cut across him. 'Listen, don't talk. Put a thousand bucks in my account and find me a place where I can rent a car in the nearest place to Mashpee. I think it's on Cape Cod, but I'm not sure. Let me know when you have done each task. Move quick, Alfonse. We're quite literally on the run from bad guys.'

I hear the low whistle from him before I end the call. Two minutes later I insert my card and check my balance. It's up by a thousand bucks.

My card limit is set at three hundred dollars a day. I could get it raised but it's wiser for me not to. On the rare occasions I drink, I tend to burn through money, so the less I have access to, the better.

Rather than raise suspicions by walking into the bank and withdrawing all the money that's just appeared in my account, I use the ATM to get my daily allowance.

Cameron goes to do the same, but again I stop him. His card will be used to hire a car. The blandest, least conspicuous car it's possible to rent. The car we get will blend in with all the other similar models on the road.

Life in Mashpee is moving with the gentle pace of a retirement village, or perhaps a vacation destination. Nobody has any sense of urgency and people are travelling around in languid fashion as they potter about their business.

Alfonse delivers the details for the nearest car rental place and as soon as I read his email I know what to do.

The guy behind the counter at the Enterprise branch hardly gives us a second glance. His attention is focussed on the red-haired, fish-lipped secretary who's using one hand to hold a phone and the other to twirl her hair.

The car we get is nothing special, but that's perfect. We're trying to hide, not draw attention to ourselves.

Chapter 40

The Bourne Bridge spanning the river, or canal, has arched metal framework. Instinct makes me want to speed across it, but I play it cool and drive slow enough for Cameron to launch his submachine gun into the crisp blue water.

The map on my cell had shown there were only two bridges that cross this river, or canal, or whatever it is. Both are ideal bottlenecks for those looking to catch up with people driving away from Cape Cod.

As I cross the bridge, I maintain the same vigilance I've had for the last twenty or so miles.

I haven't seen any person or persons who could be watching for us, but I'm not James Bond: I don't know what I should be looking for beyond the obvious. Put me in a bar and I can tell within five minutes where the trouble lies, who's most likely to kick off, and which order I should deal with people. Spotting tails, however, is not my area of speciality.

Behind me, Cameron lies across the back seat out of sight. I'm now wearing a bright red shirt, baseball cap and a pair of cheap shades. As disguises go, it's not the greatest, but it was the best I could do without wasting a lot of time.

Our passing across the bridge goes smoothly, and I am approaching the turn for a highway when my lizard brain starts dumping hormones throughout my body.

There's a car sat by the highway and there is an SUV beside it. A young woman is chatting to an older guy who is changing a wheel. Her hair flutters in the breeze and she wears her boredom like it's the latest designer outfit.

The scene is so innocuous that I look elsewhere, until something draws me to look back at the girl, and what appears to be a gallant old gent who's stopped to help her.

Neither are looking our way, but when I look at them I see her put a foot on the wheel that's just been removed from her car. Her foot rests on the tyre, and she straightens her leg until she's lifted from the ground, supported only by the foot on the tyre.

She's standing on the tyre that's just been changed because it's flat. However, the tyre doesn't buckle under her weight; it doesn't even give a little. That means it's fully inflated. Which means the girl and the guy aren't really changing a wheel.

They are a plant. A reason for the SUV to be parked by the road.

I make a point of not staring at the SUV, but I look at it as much as I can without making it obvious. There's someone in the passenger seat and he's not watching the Good Samaritan. This guy is young enough that he should be doing the work rather than the older guy.

The back windows of the SUV are blacked out, but I'm sure if I could see through them, I'd see a car filled with muscled heavies, with a penchant for mindless violence.

I take the turn and head away from town. It's bad enough that Cameron and I may be at risk, but I'm not going to speed around streets where innocents may get hurt.

My plan was to head north until I got on a road to Boston, then follow that until I found a motel where we could hole up.

With the surveillance operation on the bridge potentially identifying us, I now need to get on the back roads and do a lot of direction changes so I can throw off anyone who decides to follow us.

A glance in my rear-view mirror confirms that the SUV has re-joined the flow of traffic. It's not certain they've pinpointed us yet, but I'll know in a minute or two.

Chapter 41

I grip the wheel a little tighter and check my rear-view mirror again. The SUV is where it has been since re-joining the road.

It's three cars back and seems to be content with just following us for the time being. Although the road isn't too busy, there is enough traffic for them to worry about witnesses.

I figure they're either waiting for us to drive somewhere remote, or they're just keeping tabs on us until reinforcements arrive. Neither of these scenarios appeal to me so I decide to do what they will least expect.

There's a chance I'm wrong about the SUV, and I should stop jumping at shadows, but I need to know one way or another.

The rental car slows as I remove my foot from the gas. I check the mirror and see the car behind me indicate and pull out to pass us.

Now there's just one car between us and the SUV.

Another look in the mirror sees the final car pull out without signalling.

The SUV is hanging back. Its pace matches ours.

If they are tailing us, they'll know they've been made.

The SUV creeps past us, its driver doing a scant mile per hour more than I am. He doesn't look at us but I'm sure that, behind the blacked-out windows, his buddies are giving us a thorough examination.

I should have followed my original instinct and hidden Cameron in the trunk. When I hired the car, I pulled what I'd hoped would be an effective deception: hiring one car in my name, and a second, from a different company, in Cameron's name, using his card.

The car I'd hired in his name was an ice-blue suburban, whereas the one we're in now is a tan compact.

We dumped the suburban at a marina, two miles from the rental office, in the hope of convincing our pursuers we'd gone back to sea.

Now I realise that all we've achieved is a waste of time and money.

The SUV pulls in front of us and slows, so I have to choose between slowing further or overtaking it.

There's no way I'm prepared to let him draw us slower and slower, so I wait for a gap in the traffic, indicate, and pull over.

I draw past him at a steady pace and when it's time to pull back into the slower lane, I stomp on the gas.

The traffic ahead has thinned so it's not long before I have the compact up to seventy. I'd much sooner be driving my Mustang than this crappy rental thing, but there's no point wishing for something I can't have.

I check the mirror; the SUV has pulled into the same lane as me and, from what I can tell, the driver is trying to close the gap.

There's a turn ahead so I take it as fast as is safely possible. Again, I wish I was driving my Mustang. Not only is it fast enough to outrun the SUV, but I've put it through its paces often enough to know its limits. With the compact, I don't know how hard I can push it in the corners before passing the point of no return.

Cameron says something but I tell him to shut up and keep down as I don't have time to deal with his questions.

The SUV appears in my mirror as I swing the wheel left and head for a back road. There's a squeal as the tyres protest at my sudden change of direction, but they get us around the corner with only a little bit of understeer.

I straighten up the car and try to push the gas pedal through the floor.

A check in my mirror shows the SUV has made the same turn.

There is no point trying to cling on to faint hopes; the SUV is officially following us. Now I know for certain, I can plan how to deal with it.

'Cameron. You might as well get up now. There's an SUV behind us. I'm pretty sure it's your friends.'

My use of the word friends is laden with sarcasm, but I'm not terribly worried about hurting Cameron's feelings. If we get out of this alive, he and I are going to have serious words – once he has done right by John. Should he not say the right things, I plan to hurt a lot more than his feelings.

The SUV looms in the rear-view mirror as Cameron hauls himself up.

His face is grave, and he casts a look out of the rear window.

'I bet you wish I still had that gun you made me throw away.'

I've been thinking the same thing, but my intentions were right at the time and, if nothing else since meeting Cameron, I've learned that you can't change the past, regardless of how loud its echoes reverberate into the present.

I squeeze on the gas even harder, but the compact is no match for the SUV, which is now hanging a foot from our rear fender.

The SUV's driver knows this, and slows a little, then accelerates until the SUV's front fender rams into the back of the compact.

Chapter 42

The SUV hits us hard enough to shake the compact but, other than a little squirming, the impact isn't hard enough to cause any major problems.

I'm sure the driver will learn from his mistake. Next time he hits us he won't hit the full width of the car. He'll target one side or the other.

Maybe he'll pull alongside us and slam into the rear wheel area.

I don't intend to wait and find out.

There's a bend ahead that I take as fast as I dare. The greater weight and higher centre of gravity force the SUV's driver to ease off before he can catch us.

This teaches me a valuable lesson: he might have more straight-line speed than me, and better acceleration, but I can get around corners a lot quicker than he can.

A car appears in front of me as I throw the compact around the next corner.

I swing out, and pass it before its driver has the chance to even register I'm behind him.

When I check the mirror, I see Cameron's face. He's wide-eyed as he looks back and forward.

I'm pushing the compact to its limits and taking stupid risks as I hurl it round blind corners.

I glance in the mirror again and see only Cameron's head.

'Sit at one side or the other. I need to see.'

I hear a rustle as he moves across. There's also the click of a seatbelt being fastened. It's the smartest thing I've known him to do.

The SUV looms large in the mirror, but I overtake a panel van and use the manoeuvre to buy myself a little time.

There's a junction ahead so I swing the wheel right and join the new road in a four-wheeled drift that I've only got the merest control of.

Behind me I hear Cameron gasp in fear. He's mumbling something but I doubt it's the rosary he's saying. A selfish, conniving, inconsiderate prick like him isn't the kind of person who worships another.

Taking this turn was a mistake. We're on a wider road, which is dead straight, there's little traffic to protect us, and there are deep ditches at either side of the road.

The SUV appears behind me and I can imagine its occupants smiling as they realise there is little I can do by way of defence, let alone mounting a counter attack.

There's a crack and I hear Cameron throwing himself down on the back seat.

I take a glance in the rear-view mirror and see the guy in the SUV's passenger seat hanging out of his window.

It's the gun in his hand that gives me the greatest concern.

Chapter 43

To throw off the gunman's aim, I swerve from side to side as much as I dare. It's a risky tactic and it bleeds some of the compact's speed.

The driver of the SUV only needs to nudge the rear of the compact, at one end of my sweeping arcs, for me to lose control.

With ditches at either side I have nowhere to go but forward.

The SUV holds left as I veer right, and a surge of power from its engine sees it gain enough ground to prevent me from cutting back to the left.

I see a vicious smile on the passenger's face as he points his gun at the rear of the compact.

Whether he's trying to kill Cameron, or shoot out our tyres, is a moot point. At a range of five feet, the odds of him missing are low.

There is only one course of action available to me, so I take it.

My foot slams down on the brake, causing the SUV to fly past us. There's a shot fired by the passenger but I don't hear the bullet striking the car.

As soon as we've slowed enough to turn, I wrench on the wheel and plant my boot back on the gas.

The SUV will catch us again, there's no doubt about that, but at least I've bought us a couple of minutes.

I look in the mirror and see they have turned and are coming after us.

The move won't work a second time, but I'm not done yet.

As the SUV hangs on our rear again, a truck lumbers into view. It's laden with a large bulldozer, which overhangs its trailer-bed.

I weave a little but there is no sign of the gunman now the truck is here. I have the beginnings of a plan, but it's risky at best; downright suicidal if it goes wrong.

As I weave, I increase the amount I cross the road. The truck is still approaching, and the SUV is hanging at the centre of the road as the driver waits for the optimal time to give us a nudge that will send us careering either into the oncoming truck, or one of the roadside ditches.

I keep this up until the truck is less than fifty yards away.

The compact is on the right-hand verge of the road when I stamp on the brakes for a second time. I have to give the SUV driver credit when he reacts a fraction of a second after I do. Just as I had hoped he would.

He's too late though. We're side-by-side now, with him between us and the truck.

While he's still braking, I haul the wheel left and slam the side of the compact into the SUV.

My foot is hard on the gas and I am holding the wheel over, forcing him towards the truck.

The SUV brakes.

The truck swerves.

I keep pushing the SUV towards the truck's chrome fender.

At the final second before impact, I tease the wheel right and disengage the compact from the SUV.

It takes me a second to bring the compact fully under control, and when I look in my rear-view mirror I see the SUV's crumpled front end and the truck's brake lights.

For the time being, the SUV is out of action.

The damage to the compact will cost me at least a couple of thousand bucks when the rental company gets it back but, so far as I'm concerned, it's worth every cent. We've survived and that's all that matters.

As Cameron straightens in his seat I realise that my mouth is dry and I have sweat oozing from every pore.

Like the damage to the compact, it doesn't matter in the slightest.

It's now time to start thinking about our next step. 'Cameron. Use my phone to find out where we are and how far away Boston is.'

Chapter 44

Cameron doesn't like the way Jake has taken over, but he knows that challenging him would be a bad idea. Not only has Jake proved resourceful – saving their lives twice now – he's also beyond furious at the way his girlfriend was killed.

For the time being he has to go along with Jake, and wait for a chance to arise for him to slip away.

Since the incident with the SUV, his son has been quiet and aloof. Cameron is sure that Jake is plotting their next move, as well as trying to come to terms with the girl's death. As he knows he's due some blame, he keeps his mouth shut and tries to figure out a way to regain his control over events.

Dusk has now fallen and the faithful little compact's engine has never missed a beat as they've travelled north. When they stopped for gas they examined the car, and saw that one side and the rear end were dented far beyond the talents of even the best panel-beater. A headlamp was also smashed and the front fender now hangs lower than it should.

The car's wounds are superficial but they are noticeable, so he agrees with Jake when he parks the compact in a multi-storey car park and leaves it to its fate. As a rental car it'll have a tracking device, so the company will find it in a day or two.

They're in a town near Brockton, twenty or thirty miles south of Boston. Their exact location isn't important to Cameron. What is important, is that they have escaped their pursuers, and for the time being they are safe.

Jake uses his phone to find a motel, and his charm to borrow a charger from the receptionist. The only bags they have are Jake's backpack and the laptop case Cameron uses as a briefcase.

'First we eat. Then we sleep.'

Those six words are the most Jake has spoken to him in an hour, but Cameron doesn't take offence; he might have, if he cared what Jake thought of him.

All of Cameron's thoughts are on how to rebuild his life. With what amounts to a death sentence hanging over him, should his employer catch him, his options are somewhat limited.

Not exhausted though.

Cameron still has a few cards up his sleeve to enable him to start anew in relative safety – providing he picks the right location and deals himself the right hand.

Jake leads him out of the crummy motel and along the street until they find a diner. They look at the menus in silence, only speaking to give the bored-looking waitress their orders.

'Look, about what happened on the boat with Tanya. I'm sorry. I didn't for one minute think they'd shoot when there was a woman in front of me.'

'Her name was Taylor. Not Tanya.' Cameron sees Jake's fists clench and unclench. 'Now sit there, and don't say another word about her, because if you do, I'll be coming over this table and condemning John to death by beating the living shit out of you.'

Cameron heeds his son's warning and doesn't speak. Getting the girl's name wrong was a tad clumsy, but he's seen enough of Jake's determination and resourcefulness to know that he's more than capable of carrying out his threat.

As soon as Cameron finishes his food, Jake stands and nods towards the door. 'Let's go.'

As much as Cameron wants to discuss their next move with Jake, he can tell his son is hanging on to both his temper and his composure by the slenderest of margins. One wrong word or another ill-timed comment will be more than enough to tip Jake's scales towards violence.

On the walk back to the motel he sees a liquor store, but decides that alcohol would not be a good addition to their current situation. Not only do they both need to keep their wits about them, he doesn't want to make a drunken mistake. Plus, he doesn't know if Jake is a mean drunk.

Maybe once Jake has calmed down he can get him drunk and wait until he passes out to make his escape.

Under the shroud of darkness the motel looks even more depressing. It looks as if rooms are available by the hour, and the fact there's a titty bar across the street does nothing to give him confidence that he'll get a good night's sleep. After being awake most of the previous night, and the stress of today's attempts on his life, Cameron is starting to feel every year of his age.

If this were a normal day, and he was alone, he'd get his head down for a couple of hours, have a few drinks in the titty bar, and wait to see what offers came his way.

A jaw-clicking yawn drives that idea from his head.

Back at the motel, he washes his face in the bathroom and dries it with the threadbare towel that has been provided.

While in there he dismisses the idea of climbing from the window as it's way too small.

Cameron leaves the bathroom to find Jake unplugging his cell from the borrowed charger.

'I'm gonna make a couple of calls. You stay here.'

The second the door closes behind Jake, Cameron moves to the bedroom's only window. He tries to open it but it's jammed fast. Decades of being painted without being opened, have locked the window's sash in the closed position.

With that escape route closed, he puts his ear to the door and hears nothing.

Neither the door's handle nor its hinges squeak when he teases it open and looks outside. He turns his head left, then right.

Jake is at the end of the corridor, looking his way. Cameron gives his son a thumbs-up and retreats into the bedroom.

Chapter 45

Now I'm alone, outside the crummy motel room, I start to shake. Today has been the most intense day of my life. I have no military training to prepare me for gunfights, or life and death situations with a murderous SUV. All I have are my wits and a refusal to quit.

I want to rage and shout and scream at the world for the injustice that saw Taylor catch that bullet instead of Cameron. I also feel an intense need to hate myself – for bringing Taylor along on this crazy trip, for not protecting her, and most of all, for leaving her body on the yacht.

As much as I want to berate myself, and find a bunch of guys to fight with so I can vent the fury that is threatening to overwhelm me, I stay calm and pull my cell from my shirt pocket.

I'm dreading the first call, and what I'm going to ask the second person I have to call is beyond any call of duty, or blood. That will be the most difficult conversation of my life and I'd make the first call a thousand times before making the second even once.

I select Alfonse's name and press call.

'What's going on, Jake?'

I tell Alfonse everything in brief, clipped sentences that don't allow my voice to crack, as the grief of verbalising Taylor's death envelops me.

Alfonse's response is a ragged breath followed by soft-voiced condolences.

I don't acknowledge them. Can't.

'Right. So, you're holed up in a motel with your father and you want to get him back to Casperton ASAP for John's sake;

you're pretty sure that your father will abscond at the earliest given opportunity, and the guys who are after you are powerful enough to track cell signals. Have I missed anything?'

'Just the fact that if Cameron gives me so much as half a reason, I'll not be able to stop myself pounding on him until he's nothing but a bloody pulp.'

'I feel the same, Jake. However, as nice as the idea seems, beating on your father isn't going to get you out of the mess you're in. From what you've told me so far, you're lucky to be alive. What we need to do is work out how to keep you that way. Options for travelling back to Casperton include, road, rail and air.'

'Rail and air are out. The minute our names go on a passenger list we're at risk of being traced by the guys who are after us.'

'Agreed. That leaves road. Even if you could trust your father—'

'Please don't call him that. He's not my father. I don't want him to be my father. Call him Cameron.'

Alfonse inhales deeply. 'Even if you could trust Cameron to not run off, and shared the driving so you didn't have to stop travelling, it'd still take you a couple of days. If you're travelling with someone who's a prisoner in all but name, then you're looking at three to four days by the time you add in rest stops.'

Alfonse isn't telling me anything I haven't already thought myself. Four days of being trapped in a car with Cameron is more than I can bear.

My need to avenge Taylor's death is growing by the hour and if it takes four or more days to get to Casperton, I'm not sure Cameron will be alive when we get there.

It's time to get to the real reason for my call. 'I was hoping you could help me out there.'

'Say the word and I'm on a plane to share the driving with you.'

'Thanks, but after what happened to Taylor there's no way I'm letting anyone else join us until I know we're safe.'

'So how can I help you?'

I spend five minutes explaining my plan to him and listening to his suggested refinements.

Alfonse isn't just my best friend, he's the best kind of friend any man could have. His loyalty is unfailing, he'll drop whatever he's doing to help me and he's secure enough to tell me when I'm wrong. I'm lucky to have him in my life.

Right now, I want to do anything bar make the second call.

I take several deep breaths, offer up a blasphemous prayer to the gods of forgiveness, and hit the call button once again.

Chapter 46

The ringing of my cell wakes me from the fitful slumber I've experienced since climbing into the motel's ratty bed.

As a precaution against Cameron absconding during the night, I had positioned my bed behind the door; it also prevented anyone getting into the room without me knowing.

I answer the call and listen to what Alfonse has to say.

As always, he's come through for me and has fulfilled my request to the letter. Now it's just a case of Cameron and me getting ourselves to the collection point, and we'll be flying back to Casperton.

I look at my watch and see we have two hours to make the journey. How Alfonse has managed to get this organised during the night, I don't know. All I can guess is that he's called in some favours and promised a lot more in exchange.

Alfonse bids me goodbye. The exact details of what he's told me are sketchy in my head, but it's not a worry as I know he'll also email them to me.

My cell sounds its email tone less than a minute after Alfonse has hung up.

I open the email and start reading.

Cameron and I have to be at Hopedale Airport by 10 a.m. It's 6 a.m. now so I'm sure there will be enough time. I use my phone to check, and it's just under an hour away. Time is on our side.

I go back to the email and absorb its details, and the probable cost to Alfonse in terms of favours.

There are few implications that I can see, so I think about the person who has helped to make this possible.

Claire Knight is a rising star at the company that controls the oilfield to the north of Casperton. A good-looking woman, who's forsaken romance for a career in a male-dominated industry, she is hard and ruthless when she needs to be, yet kind and compassionate when a gentler approach is required.

That she's getting the company jet to make a detour to pick up Cameron and me, is testament to her kindness. On the other hand, she'll have extracted her pound of flesh from Alfonse for the favour.

I know from first-hand experience that Claire gets what she wants. The night she lured me into her bed is a case in point. She seduced me, set the pace, and asserted not just her body, but her personality on me.

Cameron grumbles in his sleep but I can't make out the words. As much as I'm loath to touch him, I grab his shoulder and give him a shake. 'Wake up. We leave in ten minutes.'

There isn't a big hurry, but I want to take a slow meandering journey to the airport rather than a direct one.

It's not that I think we'll be followed again, more a precaution in case we are.

Now that I've got my plans in place, and will soon be arriving in Casperton with Cameron, I have to share the information.

I can make a call or send a message.

I chicken out and send a message. The reply won't have an aggrieved tone and there will be plenty of opportunity for my character to be assassinated when I get back to Casperton.

Cameron heads to the bathroom and I hear water running.

While he's in there, I put my bed back where it should be and check how much money I have in my wallet.

There's enough to buy us breakfast and put enough gas in the compact to get us to the airfield. Beyond that, I'll be relying on my card for any expenses we run up.

Cameron exits the bathroom and I sling my backpack over my shoulder. 'Let's go.'

'Where?'

'Casperton.'

'How?'

'I've chartered a plane. Get your ass in gear.'

Chapter 47

Hopedale Airport is little more than a single runway that bisects a small industrial estate. I watch in trepidation as a small jet swoops in over the trees and touches down.

The plane taxies to the end of the runway then turns in its own length as the pilot stands on the left brake.

A door folds open and Claire Knight's face appears. Her long, brown hair flaps in the breeze from the engine as she walks down the steps. She's dressed in a pastel skirt-suit and, as is her way, wears her clothes as if they are an advertisement for her sexuality. Her skirt is at least an inch too short for the boardroom and the cut of her blouse shows a generous amount of cleavage.

This is typical of her. She does things her own way and is happy to fly in the face of convention. Anyone foolish enough to think she'd slept her way to the top would learn of their mistake when confronted with her sharp mind and instinctive cunning.

The clack of her heels can be heard over the rumble of the plane's idling engines as she marches towards us. Her expression is business-like, but I can see a mischievous sparkle in her eyes.

She gives me a kiss on the cheek and offers her hand to Cameron.

He smiles what appears to be a genuine smile and introduces himself.

'I know who you are, Mr MacDonald. Alfonse filled me in on the need to rush you back to Casperton. I think it's very noble of you to help your son in this way.'

'I insisted on helping as soon as I heard about my poor boy.'

It doesn't take a genius to work out that Alfonse has given Claire a potted version of the truth. To me it sounds like he's omitted all the unsavoury details and has pitched our need for transport as a mercy dash, rather than the hot extraction it is.

What he's said to enlist her help doesn't bother me. Desperate times call for desperate measures; without her aid there's little chance of me getting Cameron to John's bedside.

The thing that bothers me most is the charm that Cameron's displaying. As soon as he heard Claire suggest he was doing an honourable thing, he twisted the dial to maximum. Within seconds he was all smiles as he offered Claire his arm for the walk to the plane.

The fact that my father is an instinctive player shouldn't have surprised me. I was one until I fell for Taylor. I had to inherit the trait from somewhere, and I'd much prefer it to come from an absent father than a narcissistic mother.

I buckle my seatbelt and watch as Claire takes the seat beside Cameron.

The jet engines roar as we hurtle down the tiny runway. I don't know a lot about aeronautics, but to me, the runway seems too short for the jet to build up enough speed to take off.

Claire's pilot must know better. He lifts the nose of the plane and we soar into the sky.

I'm tempted to look out of the window to see how much we clear the trees, but sometimes it's better not to know.

Once the plane levels out, I unclip my seatbelt and take a few paces up and down the aisle to stretch my legs.

I make sure, when I sit back down, that I can establish eye contact with both Claire and Cameron. She might be doing us a huge favour, but she's a sexual predator who's sitting next to a slippery liar who'll do and say whatever he thinks will earn him any kind of reward.

Claire is a big girl and I know she can take care of herself, it's Cameron I'm blocking. My girlfriend died because of his selfishness and cowardice; there's no way I'm going to stand by and allow him to seduce a woman young enough to be his daughter.

I don't particularly want to tell Claire what he's really like yet. It's bad enough that she's been spun a line to help us, telling her while we're mid-air will only lead to a frosty atmosphere for the rest of the journey.

I couldn't give two hoots about having a pleasant atmosphere; however, I do want time and peace to think.

Getting Cameron to Casperton is only part of what I have to plan.

Chapter 48

I look out of the window as the plane taxies towards the low building that is Casperton Airport's terminal. I can see Alfonse's car and I know he'll have followed my instructions regardless of his own feelings.

Casperton Airport might not be much, but compared to Hopedale's tree-flanked runway its wide, open space makes it feel like JFK or LAX in size, if not in volume of traffic.

I sling my backpack over my shoulder once the plane has stopped near the terminal. There are no elevated walkways here, just flat tarmac and a building that houses the requisite amount of security guards, a fast-food outlet, and a car hire firm.

The air is hot and dry as we walk across the tarmac.

As we exit the terminal, Cameron freezes.

I know the cause of his sudden reluctance to move. To a certain degree I can understand why he doesn't want to go any further.

Tough. He's the man who walked out on my mother, my sister and me. He's the man whose actions caused the death of my girlfriend.

'Why did you have to bring her here?' Cameron looks at me with panic on his face. 'Jesus, Jake. You're ripping the piss here.'

'It's nice to see you recognise her after all these years.' I raise an eyebrow at him. If my face is giving away any of my thoughts, he'll know to shut his mouth. 'She's going to look after you. Make sure you're comfortable. You'll be able to catch up on old times.'

The one word he gives voice to has seven letters.

My reply doubles him over.

I've been called a lot worse, but when a father uses a term that implies illegitimacy to his son, I figure the only fitting response is violence.

I've thrown harder punches and, if he's mixed up with the people he says he is, it's a fair bet that at some point in his life he'll have been hit with a lot more intent. All I did was remind him to watch his manners around me.

Alfonse looks grave standing beside Mother. Compared to her though, he's wearing the expression of someone who's just checked their lottery numbers and found out they've won the jackpot. I'd expected to see a wateriness to her eyes, or a tremble in her jaw. Neither are evident.

Thirty years of hate now have a legitimate target.

None of us speak, but the look I get from Mother is sharp enough to eviscerate a concrete elephant. She's gone beyond grief and self-pity. She's now in the land of controlled fury. I swear, if she was holding a gun, she'd put it to Cameron's head and pull the trigger without hesitation.

I slump down in the back of Alfonse's car and keep my face turned away from the window. It's only a matter of time before my name is connected to Taylor's death. Her bag is still on the yacht and will contain enough details to identify her.

Once Taylor's parents have learned of her death, they'll tell the police she was with me when they last saw her.

This is not the first situation I have been in where people have died, so my name will be at the top of what I don't expect to be a long list of suspects.

As soon as I get Cameron to the hospital to be tested, and deposited at my apartment with Mother as his guard, I'm going back to New York.

Claire Knight is returning there at midnight and I've managed to talk my way onto the plane for a second time.

Mother doesn't know about my plans, but Alfonse does. He's tried without success to dissuade me.

Before I go, I need to have a brief talk with Cameron. At least I hope it will be a talk. If he listens to me, and trusts me enough to share what he knows, it'll be a conversation.

Should he have other ideas, I may have to persuade him the same way as I did Donny. I don't like the idea of using torture, or even threats of it, with Cameron. When all is said and done, I still have his blood running through my veins.

On the other hand, I'm not going to let my respect for the status of fatherhood stand in the way of what needs to be done to avenge Taylor.

My trip to New York has another purpose. It's one thing delivering vengeance, but for justice to be done I need to make sure that my innocence in Taylor's death is proven beyond doubt.

Even if I die in my attempts, I don't want my name to be associated with a murder I'm innocent of.

Alfonse parks a hundred yards from the hospital's main entrance.

I stare at Cameron and wait until he looks at me before speaking.

'Are you going to man up and walk in there like a proper father, or do I have to lay you out and carry you in?' I give a nonchalant shrug to emphasise my point. 'You don't need to be conscious for them to test your bone marrow.'

Cameron scowls and makes a growling noise.

I lift an eyebrow and point to the hospital. He may be the parent, and I the child, but we both know, in our relationship, that the young bull has superseded the old one.

As soon as he opens his door, I open mine. Alfonse follows suit, but Mother sits with her arms folded. This isn't something she wants to be part of.

We leave her to intimidate the cars in the parking lot and escort Cameron into the hospital.

Chapter 49

Cameron settles himself on the bed and looks around the room. It's spartan to say the least. There's a bed, a boarded-up window, and an ensuite bathroom. A series of indentations in the carpet show where furniture usually stands.

His stomach still aches from Jake's punch, and there's a residual numbness in his pelvis where the bone marrow sample was taken. As the numbness is wearing off, a dull throbbing is settling in.

With everything that has happened today, he's shattered, and welcomes the bed with its clean sheets and plump pillows.

Seeing Ivy again was something of a shock, but he should have guessed she'd need to be involved.

The room he's in is his son's. Before he was ushered in here, Jake had sat him down, outlined a wild plan, and asked one question after another.

Cameron had thought for a minute or two as Jake had talked, and had decided he had nothing to lose by giving honest answers to Jake's questions.

If Jake's plan works, his name will be cleared as his bosses will be either imprisoned or dead. This means he can live the rest of his life with considerably fewer looks over his shoulder.

Should Jake fail, he will die, and his death will attract all the attention, thereby giving Cameron a better chance at starting a new life. Plus, without Jake's brawn, he can easily get away from Ivy and the puny guy who'd done the driving. Noble as it would be to save a life, Cameron's priority is preserving his own.

The only way things could go bad for him, is if Jake falls into the hands of his former bosses. Jake may be tough, but Cameron doubts he's tough enough to withstand the torture he'd be sure to face.

Cameron doesn't believe his son will triumph. Jake might be a good bar room brawler, but he'll be going up against professional hoods and hitmen. They'll have guns and experience; he'll have anger and fists.

Cameron has seen enough fights to know that the man who keeps a cool head will, more often than not, beat the guy who throws wild punches and doesn't worry about defence.

All he has to do is wait to see who opens the door. If it's Ivy, he's home free. If it's Jake, he'll have to wait around to help John before he can get on with rebuilding his life.

'You make sure you get a good night's sleep, Cameron. Because tomorrow, starting at six, I'm going to read you the diaries I kept after you broke the hearts of a good woman and two innocent bairns.'

It isn't tiredness that closes Cameron's eyes.

Chapter 50

I head into my bathroom and grab a quick shower. I don't bother shaving. The clothes I put on afterwards are clean, comfortable, and importantly, if things go the way I expect them to, disposable.

I pick up my wallet, a cheap cell, and the backpack containing Ms Rosenberg's evidence.

The contents of the backpack will be handed to Alfonse, so he can assimilate all the information, scan it onto memory sticks and distribute it to all the major news channels and law enforcement agencies.

Rather than take my own cell I have bought a new one – so I can use Google and other services. No numbers will be stored in it lest it falls into the wrong hands and paints a target on the back of someone I care about.

I open my wallet – my Glasgow roots don't let me think of it as a billfold – and remove all the cards and licences from it.

Alfonse has advised me to have the back up of a credit card, but I don't think running out of money is going to be the biggest issue I have.

I pull out the handful of receipts in the back of my wallet and flick idly through them. There's a receipt for a meal Taylor and I had enjoyed, and one for a film we hadn't.

The next receipt I look at isn't one I recognise, so I look at it a bit closer. It's dated two days ago, and when I see what it's for, my breathing stops.

Somehow I manage to wobble my way to a chair and sit.

I breathe again and it feels ragged and uncomfortable. However, compared to the sudden and debilitating ache in my heart, it is painless.

Mother looks at me with concern.

I shake my head and hope I'm wrong.

On my last night with Taylor, I'd told her I loved her.

It wasn't a sudden thing; I'd just gotten myself drunk enough to realise it.

'What is it, Jake? What's wrong?'

I open my mouth, but words don't come out.

I try again but still have no success.

I give up trying to speak, and hand Mother the receipt.

She holds it at arm's length and squints at it.

Her mouth twists as she battles her emotions. Strength in the face of adversity, beats complete meltdown by the tiniest fraction.

She walks across, lays a weathered hand on my arm and looks deep into my eyes. 'Oh, Jake. I'm so sorry.'

We sit together in silence for a while then Mother leaves me to manage my grief alone. I want to scream to express my feelings, but I don't. Neither do I lash out and punch the walls or a door. There will be plenty of opportunity to release my emotions when I get to New York; hurting my hands now will achieve nothing bar shortening my odds of success.

My anger needs a temporary outlet, so I pick myself up, change into running sweats and go out for a run. I have an hour before Alfonse picks me up and takes me to the airport.

Taylor told me that a drunk man speaks the truth.

I'd spoken the truth to her and my actions had spoken louder to me.

When I close the door behind me, the receipt for the deposit I'd put down on an engagement ring is clasped between my fingers.

Chapter 51

I part company with Claire Knight outside the arrivals lounge. A town car and driver awaits her; I hail a cab and ask the driver to take me to Queens.

First on my to-do list is to get some weapons. After that, I need to hole up somewhere until it's evening.

As we drive through the streets the cab driver regales me with his opinions on the mayoral election.

It's tempting to inform him how crooked his preferred choice is, but I keep my mouth shut. When Alfonse gets the word out, the last thing I want is some random cabbie going to the press with tales of a passenger who'd told him everything they'd printed before they got the information. I have enough potential threats to my life without going public and giving people a trail to follow.

I suffer his forthright views without comment and pay him what he asks, with a tip, when he drops me off on Metropolitan Avenue.

There are a multitude of shops here, and while travelling in the cab I saw a few where I could begin to build my arsenal.

The first store I enter is an everyday convenience store. It has the usual aisles lined with food, and people shopping for groceries. A young mum pushes a trolley in which a toddler is screaming for attention while she focuses on her cell phone.

I make my way to the back of the store and check out their cookware range. Were it not for the rage inside me, I'd give a smile of triumph.

I select four knives of various sizes from the range that have stainless steel handles. I also pick up one of those little blowtorches. Next, is a ten-inch sharpening steel. Not only will it sharpen knives, it'll work as a club and is compact enough to slide inside a sleeve.

The guy who takes my money looks as if he'd rather be anywhere else than working in a convenience store. I'm all for free expression when it comes to piercings and tattoos, but with the amount this guy has on his face and hands, I guess this may well be the best job he'll ever have.

With my purchases in my backpack I start to walk along the street. There are still a number of items I need, and the newspaper I buy will help me identify the best place to complete my list of weapons.

Knives are a good weapon for a close up fight, but guns have range and a far greater threat level.

If I buy a gun from a shop, there is bound to be a registration process. The last thing I want to do is put my name against a weapon that will be used in a murder.

Only the most stupid of gun shop owners would fail to have a CCTV camera watching over their store. This means my new unshaven look will be connected with me from the word go, should the authorities trace the gun I plan to use.

To counteract this, I plan to get a gun another way. Hence the newspaper. There are some things you just can't Google.

Chapter 52

The list of businesses I got from Cameron is extensive, and I make sure I take a walk past as many of them as I can.

They are all typical looking businesses. None are remarkable in any way other than their ownership and randomness.

My walk takes me past auto repair shops, hotels, bars, a convenience store, and many other seemingly unconnected businesses.

Cameron's employer owns a wide cross-section of companies to give a legitimate front to their crime empire. He didn't say as much, but I'm ninety per cent sure that Cameron was involved in laundering money through these businesses. They are too eclectic to be anything other than laundromats for money generated from prostitution, drug dealing and other illegal activities.

I spy a traditional barbershop and walk through its door.

There's a scuffed leather bench where a row of guys are waiting their turn. A melancholic blues track is playing in the background and there's a whiff of grooming products in the air.

Four barbers are snipping, styling and shaving away at their customers.

My turn comes and I take a seat in front of the mirror. The barber I get is an old man with steady hands and bright eyes.

'Whatcha after, son?'

'Shave off all my hair and give my head a wet shave please.' I see the puzzlement in his eyes and give a shrug. 'It's my girlfriend's idea.'

He gives a throaty chuckle. 'Damn, son, you gotta give the ladies what they want.'

I sit and listen as the barber does as requested while regaling me with tales of the things he's done for the various ladies who've been in his life. Despite my serious mood, I can't help but chuckle with him, as he tells of a former lover who would only make love to him if he was dressed as a fireman. The mental image of this frail old man being swamped by a fire helmet and flameproof clothing is just the kind of thing that tickles me.

I leave the barbershop and resume my walking. As far as disguises go, a bald head and two days' worth of stubble is not what you'd call innovative, but we all have to start somewhere.

There's a different feel to having all your hair shaved off. It's more than just a change in look, I feel the heat from the sun more, and when I step into shaded areas I notice a breeze that wasn't apparent before.

Chapter 53

I find a cheap hotel and book a room for a few hours. Although I'm wired, I know I should try and get some sleep.

When I open the door to my room I find the hotel is worse than crummy. The fact I'd been able to book a room by the hour had indicated the level of luxury I could expect but, despite having low expectations, I find myself underwhelmed nonetheless.

The room looks as if it was last refurbished when Jesus was in nursery school, and the furnishings are exhausted rather than tired. Sure, it might be the kind of place where hookers bring their johns, but jeez, who'd want to have contact with a woman who'd put her bare skin on a bed this ratty?

I pull back the top sheet and get a whiff of something that was once a bodily fluid. The towels in the bathroom are damp and there's a trickle of lukewarm brown water when I turn on the tap.

That someone has bathed in this water is enough to make my gag reflex spring into action, before I crush it down and think of the person as one of life's unfortunates who is unable to enjoy the basic comforts I've always taken for granted.

The room may have been cheap, but there's no way I'm putting any part of me, other than my hands, on the bed or bedding. Instead of trying to sleep, I reach into my backpack and remove one of the knives and the sharpening bar.

It takes me a few minutes to build up the right rhythm, but I soon get things right. Once the knife is sharp enough to shave the hairs on my arm, I return it carefully into my backpack and pull out the next one.

After an hour I have all four knives sharpened to a degree that I'm satisfied with. I dare say a professional chef would have done the same job in less time, with better results, but now I've decided to forego sleeping in this room I have time on my side.

To make the best use of that time, I secrete the knives around my person and practise drawing them out at speed.

The paring knife I hide in my boot is the biggest problem. Not only do I have to bend to get it, but I have to make sure it doesn't turn and slice my foot as I walk.

I open the drawers of the dresser and find what I'm looking for. What's better is that it is largely untouched. This isn't the kind of place where the clientele will hunt out the obligatory bible therefore, other than a coating of dust, it's clean.

It's sacrilege to slice the cover from a bible but I do it anyway. My next move is to slide the piece of hard-backed cover into the gap between the bathroom door and its frame.

A little pressure and I have a ninety-degree fold. I reverse it and do the same to the other side.

I press the two folds inwards until they form a narrow cardboard sheath.

With the homemade sheath wedged between the outside of my foot and my boot, I practise drawing the knife again. It is much quicker and allows me to arc the knife several different ways as I straighten after gripping it.

The next thing I want to practise isn't something I should do in here, but I figure that the management of this so-called hotel will either curse and do nothing, or be prompted to make improvements that will only benefit the room's next guests.

I position myself six feet away from the bathroom door and throw one of my larger knives. My throw is an underhand one, aimed about four feet above the floor. The torso is the largest target on the human body, and I know I don't have time to perfect my technique enough to accurately hit someone in their throat or eye.

The knife's handle bounces off the stained wood and it falls to the floor.

I try again with the same result.

It takes another fifteen attempts before the blade strikes the door, and forty-three before it sticks in.

A half hour later, the knife blade is striking the door with every throw, and sticking in it every other time. The bathroom door is suffering under the knife's onslaught and bears a two-foot circle of chipped and splintered paintwork.

I step back and try from a longer range. It takes me a few dozen throws to get my eye in, but I achieve similar results to the first position a lot quicker now I've learned the correct amount of power and spin to put on the knife.

My next step back puts me a good twelve feet from the bathroom door. This proves to be harder than either of the previous two stances, as the ratio between power and spin has changed exponentially now that I'm throwing further.

It takes me a half hour to master this distance, but I train myself to at least hit the door with the knife's blade – even if the point doesn't stick in. The human gut is a lot softer than the bathroom door, and the knife will inflict damage whether it pierces enough flesh to impale or not.

I step forward and back again between my three points and at random intervals between them.

The bathroom door is disintegrating as the knife either digs in or gouges out yet another splinter.

I move, throw, move, throw, until I'm happy that I can change distance if necessary.

I try a few throws with my left hand but they prove a waste of time. Not only can I not get the blade to hit the door, sometimes I miss with the handle as well. Giving up on that as a bad idea, I try moving around to see what results I get. They're not great, but I take heart from the attempt that sees me whirl round from having my back to the bathroom door.

The knife embeds itself right in the middle of the destruction I've wrought on the door and wavers back and forth until its momentum is spent.

I retrieve the knife and thumb the blade.

The repeated strikes against the door have dulled its edge.

I retrieve the sharpening steel from my backpack and hone the blade to its former sharpness.

Chapter 54

Cameron unclamps his hands from his ears and marvels at the quiet. Ivy has sat outside the door, talking to him all day. Except it hasn't been a conversation. It's been a constant diatribe that has ranged from soft verbalisations of long ago feelings, to snarled abuse about the way he abandoned her and the kids.

At first he'd listened to her with an uncaring indifference, but her words had penetrated the tiny portion of his heart he reserved for feelings about others. Once the penetration was complete, she'd twisted the verbal skewers, and reiterated key points, before attempting to shame him with the results his actions had had on Jake and Sharon.

The problem Cameron has, is that he doesn't regret anything; other than the fact he'd tried to play at being a husband and father when he'd known it was a mistake from the day he'd put a ring on Ivy's finger.

He knows he's not the considerate type, that he always puts his own needs before those of others, that if he'd stuck around any longer he would have turned on Ivy and quite possibly the children.

Walking out on them was a terrible thing to do, but he's spent years justifying that it would have been worse for them had he stayed.

His second marriage was an even stupider idea. Vanessa had fallen pregnant and he'd been so infatuated by her beauty that he'd believed he could change. Six months after John was born, he'd started making plans to leave when Vanessa had told him she was expecting again.

He'd stuck around until she'd had the baby and left before she'd returned from hospital. John had been deposited at his grandparents without an explanation, and once again Cameron had done his bit to improve the lives of his wife and kids, by not being around to be a failure to them.

A pizza box slides under the two-inch section that's been cut from the bottom of the door.

Cameron opens the box and sees a pepperoni pizza. His stomach growls: it's the first food he's had since a pre-packaged sandwich at the hospital.

He picks up a slice and stuffs it into his mouth. It's not as warm as he'd like, but he's too hungry to care. As he chews on the pizza he feels his tongue and lips start to burn. There's some spicy sauce or chilli flavouring on the pizza. He's never liked spicy food and the few times he's tried it he's felt unwell afterwards.

Cameron puts the pizza box on the floor and fills a plastic beaker from the bathroom sink. It takes five beakers of water before his mouth is somewhere close to normal. So far as he's concerned, the pizza is inedible.

He closes the box lid and slides it back under the door.

Ivy's response is immediate. 'That was quick. Oh, you've not eaten it. Aren't you hungry?'

There's something in her tone that Cameron recognises from all those years ago. It's triumph. She always did like getting one over on him when they'd argued.

'You did that on purpose, didn't you?'

'Did what?'

Cameron isn't fooled by the innocence in her voice. 'You deliberately got me a hot and spicy meal because you knew I wouldn't be able to eat it.'

'Why, Cameron, what an awful thing to suggest. Why would you think I would do such a thing?'

His mouth opens but he doesn't speak. Ivy has had her petty revenge and she'll be delighting in it. He's prepared to let her have a small victory – at least for the moment.

He'll let her have her moment of triumph, and in an hour or so he'll point out that if he's to donate bone marrow, it would probably be best for John if he's fit and well. Being starved, or given foods that prompt illness, will not have him as fit as he may need to be.

'Of all the things you've done to me and my kids, do you know what is the worst?' Ivy doesn't wait for an answer. 'You've stolen my only chance of grandchildren. Sharon can't conceive, and Jake has never had a relationship that's lasted more than three months until he met Taylor. She was the only girlfriend he's brought home. She was the one he wanted to spend his life with. When you used her to save your own miserable hide, you didn't just kill her; you killed any chance of Jake ever settling down.'

Cameron pulls the pillow over his head and presses it against his ears. He can't be bothered listening to Ivy any longer. So, Jake isn't going to settle down, boo hoo. The decision to let his kids live their own lives without him had been taken, and acted upon, many years ago. To come complaining about it now, when they need him, is hypocritical. If he was such a loss to their lives, why has it taken them so long to hunt him down?

Ivy's voice carries through the door and the pillow. 'What's worse than him never settling down, is that he'll never experience the joy of being a parent. *You* may not think it's a joy, but believe you me, those kids of mine have made me proud every day since they were born. Since they grew up and left home, all I've ever wanted for them was to be happy, and to have the love and pride for their children that I have for mine. Jake will never settle now. Never experience that joy. You took that from him and, despite everything else you've done, that's what I hate you for most of all. You may not know it, but you're a grandfather thrice over. Your other son has two girls and his sister has a son. You've turned your back on your grandchildren the same way you turned your back on your children. Can you imagine how much it hurts me to know that you have grandchildren you don't want, while I want the grandchildren I'll never have?'

Cameron knows he should feel shame, or self-loathing, or something other than what he's feeling. He doesn't though. He just feels hungry.

Chapter 55

The young woman, who opens the theatre's back door an inch, gives me the once-over with a brown eye and a suspicious expression.

I give her a smile, and the false name I used when making this booking.

She nods and the door opens a foot. 'Sorry about that. You gotta be careful.'

'I can imagine.'

The theatre isn't in the best of areas and I'd say it gets used more by community groups than budding impresarios.

'I'm Melody. Come on in.'

When the door opens I see she's had a friend provide backup. He's a hippy type with lank dreadlocks, and provides the same level of intimidation as a goldfish. Unless he's a closet martial artist, he'll be easier to drop than the proverbial hot potato.

I follow Melody to a dressing room.

There's the obligatory bulb-surrounded mirror, and a clothes rack with a variety of different costumes hanging from it. A toolbox is open on the worktop and while it looks well stocked, it doesn't allay my doubts that Melody isn't as good as she makes out on her website.

The rundown theatre and the fact she's nervous don't give me confidence in her professional skills. However, it's too late to find an alternative, so I either have to let her do her stuff, or forego this part of my disguise.

'Have you just had your head shaved today?'

'Yeah. Why?'

'The skin on your head is a different colour to your face and neck. I'll need to match the colour because it looks a bit odd.'

'Okay.'

Melody arranges me in a chair by the mirror with the bulbs and flicks a switch. She gives an embarrassed grimace when only three of the bulbs light up.

As she goes to work, Melody gives a running commentary while I watch her actions in the mirror. I feel her draw a short line on the back of my head, then she opens a vial of liquid that has a brush fitted to the lid.

A strong, unpleasant smell fills the dressing room and makes my nose wrinkle. It's similar to the chemical scent of lacquer. Melody doesn't react to the smell – other than a fast disappearing smile at my reaction.

She paints the liquid several times over the same area that she'd drawn the line, blowing gently on the back of my head to dry it between each new layer.

The sensation of her warm breath is accompanied by what I can only describe as a contracting of my skin in the area where she's applied the solution.

Melody works quickly and without hesitation. More products are retrieved from her toolbox and applied to the back of my head.

'Done.' She turns me to face the mirror and, like a barber, uses a second mirror to show me the back of my head. 'What do you think?'

'Looks good to me.'

The scar she's drawn looks so realistic I want to reach back and touch it, feel its rough edges and caress the puckered skin of what looks like a scar I've had for years.

The scar she creates on my cheek is even better, although she makes it look as if it's a recent addition.

As she's using the foul-smelling liquid on my cheek, I have an idea. It's an impertinent one, but I'm long past the point of worrying what other people think of me.

I wait until she's finished doing the second scar, and ask a few questions about the liquid. It turns out to be a specialist scarring product called Rigid Collodion.

Melody explains that as it dries, it puckers up loose skin to form the effect of scars on flesh.

My idea is beginning to look as if it might just work. 'Could I buy the rest of the bottle from you?'

'Sure.' She looks a little apprehensive. 'It'll be twenty bucks though.'

'No problem.'

The look of relief on her face tells me that Melody has just overcharged me. I'm not worried, I'd have paid fifty bucks if she'd asked.

I thank Melody, pay her the agreed price for my makeover, and leave.

The alley at the back of the theatre is deserted, so I paint my left forefinger with a liberal amount of the Collodion. Once it has dried, I wipe the screen of my cell on my shirt until it's clean and press my left forefinger against it.

As I'd hoped, it doesn't leave a fingerprint.

Chapter 56

With my disguise complete I have one more part of my plan to finalise before it's time to go on the attack.

I may well have a disguise, and a minor level of proficiency at throwing knives, but the people I'm going up against can track cell phones, bring in a sniper, and will have countless goons in their employ. I need a gun before I engage in any conflict with them.

I'm sure buying a gun is easy enough, provided you have the right kind of ID with you. Mine has been left in Casperton on purpose.

There is always the black market, but it will take time I don't have to identify the right person and establish my own credentials.

As always, there is another solution. One that involves me finding someone who has a gun they no longer need.

First though, I stop at a twenty-four-hour mini-market and buy myself a hoodie. The scars have given me a much tougher look than I normally have, and I need to hide them if I want to get mugged.

The newspaper has given me a location that will heighten my chances of being rolled over, and as I stride towards it I feel my jaw setting and my heart blackening.

I stop at a bar, a half block from Union Hall Street, and order a whisky.

Rather than drink it, I dip my fingers in the liquid and dribble it on my neck and rub it into my clothes.

Now that I stink of whisky, I put my hands beneath the table and paint all my fingertips with three coats of the Collodion.

The smell of the scarring agent causes one or two of the bar's patrons to look at me, wrinkle their noses and move seats. I figure they think I've soiled myself. They can make whatever assumptions they like.

I leave the bar and make my way towards Union Hall Street. According to the newspaper's reporting of crimes, it's one of the worst areas in Queens. If I can't get mugged here, I can't get mugged anywhere.

With my hood pulled over my head, I stagger and lurch my way onto Union Hall Street. It's a residential area and it wouldn't look too bad were it not for the occasional boarded window, and the basketball courts encased by rusty, broken, chain-link fences.

Some young punks loiter across the street, and there are a few knots of girls – three parts attitude, one part scared children – who've been forced by circumstances to grow up way quicker than is natural.

None of them look like they'll tackle me, so I cut through a side street and find myself in a different kind of place.

The buildings here are taller and closer together; there is an air of menace, and those who inhabit these streets are older and meaner than any of the kids on Union Hall Street.

Beneath the cover of my hoodie, I smile.

Chapter 57

I exaggerate my lurch into the alleyway. It's dim, dark, and has piles of garbage everywhere. Most people would have more sense than to go anywhere near a place like this, but I feign a stagger as I walk halfway along it.

I pause by a dumpster, undo the zip on my jeans, and widen my feet to shoulder width. Anyone looking at me will think I'm taking a whizz. Anyone who wants the contents of my wallet will think all their Christmases have come at once.

I hear footsteps behind me but I don't give a visible reaction. Instead of turning my head, I'm listening, and calculating how many would-be muggers there are and where they are positioned.

A hand grips my shoulder and I smell breath that's even fouler than the stench coming from the dumpster.

'S'matter? Can't a dude take a whizz?' The slurring I add to my tone isn't perfect, but it should be good enough to convince the hand's owner.

I feel something press against my right kidney, and get a second, stronger, blast of the foul breath.

'You forgot to pay the tax, buddy. Just hand over your wallet, cell and watch, and you can walk outta here.'

The speaker's accent is low and guttural. There is no refinement in his voice, no suggestion that he's had even a half-decent education. The wisecrack about the tax shows as much. It's the kind of line you'd get in a bad movie.

From the corner of my eye I see a second person. If Bad Breath is at my six o'clock, Compatriot is at eight.

The fact they've pulled a weapon so early on, neutralises any qualms I have about hurting them.

The hand on my shoulder removes itself, as Bad Breath waits for me to turn round.

When I do turn, it's a lot faster than he's expecting; I drive myself round and throw my left elbow towards his head. As I spin, my body whirls away from whatever weapon he's holding against my right kidney.

My elbow catches the side of his jaw; whether it's dislocated or broken isn't important. My right hand follows up and slams into his temple.

As Bad Breath is collapsing, I'm stepping towards Compatriot.

He pulls a knife from his pocket and waves it in front of my face. I raise my hands into a boxer's stance and watch his eyes. There's uncertainty and fear.

I feint a jab. He slashes his knife wide.

A fraction of a second later, my hand is on his wrist and I've got it twisted until he's in an armbar.

I drive the heel of my hand into his elbow and hear the double crunch of breaking bone and tearing sinew before he howls in agony.

Compatriot drops to his knees so I introduce his chin to my boot. They don't get on.

I search the two prone bodies for weapons, and find two knives and just over a hundred dollars.

The knives get tossed into a dumpster and the money goes into my pocket. I'm not a thief and this is the first time I've ever taken something that wasn't freely given to me. The money I've taken from them will find its way to a charity. I've only taken it as it seems like poetic justice to mug the muggers.

The next two alleyways I walk down see me collect another one hundred and fifty bucks for charity. The nearest emergency ward also got another three patients, but hey, while I may have intimated I was an easy target, I didn't force them to mug me.

I pass an alleyway between two apartment blocks but choose not to go down it. There's too much light and there is nobody around to follow me.

Perhaps the local muggers have seen me followed three times already, and emerging unscathed. If that's the case I may have to give up on my plan.

I decide to give it one more go and cross the street. There's an alleyway on the left that I stagger along. I have one hand on the coarse brick wall, and I'm going through my taking-a-whizz routine when I hear footsteps.

I stay in position and wait to see what happens.

'Yo.'

I don't answer.

'Yo, dude. I'm like, talking to you.'

I turn around and see three people. All are wearing hoodies that shade their faces.

Their faces don't matter.

What matters is the gun the one in the centre is holding. It's pointed at my nose and he thinks he's being cool by holding it at ninety degrees from upright, but he's being stupid and reducing his chances of firing with any great accuracy.

I give up the pretence of drunkenness and address the man whose gun I plan to steal. 'I'm listening.'

'We been watching you, dude. You think you can come here and take my bros down? You think you're some vigilante? Man, you are sooo wrong.'

He adds an insult which suggests I have intimate relations with my female parent.

I'm from Glasgow, where the c-word is used as a term of endearment. If he wants to insult me, he's going to have to try a lot harder.

'I'm not a vigilante. I've just come here for something, and I'm not leaving until I get it.'

The calmness and certainty in my voice triggers something in him. He steps forward so his gun is three inches from my nose.

'All you're getting, is your ass well and truly whupped.'

As Gunman speaks, his buddies circle round from behind him.

'You're wrong. Let me tell you what I want, and if you give it to me, I'll let you walk away unhurt.'

Gunman's buddies halt. Maybe it's the fact that I've kept my tone conversational, or that I have never flinched, despite having a gun inches from my face. Whatever the reason, it's enough to make them cautious.

'Before we kick yo' ass, you can give us a laugh and tell us what you want. Whatcha after, Mr Vigilante? What's down here that you want?'

I duck my head left as my right hand grabs the gun and twists it upwards, breaking the finger he has in the trigger guard. As he drops the gun, I smash an elbow into the face of the guy on the left. The guy on the right is coming for me with balled fists, so I let him throw a wild punch and counter with a hard shot to his gut.

The gunman is kicking at me, so I grab his raised foot and twist it until he flips and lands face down. My boot connects with his genitalia hard enough to score a fifty-yard field goal. His buddies have recovered enough to straighten up, and the guy on the left is pulling something from his jacket.

I charge at him and drive him backwards towards an abandoned shopping cart. He falls over it and smashes his head on the hard cobbles of the alleyway. While he's still groggy, I arrange a meeting with my boot for his already shattered nose.

A hammer blow to the back of my head has me reeling forward. The guy I turn to face is the one who thinks he's a boxer. Tempted as I am to prove him wrong with a sustained series of punches, I just want to get this over with.

His right hand snakes towards my head, I duck back and use the toe of my boot to lift his kneecap upwards. He yelps, and hops on his good leg with both hands wrapped around his broken knee.

One quick punch to his temple crumples him into an unconscious heap.

It's taken me no more than ten seconds to drop these three, and it takes me another twenty to search them. I get the best part of five hundred bucks for charity, one gun, and a collapsible baton.

The collapsible baton goes in my pocket as I walk towards the entrance of the alleyway – I need more light for my next task.

I position myself where I can't be ambushed and check out the gun. It's an automatic. Guns are not my area of interest and as such I don't know a lot about them.

I fiddle with it and find a lever that releases the magazine. I count the bullets in it. All seven of them.

There's another lever, which I presume is a safety catch, but in this light, I can't see which way is on and which is off.

I return to the three bozos and reach into the right pocket of Gunman's hoodie for the lighter I'd felt earlier.

It sparks on the first flick of the wheel, and illuminates the gun enough for me to ensure the safety catch is on. I stuff the gun into the waistband of my jeans, cover it with my shirt and, for the first time in my life, set off to commit murder.

Chapter 58

I dump my hoodie in a trash can and cross the street. The neon lights of The Elite Club flash in a cursive script that suggests familiarity and welcome.

Like titty bars everywhere, there's a person on the door who resembles a gorilla that's been levered into a suit, and fed a regular diet of steroids until the suit bulges at every seam.

There's red rope hanging from brass pedestals to give the illusion of class. As if class can be associated with disillusioned women painting on fake smiles and stripping for men they would normally cross the street to avoid.

A bunch of guys wander towards The Elite Club and the gorilla lets them in. I might be a half block away, but I can tell from the way they're shouting and laughing that they're liquored up.

I approach the door and wait for the gorilla to step aside. He gives me a long, hard look; I know he's looking at my scar, trying to work out how much trouble I might be. I keep my face neutral and voice polite when I ask what the entrance fee is. The last thing I need is for him to refuse me.

The gorilla moves out of my way, so I pay the bored-looking woman in the kiosk and walk into the strip club.

It's as bad as I'd expected. All the tropes are there in evidence. Red flocked wallpaper adorned with pictures of models who'd refuse to set foot in here, let alone perform a strip.

The bar is long and in need of some maintenance, let alone a thorough cleaning. When I look at the seats I see a synthetic covering that may, just may, have resembled leather when it was installed.

Bad music is blasting out with an emphasis on the bass. I guess it's that way to give the dancers a rhythm, or it would be if any of them were actually in time with the music. Every one of them is dancing to a different beat with a fixed smile and a marked lack of sensuality.

I buy a soda and take a seat at the back of the room to observe things. The girls range from nearly pretty to somewhat attractive. They aren't ugly, they've just buried their true selves beneath a thick layer of cosmetics.

An inspection of the security arrangements confirms two roving doormen, six CCTV domes, and a pair of doors with electronic keypads.

Another look at the bar makes me reassess my count of the doormen – two of the bartenders are also big enough to stop most patrons who decide to act out.

I take a sip of my soda and ponder on the cliché that is organised crime and strip clubs. It's like one can't exist without the other. I guess it's because they are a good way to launder money, and recruit girls into prostitution, while providing criminals with a steady income.

Whatever the case may be, The Elite Club is owned by Cameron's employer and is the place he was always summoned to when his boss wanted him.

Alfonse has done a thorough search on the name Cameron gave me. Olly Kingston features on a few business pages here and there but, even when Alfonse had dug deep, he'd found nothing to suggest that Kingston was anything other than a self-made man. This tells me he's clever, well-connected, and has enough steel about him to hold an elevated position in a very dangerous industry.

The one thing Alfonse couldn't find, was an address. Cameron was no use on that front either – he'd always met Kingston at one of his businesses. He may have been trusted – wrongly, as he proved – but he either wasn't close enough, or liked enough, to be invited to his boss's home.

Cameron's insistence that Kingston likes to be known as The King, implies delusion regarding his status, or a serious obsession with Elvis Presley.

I see one of the girls wander among the rows of seats. Her eyes flit back and forth as she seeks out a likely target. I'm given a half-second glance as she moves on to the bunch of guys I'd seen entering before me.

A moment later she's leading one of them by the hand towards the private booths.

They emerge a song later with him grinning like someone who's just been promoted from village to town idiot, and her already looking for her next mark.

Chapter 59

A dancer approaches me and introduces herself as Mandi-with-one-I. Despite her having two eyes, I can't help but think of her as Cyclops.

'You okay, sugar? You been sat here all on your lonesome and you ain't had no company.'

'I'm fine.' I give her a tight smile.

'Sure you are.' The hand she lays on my leg is warm and has false nails that resemble talons. 'A twenty buck dance from me will make you even better.'

If I let her dance for me, I'll blend in.

'Thanks, but no thanks.'

Not only do I want to stand out, but strip bars have never been my thing. I have no interest in paying a woman to take her clothes off for me. Even less so when I'm avenging a murdered girlfriend.

I watch Cyclops as she walks away. She turns her head to the barman and gives it a little shake.

The barman plays it cool, but two minutes later he's chatting to one of the roving doormen.

It takes a few minutes, but the roving doorman eventually speaks to a dancer who is wearing a long silky dress.

She doesn't look my way, but she does work her way round the room until she's heading in my direction.

As she approaches me, I give her a thorough appraisal. She's the most attractive girl in here by a considerable distance. She moves with a seductive sway and she has the quiet confidence of a woman who's used to manipulating men. In another time and place, I know I'd find myself attracted to her.

When a guy goes into a titty bar and doesn't engage with the titties, or the bar, people notice. When the right people in a bar notice something, they get antsy. When people get antsy, they react. Sending the best-looking girl in the place over here, is their reaction.

She takes the same seat that Cyclops had and crosses one leg over the other, causing the slit in her dress to part enough to give me a good view of her upper thigh.

She doesn't speak as she returns my appraisal. Her eyes lock on to my new scar; that's the reason the scar is there.

It's a focal point, not just for the eyes, but also the memory. Anyone I encounter tonight will be able to describe my scar in detail, but when pressed about the shape of my nose and jaw, or the colour of my eyes, they'll struggle to recall details.

She curls her lips apart and uses a forefinger to caress them, before dropping her hand back in her lap. 'You've got us puzzled, mister.'

Her words are an opening gambit, in what I'm sure will become a discussion about why I'm not having any dances. Or why I'm not sitting near enough to gawp at the girls doing lazy gyrations on the stage. Perhaps she wants to know why I'm not drinking alcohol.

'I'm a puzzling kind of guy.'

'You sure are. You're not interested in the girls, and you're not hitting the beer – despite stinking of whisky.' She slides her tongue from left to right between plump lips. 'So, Mr Puzzle, why are you here?'

'I'm looking for someone.'

'Who?'

'Nobody you know.' That might be a lie, but while I have no cares about henchmen and muggers getting hurt, I don't want to see any innocents harmed.

'Are they meeting you here?'

'Possibly.' I give a nonchalant shrug and adjust my position so the gun isn't digging into my back. 'I'm waiting to see what happens.'

She gives a nervous smile. 'Can I interest you in a dance?'

I shake my head.

The girl stands and leans over me. At first, I think she's trying to use the view I'm getting down her dress to change my mind about the dance, until she opens her mouth. 'Please leave. They'll hurt you if you don't.' Her words are little more than a breathy whisper.

'Thanks.'

I wait until she's crossed the room then haul myself to my feet. It's time I got another soda.

Chapter 60

I watch as one of the bartenders leaves the bar and speaks to a roving doorman. As soon as the bartender pulls back a half step, the doorman walks to the entrance.

The suited gorilla walks in and scans the room. His eyes find the bartender, who's standing by the DJ's booth.

A moment later the bartender is walking my way, with the gorilla following at his heel like a well-trained puppy.

He stops a respectful distance away and gives me the once over. It's nothing more than a show. He's sent two dancers my way, so he's aware of what I look like and has the information I want him to have.

The gorilla at his heel is also for show. He wants me to feel intimidated. If he thinks that King Kong's baby brother is going to scare me, he's very much mistaken.

'Good evening, sir.' The bartender motions at the seat opposite mine. 'Do you mind if I join you for a brief chat?'

'Be my guest.' I slump back in my seat to show how unconcerned I am. 'What would you like to chat about?'

'Your presence here. You've told my colleague that you're waiting for someone. May I enquire as to whom it is you're waiting for?'

Like his polite words, the tone used by the bartender is neutral and respectful. This informs me that I'm not yet deemed a threat. The gorilla is there to make sure I don't become one. Or at least, that's what he expects to happen.

'Actually, he's just arrived.'

The bartender looks over his shoulder, then back at me with a puzzled expression.

I clear up the confusion by pointing at him. I'm still mostly prone on the fake leather couch so he gives a thin smile.

'If you were looking for me, then you coulda just asked someone. The guys here know who I am.'

I nod. 'True. Problem is, I didn't know your name. Still don't. Didn't even know it would be you that I wanted to speak to.'

'I'm sorry, but you've lost me. Is it me you're looking for or not?'

'I'm looking for the person in charge of this place. If it's you, then I've found who I'm looking for. If not, I'll have to ask you to lead me to them.'

His expression darkens, and he straightens up. 'I'm in charge. What do you want me for?'

'To see how much this place is selling for.'

He throws back his head and guffaws. The gorilla laughs too, although I doubt he's bright enough to have understood the conversation.

'You've had a wasted trip, buddy. The Elite Club. Is not. For sale.'

I figure he's emphasised those last four words for the gorilla's benefit rather than mine.

My eyes never leave his as I give a series of slow nods. 'I think you'll find that it is for sale. The people I represent have decided that they would like to buy The Elite Club. Therefore, it is for sale.'

'And exactly who do you represent?'

I toss him a name. It's amazing what you can find on the internet when you have a friend who's as good at running searches as Alfonse is.

The bartender blanches and I don't blame him. He works for a guy who runs a sizeable portion of Queens. The name I've just given him controls all the Bronx.

There's a change in the bartender's expression. All pretence of politeness is gone as he looks at me with a shrewder focus.

'You're not one of their men. There's no way they would employ an Englishman.'

I raise a hand in a halting gesture. 'I'm Scottish. And if you ever call me English again, I'll pour a pint of gasoline down your throat and throw lit matches at you.'

The gorilla takes a step forward, but the bartender waves him back. 'I apologise. I took a guess. No offence was intended.'

His words would be mollifying were it not for the look in his eyes. He doesn't trust me.

'I am who I say I am, and if you want to sit there insulting me, then I won't bother suggesting that we buy this place.' For the first time in the conversation, I add a snarl to my voice. 'Instead, I'll prepare a hostile takeover.'

The bartender doesn't flinch.

'Nice try, buddy, but I'm not buying what you're shovelling. There isn't going to be a sale, or a hostile takeover. This place isn't on the market. If it were, I'd know.'

I hand him my cell. 'Call The King and tell him what I've just told you. Then we'll find out if this place is for sale.'

'I'll call him, but not here.' He stands. 'I'll call him from the office; you're welcome to listen.'

His words are a direct challenge. If I were who I'm implying, I wouldn't fear going somewhere private with him and his pet gorilla. On the other hand, if I'm some random chancer, there's no way I'd be stupid enough to take that level of risk.

It's a lot of years since I backed down from a challenge.

I stand and put a happy expression on my face. 'Finally, we're getting somewhere.' I gesture towards the two key-padded doors. 'After you.'

He leads, I follow. The gorilla follows me.

By the time we get to the office, one of the roving doormen has fallen in behind the gorilla.

Three against one isn't the worst odds I've faced but, in a cramped office, there isn't a lot of room for manoeuvre when one of the room's occupants fills almost half the space.

I lean nonchalantly against a wall as the bartender goes towards the cluttered desk. The office is a functional one. It has painted block walls and a number of filing cabinets. Cameron told me about a second office, which has a boardroom table, where he would meet Kingston and his lackeys whenever a face-to-face was required.

As soon as the barman hears the click of the door closing behind the roving doorman, he whirls and throws a shot at me.

He connects.

But not with me.

I'm wise enough to anticipate a sudden attack, so I push myself backwards in time for him to miss me, and thump his fist into the block wall.

The crack of his knuckles breaking is followed by a yelp of pain.

As the bartender is cursing I throw a kick at his knee and an elbow towards the gorilla.

The kick connects but the elbow doesn't.

Something akin to a freight train collides with my ribs, and I see a cheerful smile on the gorilla's ugly face. This is what he likes: attacking smaller men and inflicting pain on them. He's even got a buddy as backup should he need any help. Perhaps the buddy is just here to observe the beating so the gorilla has someone who can support his retelling of the event.

I bounce off the wall and back towards the gorilla. Using my forward momentum, I arch my back and plant my forehead on his chin. Head-butts are best aimed at the nose but, short of jumping, there's no way I'm tall enough to connect.

He roars and comes at me with his arms held wide.

I don't have time to do much but drop to my knees. As the gorilla's arms swoop over my head, I throw an uppercut at his balls.

He grunts and doubles over. I repeat the blow and force my way up between him and the wall.

I push the gorilla and he falls over the prone bartender.

With them both vulnerable, I whip the sharpening steel from my sleeve. I'm just about to crash it down on their limbs when the roving doorman speaks.

'That's enough!' His voice isn't quite a yell, but it's not far off. 'Drop the weapon.'

I glance at him and decide to do what he says. After all, he's the one with the gun.

There are soft moans coming from the gorilla, and curses from the bartender, but it's the roving doorman I'm listening to.

I think about the gun nestling in the small of my back. It's accessible, but I don't for one minute think I can whip it out, take aim, and shoot the doorman before he pulls his trigger.

He motions for me to sit in the office's chair.

I sit.

He throws a left cross at me that reopens the split on my lip and loosens a tooth. Considering it's his weak hand, it's a good solid punch.

I straighten my head and look at him. 'Is there any need? Your buddies jumped me. I defended myself. Now you're waving a gun around like you're John Wayne.' I shake my head and make sure I have eye contact with him. 'The people I represent will not be happy about this. You can make it easy on yourself by putting that gun down right now.'

'No way.'

There's uncertainty in his tone, so I try again. 'I'm telling you. Keeping that gun on me is a very bad idea. Either you'll shoot me, which will start a turf war, or you'll miss me, and I'll kill you before I leave this room. The longer you have that gun aimed at me, the shorter your life expectancy gets.'

His eyes flick to the floor, and the gun droops an inch, before his attention is snapped back to me and the gun's aim returns to my face. I guess he got a signal from his buddies.

It's the second time tonight that a fool has pointed a gun at me. I'd rather there wasn't a third.

If the guys on the floor are sending the doorman signals, it means they are recovering from the damage I inflicted upon them. With a gun on me, and two pissed-off guys seeking retribution,

I don't much fancy my chances of leaving this office without a serious injury.

As I look at the gun, it's being traversed up and down my body. One minute it's pointing at the top of my head, the next my balls. I should be scared that the doorman is picking his spot.

Instead I'm glad he's so cocky.

As he gets to the top of his range I make a mental note of the position of his arm, and wait while he goes down and up again.

I throw myself under his arm as the gun's aim passes my nose and is still moving upwards.

By the time his brain has told his finger to squeeze, I'm below the bullet's path and am driving him against the wall with my shoulder. The gunshot exploding so close to my head is deafening, but now isn't the time to wiggle a finger in each ear.

I wrap two hands around his gun wrist and twist his arm to the point of dislocation. And beyond.

He screams as he drops the gun.

I keep hold of his wrist and swing him round until his head collides with a wall. He drops in an untidy heap so I turn my attention to the gorilla and the bartender. The gorilla is holding both hands against his gut and there is blood seeping between his fingers, while the bartender is trying to pull his leg free from underneath the gorilla.

I guess the shot fired by the doorman has hit the gorilla.

I retrieve the gun and aim it in the general direction of the bartender as I pick up my sharpening steel. My next move is to slam the steel against the knees of the doorman, before I use it to knock the gorilla out cold.

The bartender eyes me with fear as I approach him. He's still trapped by the gorilla's bulk as I use the sharpening steel to smash his right elbow.

I sit myself back in the office chair and wait for his groaning to subside. When it turns into pleas for mercy, I hold a finger to my lips.

He shushes.

'Where can I find The King?'

He shakes his head. 'I can't tell you that. It's more than my life is worth.'

I could point out that his life isn't worth anything to me, but I don't think he'd appreciate my honesty.

'I'll only ask you nicely once more. Where can I find The King?'

He doesn't answer. There's defiance in his eyes.

I walk the two steps towards him, place a boot on his left wrist and open my backpack. The chef's blowtorch fits nicely in my hand.

I press the button and a blue flame springs from its nozzle. I show it to the bartender, see the terror in his eyes, and take a sweeping pass of his fingertips.

He yelps, but otherwise remains silent.

I bend to take another sweep and his hand curls into a fist. Improvising has never been an issue for me, so I hold the flame against his knuckles for the count of three. I can see his skin blistering as the air fills with the smell of burnt pork.

He howls and tries to wriggle free, but my boot holds him in place.

I hold the unlit blowtorch in front of one of his eyes. 'Where can I find The King?'

'I ... I ... I don't know. If I need him I have a number to call.'

He gives me the number.

I write it down on a piece of paper that gets stuffed in my pocket, and take a roll of duct tape from my backpack. Tying people up with duct tape might be an overused cliché, but hey, it works.

Five minutes later I have the three of them tied up and I'm leaving the office. Had they not started throwing punches around, and refused to answer my questions, they would be in a lot less pain. They struck first so I feel no guilt about their various agonies.

I now have two guns stuffed into the small of my back. I've checked the new one and it has eight bullets in its cartridge.

Fifteen bullets, when you're as inexperienced with guns as I am, isn't a lot, but it's eight more than I had. If things go the way I've planned, I won't be getting myself into any gunfights.

Rather than let any of the staff release the bound men and alert The King, I find one of the roving doormen and tell him that The King is coming for an urgent meeting, and that he's to close the place for the night and send all the staff home. He tries to resist me giving him orders, but I drop the wrong kind of name and he does as I bid.

It takes him twenty minutes to get the doors locked, but finally the last member of staff leaves.

I make sure the club is secure and let myself out of a side door.

Chapter 61

I take a zig-zag route away from The Elite Club until I find myself on a busy street. There's a club across the road where throngs of people are hanging outside, chatting and smoking.

The scene is one I see three nights a week while tending door at The Joshua Tree: Casperton's rock bar, where even the music has to be twenty-one or older.

The club will be noisy and filled with laughter, arguments and people shouting into their friends' ears to be heard over the music.

I need somewhere quieter, but not so quiet that my conversation is overheard.

I look along the street and see a collection of bars. I head towards them in the hope of finding one with a working payphone.

Two girls are walking towards me; one is carrying her shoes, while the other totters on impossibly high heels. They see me walking their way and cut their giggling.

While it's not my intention to frighten innocents, I guess my scars are doing their job. I also figure that my recent fight, on top of all the other events, has left me looking a lot grimmer than usual.

I reach the row of bars and look for the least classy. It'll be the quietest one, devoid of shrieking laughter and booming music.

When I enter, I see the kind of place that's been around for decades – one that uses its original features to give it character. The problem is, this bar has all the character of a speakeasy that's fallen silent.

The fittings may tell of a bygone age, but they also tell of a bygone cleaner. Every piece of chrome or brass is pitted with rust spots and discolouration. The furniture is the uniform brown of dirt accumulated by a century of use, and there's no way I would drink from any of the glasses behind the bar.

I order a bottle of soda from a bartender, who appears old enough to have been Methuselah's headmaster, and ask if they have a payphone.

He puts my drink on the counter without a napkin, and points to a cubbyhole. 'Phone's in there. Don't know if it still works. It's been a while since it was last used.'

I wipe the rim of my soda bottle as I walk to the cubbyhole.

The phone has a dial-tone when I lift the handset, so I feed a handful of coins into it and punch Alfonse's number into the keypad.

Sure, I could have used my new cell to call him, but this phone is anonymous, and therefore won't leave a trail pointing to him should the worst happen to me.

Alfonse picks up on the second ring.

I spend two minutes talking to him and hang up.

To avoid suspicion from the biblical headmaster, or the bar's four patrons, I finish my soda and head out to the street.

There's a bar across the street that looks like the one I've just left, so I head over there to kill the ten minutes Alfonse has told me to wait before calling him back.

This bar is only half as old as the other one and, when I check, on a fake trip to the bathroom, the payphone has a dial tone.

Chapter 62

'You're nothing but a waste of space. I can't believe I once loved you. Do you hear me, Cameron? You're a waste of space. A complete and utter bawbag, whose only achievement in life is the infliction of misery upon those foolish enough to love him.'

Cameron gets a pang of nostalgia at Ivy's use of the Glaswegian insult, bawbag. Her abusive rants have lasted so long he's now immune to them.

If he cared about her opinion of him, he'd have been wounded by her words, but he'd lost the few feelings he'd had for her a long time ago. Now she's nothing more than a distant echo, shouting back at him from the cavern of history.

He'd thought about telling her that he wasn't listening, but decided against it. Knowing her, she'd just raise her voice.

A part of him feels sorry for her. Not for the damage his actions have wrought; more for the years she's spent accumulating bitterness. Emotions like that eat into happiness the way a starving lion gorges on a fresh kill.

Just two days after losing the fortune that would have funded his retirement, he's cast aside any thoughts of allocating blame for his misfortune, and is looking forward rather than back.

'You remember when your mother contacted me saying you wanted a divorce? That was the day I found out what you really were. She cried on the phone to me that day. Have you any idea how often we pictured your body being found somewhere? How many times we speculated that you'd been killed, or committed suicide? Were you even aware that your mother aged twenty years in the two years it took for you to get in touch?'

Before he can stop himself, Cameron rises from the bed and bangs on the door. 'That's enough, Ivy.'

Cameron hears a throaty chuckle. 'So that's your weak spot is it? Your mother? Not your kids. Not your wives. Your mother. You're a pathetic excuse for a human being. The thought that I ever let you touch me makes my skin crawl. You broke my heart and those of my kids. Not content with breaking three hearts, you did the same with your other wife and kids, and yet, big tough guy that you are, you're only bothered about your mammy.'

'You've said enough, Ivy. Leave my mother out of this.'

'Why, what you going to do? I saw the pain of worry age her. I remember the haunted expression she took on after you'd scarpered. She's a good woman who loved the bawbag that was her son. You've never cared about your children, but you listen to me: just like your mother, I love my children. I'm proud of them and their moral fibre. They are fine, upstanding citizens who've thrown off the grief of being abandoned by a worthless bag of skin that's not fit to *say* the word father, let alone behave like one.'

'You're full of pish, Ivy. You don't know your boy as well as you think.' Cameron slams the heel of his palm against the door. 'Do you hear me? You have no idea what Jake is doing now, but let me tell you, there's nothing about murder that speaks of moral fibre.'

'What do you mean murder? What does homicide have to do with anything?'

The American word sits odd in Cameron's ears when delivered in a thick Glaswegian brogue. He gives it a moment's thought and remembers how Ivy had always tried to fit in. Her using the local terminology would be natural for someone who'd been out here as long as she had.

'Jake hasn't gone back to New York to speak to the police about what happened. He's gone back to kill the person who shot his girlfriend. He's going to either get himself killed, or arrested and jailed for murder. I said my goodbyes to him a long time ago, Ivy. It's about time you got ready to say yours.'

As Cameron lies back on the bed he can hear Ivy's sobbing recede as she walks away. He lays his head on the pillow and closes his eyes. A part of him knows he should feel cruel for shattering her illusion of Jake. Another, larger part, wishes he'd thought of it sooner as it has shut Ivy up and he can now get some peace to sleep.

Chapter 63

I make the second call to Alfonse and listen as he gives me a location for Kingston. He's as succinct as ever with his report, but I feel there's something nagging at him. He gets to the point and tells me that Mother has been in touch with him, demanding that he tells her where I am, and that he's to tell me "to return home immediately before I do something stupid".

I thank him for his help and end the call. He knows me well enough to know I won't go running just because Mother has told me to come home.

Alfonse has yet to share his opinion on what I'm planning to do. The fact he has held back from telling me, lets me know he at least agrees on some level that a biblical eye-for-an-eye justice should be delivered, rather than one meted out by a court.

It's a big step, planning to kill someone, and the aiding and abetting of a planned assassination will incur stiff penalties for him should I get caught or be killed. This is why I'm doing everything I can to isolate his involvement from my activities.

His digital searches will be registered on his computer, but he's more than smart enough to erase them in case anyone should come looking for him as my accomplice.

That mother has found out about my mission is disconcerting to say the least. While she and I may have a tumultuous relationship, we still love and respect one another.

It shouldn't surprise me that Cameron has told her what my plans are. He's possessed by a self-interest that makes Mother's narcissism seem charitable. Plus, I'm confident that she will have relished giving him a piece of her mind.

Thirty years is a long time to store hate, and there are few things Mother likes better than delivering a well-deserved bollocking.

There's no doubt in my mind that Mother will have heaped abuse and derision on him from first light until last. Mother may well be in her sixth decade, but she's still got enough fight in her to see her take on far greater targets than Cameron.

In my mind's eye I can picture them either side of the door. Her, furious and vitriolic as she lambasts him for all his failings; him, aghast and repentant at the hurt he's caused.

It's an idea that gives me the greatest of pleasure. There are few people in this world that I hate, but my father tops the list. A day or two having Mother give him a good old-fashioned Glasgow slagging is the least he deserves.

I know my mother though. She'll go too far. She always does.

Cameron telling her that I'm planning to kill is a sure-fire indicator that she's already crossed his red line. Alfonse telling me that Mother has just called him advises me that the line has only been crossed in the last few minutes.

It's a worry I have to shelve. I can't be thinking about what Mother will say, when I'm storming The King's castle.

Chapter 64

The cab drops me a quarter mile from Olly Kingston's house as I don't want any witnesses.

His house is a good one. It sits on a good street, in a good neighbourhood. It's almost a shame I plan to do bad things in it.

I scout the house from the road at first. It has a seven-foot wall – like most of the houses in the street. There's also a pair of wrought iron, ornamental gates that look strong enough to resist anything less than a bulldozer. A plaque on the wall bears the name of the house.

It isn't Graceland, so I decide that The King has delusions of grandeur, rather than a love of a certain rock and roll star.

I'd jump up and take a peek over the wall were it not for a fear that the concrete coping stone was layered with broken glass.

A walk past the gates shows the house to be ablaze with lights and the drive littered with expensive cars. There's a little gatehouse to the right of the opening and I can see a pair of feet and a screen.

A party is not what I was expecting, and the presence of a goon at the gate makes entry a little bit tougher. The gates can be climbed in a matter of seconds, but having someone shouting the alarm will not simplify things.

I dare say I could try and bluff my way in as a late guest, or as an employee of someone attending the party, but those paths are filled with hazards. There's no telling whether the party is for legitimate or illegal friends and, either way, if I was escorted into the house and the party, I'd be recognised as a stranger as soon as they saw me.

The scar on my face will go against me, should it be a legitimate party, and I'm confident there will be guns pointed at me if The King and his associates have learned what happened at The Elite Club.

I continue my walk until I'm two houses along from The King's. Neither of his neighbours, nor the houses opposite, have lights on – except external ones.

This gives me hope that the party is a legitimate one, and that his neighbours are on the guest list.

I double back to his nearest neighbour's house, and peer through their gate. The house looks to be asleep, so I ignore the pain in my ribs from the gorilla's punch and clamber up the wrought iron framework of the gate. When I reach the top I cast my eyes towards Kingston's house.

It's not the house I'm looking at, but the wall surrounding his garden. There's no glint of reflected light from any glass embedded into the top of the wall. I tell myself to get with the times and stop looking for things that went out of fashion thirty years ago. Any security arrangements Kingston has will be modern ones, backed up by gun-toting henchmen.

I'm listening for the bark of dogs, or the howl of sirens that have been triggered by a hidden alarm. Hearing neither, I creep my way through the bushes until I'm halfway along the wall between this house and Kingston's.

My next move is to get on the porch and climb slowly onto the veranda rail. As I straighten myself, my eyes are watching for anyone looking out of a window at Kingston's house.

There's nothing to see but, until the party reduces itself to the last few guests, I can't begin to think about crossing the wall.

I climb down and prepare myself for a wait, as I listen for the sounds of people leaving.

As I wait, I put myself through a series of stretches so I'm as supple as a man my age can be. A pulled muscle will almost certainly make the difference between life and death.

I marvel at how steady my hands are, and how controlled my breathing is. I should be a shaking mess, fighting my emotions and the adrenaline that's pumping its way around my body, but I'm not. The only thing I'm afraid of tonight, is failure.

My anger has robbed me of my instinct for self-preservation. I'm not suicidal; I have a mission to carry out, and I'm not afraid for my well-being so long as the mission is a success.

Chapter 65

When I hear a series of car doors slamming, followed by the sound of engines purring and the crunching whisper of tyres on fine gravel, I shin up the first few branches of a tree and peer over the wall.

There's little sign of life from Kingston's house. The drapes are pulled and only half of the rooms that were previously illuminated now show lights.

With just a few guests left, I figure I should get myself over the wall before he switches on any electronic security.

I drop from the tree to the ground, and leap up and grab the top of the wall with my hands. It takes a little scrabbling with my feet, but I manage to haul myself up and over the wall.

My feet land in the soft soil of a flowerbed, as I intended, and I pad over to the house's outer wall, pressing myself flat against the stonework.

A quick check reassures me that I still have all my weapons in place, so I creep towards the rear of the house – taking care to duck below any lit windows. When I near the corner, I inch myself forward so I don't walk right into someone's view, and so I can observe each new part of the garden as it is revealed.

There's a swimming pool, which is lit with underwater lights; while it may be too late in the year for swimming, I guess Kingston has made sure his pool is lit up to impress his guests. Like every other part of the garden, the area around the pool is manicured and sculpted to perfection.

I press forward a little further and see an empty sunroom attached to the back of the house.

As I round the corner, and crawl towards the sunroom on my hands and knees, I adopt caution as a middle name.

A quick bob of my head confirms it's still empty, so I manoeuvre myself to the door and tease the handle down. The door opens without a sound.

I get inside the sunroom and crouch beneath a rattan couch that sports cream cushions. From here, I can see the sunroom is connected to the house by a hallway, which has openings left and right and runs through the main building.

This is bad. Whichever way I choose I'll be leaving myself open to an ambush from a minimum of two directions.

On the other hand, should I need them, I'll have three escape routes.

A more immediate worry is that the door from the sunroom to the hall could be locked. I get up and move towards it with a blend of speed and silence.

This handle is stiffer than the other, but it opens with the faintest of noises when I put a bit more weight behind my hand. Before I step into the hallway, I crane my head left and right while listening for movement.

Of the three doors leading from the hall, only the one to my left has light showing beneath it.

As a precaution against ambush I open the door straight ahead, and the one to my right, but find a large empty lounge and a deserted kitchen that looks more like a showroom than the heart of a home.

With Kingston's money, it's probable that he dines out most nights, and for an event like tonight's he would hire caterers.

I pull both guns from the small of my back and make sure their safety catches are off. I tuck one under my right armpit, while I grasp the door handle, and with a deep exhale I throw the door open and stride into the room.

'Nobody move.' My voice is raised, and I have both guns pointing at the men sitting round a large dining table.

One of the men disobeys my command and rises from his seat. As he stands, his right hand dives beneath his jacket. I pull both my triggers twice, and see a spurt of red leap from the side of his neck. As he falls to the floor a thick geyser of arterial blood sprays the guy next to him.

I keep my face stern and try not to show relief that I've hit him. I'd aimed at the centre of the guy's stomach; therefore, I'd missed my target by between fourteen and eighteen inches. Another inch to the right and it would have missed him altogether.

With four bullets gone I have eleven left. A quick head count shows there are six men seated around the table.

The air hangs with expectancy and cigar smoke.

I lay down the gun in my left hand, and cover the men with the one in my right, as I fish the roll of duct tape from my pocket.

'You.' I point at the nearest man – a thin streak of nothing with a greasy ponytail – as the roll of tape flies towards him. 'Bind your buddies. If any of them manage to escape, I'll shoot you first. Understand?'

He goes to work, and the man I've recognised as Kingston slowly rises to his feet with his hands above his head. He looks a little older than he does in the only picture that Alfonse was able to find of him on the internet. His jowls hang lower and there's less hair surrounding his baldpate.

'You've made a grave mistake, Buster.'

I point one gun at him while keeping the rest of them covered with the other gun in my right hand. 'Really? I could say the same about you. You are behind the death of someone very dear to me. That's something I take exception to.'

The calmness I felt earlier is still there and I have to fight my amazement at it. To me, this feels right. I'm here to deliver justice and to make sure Kingston pays for his part in Taylor's death.

I glance at the men and see that Ponytail has secured three of them and is working on the fourth. Once he's finished the next guy, he'll only have Kingston left. My plan is to knock Ponytail out and bind him myself.

I'll have plenty of time to persuade Kingston to tell me the name of the man who pulled the trigger. I am certain that, while he may have instructed the man to shoot, there is no way he did it himself. To do that would implicate him in ways that are undeniable to law enforcers.

'FREEZE!'

If the shout doesn't make me obey, the gun pressed against the back of my neck makes it a no-brainer. I have no option but to allow Ponytail and Kingston to take my weapons from me.

When the gun is removed from my neck, I see a woman whose face is a rigid mask; it's either Botox, or Kingston's wife is more than a little miffed with me for getting blood on her carpet.

Chapter 66

Credit where it's due, neither Kingston nor his men do anything to harm me as they drag me to an ornamental steel pillar, which supports an ornate staircase, wrap my arms around it and bind my hands with duct tape.

I'd expected a few cheap shots on account of the man I'd killed, but not only are they professional, they're obedient, and follow Kingston's quiet commands without question.

They've positioned me so that my back is to the room and they have me at their mercy – the only defence I can mount is mule kicks.

A fist slams into my kidneys and sends spasms of pain throughout me.

'Okay, boys. You all get one punch each, and then we'll see what Buster has to say for himself.'

It's not Kingston's words that scare me, it's the matter-of-fact tone they're delivered in. This is all in a day's work for him. A man has been shot dead at his dining table, by a gun-toting stranger, and he's speaking in the calm, measured fashion that I used when I met Taylor's parents for the first time.

Four more blows land on my kidneys, but it's the final punch that does the most damage. It lands on the back of my head and drives my forehead against the ornamental pillar. I hang on the edge of consciousness with my arms supporting me where the duct tape has snagged on a decorative feature. The sudden halt as I fell was akin to having my arms yanked upwards.

It could be worse. The clock had struck twelve long ago, and there are enough whisky fumes in the air to suggest that these men have all had a good drink. Therefore, they're not at their peak when it comes to punching. Even if their target is bound and unmissable. Had they been sober, I dare say I'd be on my knees by now.

I force myself to my feet, as much to relieve the ache in my arms as to show defiance.

Two goons turn me so Kingston can see my face.

'So, Buster. Who are you, and why are you here?'

'I'm a friend of a friend. I heard you were looking for staff.'

My answer is a shock to me, but there's no way I plan to tell him the truth.

'So, instead of applying for a job, like any normal person, you sneak in here and kill one of my associates?'

'He killed himself when he didn't listen. It's not my fault you hired a moron.'

There's a curse, followed by rapid footsteps. I brace myself for the blow, but a word from Kingston is enough to make the aggressor stop.

'Forgive William. The man you killed was his brother, so it's only natural he's rather upset with you.'

I don't say anything. William may be controlled by Kingston, but there's no point in pushing him further. Should I say the wrong the thing, William may just ignore his boss and kill me.

'So then, Buster, do you have a name?'

There an oddness about Kingston calling me Buster, and his polite tones. It's like he's either struggling to shake off his roots, or is dumbing himself down so his men don't feel inadequate at his superior intelligence.

'Buster is as good a name as any.'

Kingston looks over my shoulder and does the peace sign. 'William, if you'd do the honours, please?'

Unsure of where the blows will land, I tense my body and make sure my head can't be knocked against the pillar for a second time. William's fists collide with my kidneys.

My right kidney has taken more damage than the left one, but I can tell that William is left handed from the power of his punches. It's a fact that may or may not come in useful.

'I think William would rather like it if you don't tell me your name. Do you want to make him happy, or do you want to tell me your name?'

I've held on to this minor detail for long enough. While I'm taking a pounding they're not killing me. The longer I can draw this out, the better my chances are of finding a way to escape, or at least killing Kingston before his goons kill me.

By the same token, I don't want to stretch credibility by not giving up a fact as inconsequential as my name. So long as I seem to give them each piece of information they want with a grudge, it will add a layer of validity to the lies I tell.

'My name is Brian Johnson.'

I'm not sure if they're fans of AC/DC. In a lot of ways, I don't care. Even if they do recognise the singer's name, Brian Johnson is the kind of everyday name that is believable. Had I told them my name was Mick Jagger, or Axl Rose, I would have given them such grounds for disbelief that I may as well beat myself up.

'So, Brian, you said you came here looking for a position within my organisation; perhaps you can enlighten me as to your qualifications? Also, tell me, who is this friend of mine who suggested you come and see me?'

The way Kingston says "Brian" suggests he doesn't believe it's my real name. He doesn't push it though. I suppose in his line of work, false names are given more often than real ones.

A bigger issue is that he wants to know who has sent me. Cameron's name will get me a bullet in the back of the head, and I don't know any of Kingston's friends who might have made a genuine recommendation.

However, I'd always known this moment may arise, and I've taken a few steps in preparation.

I give him the name of the man who controls the southern half of Staten Island.

Kingston purses his lips and takes a seat as he thinks about the name I've given him. He keeps his head down so his face can't be seen.

Federico Peccia is not a name to be said without reverence. I only know about him because I had Alfonse dig into the files of the NYPD to find the three-letter agency that deals with organised crime, and get me their most wanted list. I might never have been a boy scout, but their motto of "be prepared" is a good one.

Peccia is known to be one of the most ruthless of the various crime lords. His signature punishment is to flay his victims, roll them in salt, and dispatch them with a bullet to the back of the head when he tires of hearing their screams.

Kingston may, or may not, have met Peccia, but the two men will be aware of each other. They're far enough apart territorially for there to be no encroaching of boundaries, but while Kingston may be a big fish in his own area, compared to Peccia he's little more than a shrimp.

He'll now be thinking about his life expectancy and trying to work out if my presence here is enemy action, along the lines of infiltration, or if my story is genuine.

I let him think for as long as he needs. If he's thinking, nobody is punching me.

His goons are silent and there's no noise other than the faint echo of music. I can't say I know anything about classical music, but the tune I hear is dark and brooding, and I can tell it's building its way towards a thundering crescendo. I hope it isn't symbolism at work.

Kingston lifts his head and licks his lips. His expression is grave when he addresses me. 'Buster, you don't know much about Peccia if you thought you could come here saying he sent you. He doesn't do favours. Not for you, not for me.'

'I didn't come here because of a favour.' I make sure there's plenty of scorn in my voice. 'I'm here because I get around and I hear things. A lot of what I've heard is not good news. At least, not for you.'

'So, what have you heard?' Kingston picks up one of my guns and points it in my face.

I try not to show fear. 'Shooting me won't get you the information that will save your life. It might be Peccia that's coming for you, it may well be someone else.'

'Gentlemen, we are saved. Brian here, has come to rescue us from our enemies.' Kingston turns to his goons and laughs until they join in, like the good little sycophants they are. It's a false laugh, derived from fear and uncertainty.

'You made a mistake killing the girl on the yacht. That's brought you a lot of attention. Trust me, it's the wrong kind of attention.'

Kingston's laughter stops dead and his eyes narrow. 'What do you know about the yacht?'

'Everything.'

'Would you care to elaborate, or do I have to ask William to encourage you?'

'You got shafted by one of your own. Gave chase, killed the wrong person, and became a laughing stock when the guy you were after disappeared.'

Kingston puts the gun on an occasional table, three feet to my right, and returns to his chair. 'You seem well-informed, but only to a point. We didn't make it public knowledge, but we got the guy we were after, and his buddy. Therefore, your information is wrong.'

I'd laugh if my life wasn't in imminent danger. Kingston is bluffing and his face says he believes the lie. Perhaps he's been told it as a truth, by men who're afraid to give him bad news.

It's time for me to ramp up the tension. 'What about the girl? My sources tell me she was the daughter of a senator. I shouldn't think the police will be allowed to not solve her murder.'

'She's a senator's daughter, is she?' His face changes. 'It would appear to me that your sources are less than accurate. Either that, or you're being economical with the truth. William, if you'd care to go first, I think two blows each this time.'

I hear footsteps approach me and I tense myself, ready for the pain that may well be coming my way.

Chapter 67

I'm not looking forward to getting hit ten times, so I attempt to make a bid for freedom. I lift my hands as high as possible, and drive them down with as much force as possible while tucking my elbows into my sides as they descend.

Just like the books I've read suggested, the motion is enough to free my hands from the duct tape binding them.

I feel William's fist collide with my left kidney. Now I'm free of the restraint provided by the pillar, the blow is enough to send me staggering.

This is a good thing, as it propels me towards the gun that Kingston laid on the occasional table.

As I snatch it up I look at it and assess which one it is. It's the one I got from the mugger in the alleyway. That means it has three bullets.

Six opponents, three bullets and one bad shot: me.

Those aren't good odds, but they are better than the ones I was facing when bound to the pillar.

As I whirl round to face them, I bring the gun to bear and pull the trigger.

Three deafening shots ring out and three of the men fall to the floor. Not that I hit them with a careful aim: they were so close to me it would have been harder to miss.

I don't waste time checking the severity of their injuries. Instead, I point the gun at the nearest man, who is stumbling over his buddies.

Momentum is carrying him forward, so I slip my finger from the gun's trigger guard, and use the palm of my hand as a hammer to smash it into his face. I follow up with a left cross to the temple.

As he's falling, I weigh up my last two aggressors.

One of them is Kingston. Like the hero he is, he lets his goon come at me first. I can see the snarl on the goon's face, as Kingston heads towards the dining table where my other gun still rests.

The goon has to go down quick if I'm to stand any chance of catching Kingston. Because of the bodies on the floor, he takes a circuitous route to get to me.

I use the time he wastes to grab a chair and throw it at Kingston. The chair hits the back of his legs and he stumbles to his knees.

The chance is too good to waste, so I launch myself forward and plant the toe of my boot in Kingston's unmentionables.

As I take a step towards the gun, a strong arm wraps itself around my throat and hauls backwards to exert maximum pressure on my larynx.

I throw my elbows back, but the guy holding me has positioned himself to use my body as a shield.

He has me standing on my toes, so it's no use trying to use my weight to draw him to the ground – he's too strong for that. Instead, I swing a foot forward, as far as it will go, and thrash it backwards with enough force to break his shins.

My foot misses his leg, but I'm not worried. My leg flies past his and alters our balance. Instead of me being stretched back against his chest, he's now hunched over my back.

I twist, and let my standing leg go weak.

I throw my head back as we are falling, and it collides with his as it lands on the polished wooden floor.

His arm loosens its grip on my throat long enough for me to break loose. I spin round and crash my forehead into his nose. His head goes back and presents me with the target I've been looking for.

I punch the goon with my knuckles extended. He may recover from the blow to his larynx, or he may spend the next couple of minutes gasping his way to his grave, that's his problem; for now, he's out of action.

I look for Kingston and see he's picked himself up and is reaching for the gun. I charge towards him and hit him with a running tackle that slams him into the table and drives the breath from both of our bodies.

The table overturns and I hear the gun skittering away. I'm gasping for air as Kingston picks himself up. He's unsteady on his feet but, after the punishment I've taken tonight, he's in better shape than I am.

He lifts a chair above his head and crashes it down on my chest.

What little air there is in my lungs gets driven out.

Chapter 68

I'm fighting to breathe and I see Kingston take a frantic look around him. I guess he's looking for a weapon and pray he doesn't find one.

Kingston's eyes don't rest anywhere for long. Some air enters my lungs and I feel strong enough to move, just as he launches himself towards the door that I came through.

I know, if I let him out of my sight, I'll have to leave with my mission unaccomplished. There's no way it would be safe to look for him in his own house. He'll know where his weapons are, and the best places to ambush me.

Somehow I haul my aching body upright and stumble after him.

He's ten feet ahead of me as he goes towards the door that leads to the kitchen. The door hangs open behind him and I see him reaching for the knife block as I enter.

His fingers grasp a large carving knife and he gives a vicious smile. 'You're a dead man, Buster. Even if I don't kill you right now, my men will hunt you down. Nowhere will be safe for you. You'll die screaming, begging for the pain to end.'

I ignore his taunts. He doesn't know who I am or where I'm from. There's no way his men can find me once I leave here. All he's trying to do is goad me into going for him, putting myself within reach of the knife he's holding.

He advances towards me as I round a granite-topped island that has a sink in the middle.

I throw various items from the worktop at him, but none are substantial enough to do any damage.

He tries to come around the island at me, but stops when he realises I'm circling round to where the knives are. I glance over my shoulder and see a full wine rack.

I grab two bottles by their necks.

As weapons, they are not the greatest, but they're strong enough to deflect a blow from the knife, and heavy enough to numb a muscle if I can get sufficient power into my swing.

Now it's me who advances.

'Come on then, prove you're The King. I've dropped all your henchmen, this is your chance to prove to them why you're known as The King. If you can take me down you'll become a legend.'

I see the flicker of excitement in his eyes. He wants that veneration; he wants to be classed as better than his thugs.

Inside me I know this has to end soon. If we get drawn into a long battle, the beating I've taken will give him the advantage. There's also the fact that one of his goons may not be sufficiently hurt to stay down for any length of time, and his wife could make another appearance. She'd looked wasted earlier, so I'm hoping she's passed out in her bed.

Kingston takes a dancing half-step forward, flashes his knife, and leaps back two steps as I retreat a pace. His move works for him and he grabs another knife from the block.

We face off against each other: him with a knife in each hand, me with a bottle of wine in each of mine.

He flashes his knives in front of my face in a steel blizzard as he advances on me.

I throw the bottle in my left hand at his head and, when he lifts his knives to deflect it, I strike forward with the bottle in my right. I don't care what I hit, so long as I hit something.

The bottle crashes against his left forearm causing his fingers to involuntarily open. His knife clatters to the ground.

He still has the advantage of knife against bottle, but now I've had a chance to judge how quick his reflexes are.

They are good, but not necessarily good enough.

I transfer the bottle to my left hand and wait for him to slash or stab at me.

When he does move to attack, it's with a mixture of short controlled movements that could become a slash or a stab at any time.

I swing my bottle towards his knife, deflecting it away from his centre, as I wheel inside his arm and throw an elbow at his head.

The bottle slips from my fingers and falls to the floor, sending broken glass and red wine across the cream tiles.

My elbow collides with something that's too hard to be anything other than his forehead. The pair of us slump to the ground, fighting for control of his knife. I can feel pieces of glass digging into my back as he wrestles himself on top of me.

Instead of defending myself, I use both my hands to twist his knife arm until I feel him release his grip. While I'm doing this, his free hand is throwing short hard punches at my face.

I feel my nose burst and my lips split, but I don't change my tactics.

With the knife released from his hands, I writhe and twist underneath him until I can buck him off me.

I straddle him and throw punch after punch at his face, turning it into a bloody pulp. I feel a sharp pain in my leg and see he's grabbed a knife and stabbed me.

As he pulls it out to stab me a second time, I twist his arm until the knife drops and I hear the crunch of his wrist bones breaking.

I deliver a thundering punch to his jaw that leaves him fighting consciousness.

I lever myself off him, open a cupboard, and pull Kingston into a position where I can rest one of his legs on the bottom shelf.

I stamp down hard enough on his shin to break the bone.

I kick anything that could be used as a weapon away from him, and return to the dining room. One of the goons has gotten himself into a sitting position, but the others are all lying where I dropped them. Four chests are rising and falling, which tells me only one of them is dead.

The guy sitting up watches me in fear as I gather up my jacket, backpack and the two guns.

'I'm going to talk to Kingston. Are you going to be stupid enough to interrupt our conversation?'

His answer is the defeated shaking of his head as he presses his hands against a bloody stomach wound.

Chapter 69

I arrange Kingston into a sitting position, fill a bowl with cold water and throw it in his face. A second bowlful of water gets tipped over his head.

He needs to be awake and fully alert for what I'm about to do.

I place my backpack on the floor opposite him and drop my denims before I sit beside it. He's watching me with confusion in his eyes.

I get my supplies within reach and stare at him. 'Pay attention.'

He doesn't say anything, just watches me as I remove the lid from his bottle of cognac and pour the contents on the stab wound on my right thigh. I don't know what damage has been done, I just know there's more blood coming out than I'd care for.

The brandy stings, but it's nowhere near as bad as the pain I'll feel in a minute.

My next move is to empty a bowl of water over the wound to cleanse it and wash the brandy away.

Kingston's eyes widen in surprise when I remove the blowtorch from my backpack and put one of his wooden salad forks between my teeth.

I wet the fingers of my left hand and use them to prise open the wound in my leg.

The blowtorch crackles into life; the blue flame, an inch and a half long, hisses with contempt.

My mouth tightens, and I almost chicken out of what I'm about to do, but a memory of Taylor spurs me on.

I point the tip of the blue flame into my stab wound and hold it there for two long, agonising seconds.

I clamp my teeth down on the salad fork as the pain becomes unimaginable. Were it not for the fork, I'd be screaming. Beads of sweat appear all over my body.

I put down the blowtorch and look at my leg.

The sides of the wound are red and inflamed but that doesn't worry me, it's only pain. What's important is that the blowtorch has done what I'd hoped it would do, and cauterised the veins split by Kingston's knife.

I pull some antibiotics, which I got from a pharmacy, out of my backpack and take a handful to counteract any infection that may have gotten into the wound.

Next I use my T-shirt to form a rudimentary bandage.

I pull up my denims and look at Kingston as I button my shirt. His eyes show a mixture of respect and revulsion.

'You've seen what I'm prepared to do to myself. Can you imagine what I'll do to you if you don't answer my questions?' I lift the blowtorch. 'Who shot the girl on the yacht?'

Kingston swallows and looks to the door, hoping for a rescue that doesn't come.

'So that's what this is about. She was your girl.'

'You have five seconds to give me an answer.' I don't bother telling him what the consequences will be if he doesn't. The blowtorch hissing in my hand is enough of a threat.

'She wasn't meant to die.'

'Four.'

'It was Henderson who was supposed to die.'

'The Scottish guy? Three.'

'Yeah.' Kingston squints. 'Hey, he looks a bit like you.'

'He's my father. It was me on the boat with him. Two.'

Kingston swallows and shakes his head. His eyes show fear.

'One. Who pulled the trigger?'

'It wasn't one of my men. They're okay with a pistol, but I needed someone who could shoot a rifle.'

I move the blowtorch until its flame is two inches above his shattered leg. 'Zero.'

I pull back the leg of his trousers.

'Wait. It was a guy I hired from a business associate.'

'Names.'

'The shooter is known only as The Mortician.'

'And the man who gave you his number?'

The name he gives sends my blood cold. It's not only that the guy is connected, it's also the people who are connected to him. Of all the gangland figures in New York that Alfonse had named for me, Genaro Chellini's name topped every list – whether you looked at wealth, influence, reputation or reach.

He is not the type of man who'd hire an amateur. Therefore, The Mortician will be a deadly foe.

I hold the blowtorch near enough to Kingston's ankle for him to feel its heat without being burned.

'Who was the trigger man and how did you find him?'

He repeats the names, and the fear in his eyes indicates that he's telling me the truth.

'How can I find this Mortician?'

He tells me the name he's stored The Mortician's number under in his cell, and pulls an iPhone from his pocket.

'Thank you.' I put down the blowtorch and look him in the eye. 'You set The Mortician after my father and got my girlfriend killed. That's not something I can forgive.'

I plunge one of my knives into his heart and watch the light fade from his eyes.

It doesn't feel good, but it does feel like justice has been served.

Chapter 70

I grab a set of car keys from a bowl at the front door and make my way out of Kingston's house.

I press a button on the key fob and the indicators flash on a Bentley. I climb in, fasten my seatbelt, and listen to the engine burble as I let it crawl its way to the gates.

The guy in the gatehouse doesn't look up as I pass through.

I drive without aim, until I see a sign for a subway station.

I stop by the sidewalk, spend a few minutes checking Kingston's cell, and put my plan into action. A search for "me" in the contacts gets me Kingston's number. I test it with my cell and his phone rings.

His call history doesn't show any contact with The Mortician, but I didn't expect it to. Text messages also come up blank.

Next I check his apps and see he has Snapchat. The criminal's favourite app: once a message has been viewed, it disappears.

Or at least that's the theory.

The reality is quite different. Someone with Alfonse's skills can access a person's Snapchat history and see every message. All he needs is a phone number.

I use my burner cell to call him. He answers on the fourth ring and is groggy with sleep. He sounds pleased to hear I'm alive, but I still detect a large amount of worry in his voice.

I spend five minutes giving Alfonse a combination of requests and instructions. He promises to have answers by 9 a.m.

I look at my watch and see I have five hours to kill. Some rest, a new pair of denims, and a few proper dressings for my wound are the order of my day.

It's time for me to move on. The longer I stay in one place, with Kingston's phone and his Bentley, the greater the odds are of any pursuers being able to find me.

A couple of young dudes are lurching their way towards the subway, but I don't think they're worthy candidates. Instead of bequeathing the car to someone, and possibly having Kingston's goons hunt them down, I leave the key in the ignition and his cell on the passenger seat.

I dismantle my burner as much as I can. Each piece will find its way into a different garbage bin in the subway.

I'm only halfway through the subway's entrance when I hear the roar of a large engine. Someone has already claimed the Bentley. Perhaps Lady Luck will allow them to keep it.

I plan my route back to Brooklyn and think about what I've learned. It would have been far better if the trigger man had been one of Kingston's own men.

Now The Mortician has become involved, things have ratcheted up another level.

He is a professional killer; I'm a doorman.

He will be calculating; I'm following a loose plan and improvising as I go along.

He will have a cool head; I am filled with a burning rage.

He will probably have had some military training; I was taught to fight in a garden by my grandfather.

He will have access to a personal armoury; I have three knives, one blowtorch, one gun with six bullets and a second gun with none. I don't even know what ammunition it takes so I can't buy any more; I'll get rid of it in the first drain I pass in a secluded area.

None of The Mortician's advantages are enough to make me think about giving up. Not one of them compels me to return to Casperton rather than risk my life.

The Mortician killed Taylor. I can't rest until I've killed him.

Chapter 71

The guy behind the counter at the all night convenience store looks more tired than I do. There are bags under his eyes big enough to be slung between two trees and used as hammocks, and the pallor of his skin doesn't suggest good health.

Those are his issues though.

I pay for the antiseptic cream, bandages, a new pair of denims and a packet of power bars, and limp out of the store.

My leg has been a constant source of agony since the adrenaline rush I experienced at Kingston's house dissipated. I could have added strong painkillers to my shopping list but I don't want anything to dull my wits.

The only hope I have of beating The Mortician is to outsmart him, and to do that I need to be sharp.

An all-night diner provides fuel for my body, and their coffee is stewed enough to resemble treacle. In my weakened state it's just what I need.

I have an hour to wait until it's time to call Alfonse. I've worked out what my plan should be and what I need Alfonse to do to make it happen.

My plan isn't foolproof, of that I'm sure, but it will be good enough to give me a chance to kill The Mortician. That's all I ask.

Also on my shopping list is a replacement burner.

There is the possibility that The Mortician will not fall for my ruse. Should that happen, I will have to hunt him in a different way.

The base of another plan forms in my head, but it's riskier than the first one, and may well require me to recruit some assistance.

I return my thoughts to plan A, and cross-examine it for flaws. There are far more than I am comfortable with, but I have time to smooth out some of the wrinkles. Should other failings arise, I will have to improvise as best I can.

Despite all the coffee I've had, tiredness is threatening to overtake me. As soon as I've called Alfonse, I will find myself a bed and get some rest.

Chapter 72

Cameron rubs at his eyes and lifts his head from the pillow. His watch shows he's slept for a solid eight hours. In years past he'd always needed a minimum of seven hours sleep before he could function at a reasonable level. Now he is getting older, five hours tends to be as many as he can get.

He glances around the room and sees nothing has changed since he closed his eyes. A plate appears through the gap under the door. It has two slices of buttered toast, with a blob of what he presumes is jam on it.

He lifts the toast and sniffs it. There's no hint of spice or pepper, so he takes a tentative bite. His mouth isn't set on fire, so he chomps the rest without fear.

'Good morning, Cameron. I'd ask if you've slept well, but if I'm honest, I'd prefer it if you'd tossed and turned all night, wracked with guilt.'

'Sorry to disappoint you, Ivy, but I slept like the proverbial baby.'

As soon as he'd said it, Cameron knew he'd made a mistake. Goading Ivy is not a good idea; giving her ammunition is a terrible one.

'So, you slept like a baby, huh?' Even through the door Ivy's tone is cold enough to deliver frostbite to uncovered flesh. 'Your firstborn child is out there trying to avenge a girlfriend who was killed due to your cowardice, and while he's risking his life at every turn, you get a solid night's sleep. Tell me, Cameron, when you look in the mirror do you see a man, or a selfish bawbag who'd be doing the world a favour if he took his own life?'

'Jake is a big boy. He makes his own decisions, same as you and me. Of course I don't want anything to happen to him, but let's be honest here, I haven't been part of his life for thirty years, and he hasn't been part of mine.'

'He's my son. He's *your* son, you pig. For all we know he could be dead or dying right now, and you're bragging about having slept all night. If not for his sake, or your own, consider me. I'm the wife you abandoned, the woman who brought your kids up alone. My boy is out there doing God knows what, and I can't help him. Every second I don't hear from him sees me imagining his death. You might not care about him, but right now, at this specific moment in time, he's the only thing I care about.'

'So, you haven't heard from him. That's a shame.'

Ivy is silent for a minute, then she speaks. 'Why do you care if we've heard from him?'

As tempting as it is to give a trite answer, Cameron picks his words with care. 'Of course I don't want anything to happen to him. Plus, the sooner he returns, the sooner I can help John and be on my way. Let's face it, Ivy, none of you want me to stick around, and I don't have a reason to stay where I'm not wanted.'

'He's been in touch with Alfonse a couple of times during the night. The last time was at four a.m.; that's five hours of worry for me. Five hours of sleep for you. Jake has now got the name of the man who pulled the trigger and he's going after him. My boy is going after a killer, and it's all because of what you've done. If he survives this he'll probably spend the rest of his life in jail, and it will all be your fault.'

Cameron listens to the rustle of clothing and pictures Ivy slumping to the floor, aghast with worry. While she had only made him happy for a brief period, he'd never grown to hate her. She was, and still is, a good woman with a kind heart and generous nature.

Ivy may have a strong sense of narcissism, but she would have been a good mother, and he is sure that her morals will have been passed on to her children. He knows he should think of them as his children as well, but after so many years of separation he feels detached and remote. Yes, they are his children, but he's never had a connection with them, and as the years had passed, the less thought he had given them.

'I'm not going to lie to you, Ivy. The people Jake is going up against are dangerous. But, see when he was with me, before and after the girl was killed, he was something else. He took on three guys and won. He made the right decisions and kept us both alive when it seemed we were sure to be killed. I can't claim to know him, but I've spent a lot of my life around dangerous people, and Jake is right up there. He's smart, resourceful, brave, and when necessary he's more than capable of winning a fight.'

'Is that supposed to comfort me? Are you saying my boy is good enough to survive this stupid revenge mission he's on?'

Cameron licks his lips and decides to tell his ex-wife the truth.

'I'm saying he has a chance, that's all. Perhaps not fifty-fifty, but still a chance. I don't know anyone else I'd be able to say would have better odds.'

The only answer he gets is a sob.

Chapter 73

I find a payphone and call Alfonse. He punctuates our conversation with huge yawns but, as always, he's come through for me.

He gives me the information I've asked for and I give him an outline of plans A and B. He likes A better than B and I agree with his assessment.

When I ask him if something else is possible, he falls silent. I wait him out, aware he's thinking through my request and the best way to do it.

He says it's possible but it'll take a few hours.

I tell him I'll do things at my end and will be in touch.

The hard part of our conversation centres around Mother, and her insistence that he passes on her instructions to give up my foolish mission and return home.

When we say goodbye, he doesn't waste his breath telling me to take care of myself. He knows I'll do what I need to do.

As sensible as it would be to return to Casperton and resume my normal life, there's no way I can do that until The Mortician has paid, with his blood, for taking Taylor's life.

Anyone who is a hitman for criminal gangs deserves to die. His moniker of choice tells me everything I need to know about him. That he's chosen such a macabre name will be, I'm sure, standard in his profession. Whether he is a mortician, or just likes the nickname, is neither here nor there.

The mental image I have of him is a tall, thin man, dressed like a 1920s undertaker, with a long, cadaverous face. I know I shouldn't assign a look to him, as I may fail to recognise him when the time comes, but I can't help myself.

I find a store where I can buy a new cell without a contract, and five minutes later I've let Alfonse know its number from a payphone. I may be paranoid, keeping this level of separation, but if last night's events have taught me anything, it's that things can turn bad in the time it takes to say my name.

Walking around isn't helping my leg so I find a hotel. The room is a little spartan, but that's not important; it's clean and that's all I care about.

I strip off and take a shower, making sure the wound on my leg is as clean as I can get it. Once I have smeared it with antiseptic cream and bandaged it up, I lie on the bed and close my eyes. As much as I'd like to picture Taylor as I fall asleep, I can't rest for too long. Instead of her, I create a clock in my mind's eye and position the hands to indicate one o'clock. Three hours of sleep isn't a lot but it'll do for now.

I've used this method of sleep management before and have learned to trust my body's internal clock. Quite how it works is beyond me, I just know that it works.

Chapter 74

I wake and scowl at the world. My leg has stiffened, and even doing something simple, like swinging my feet to the floor and standing up, sends waves of pain shooting from my toes to my hip.

My teeth are clamped firmly together and by the time I've pulled on my new denims, and tied the laces on my boots, there is a sheen of sweat on my forehead.

I sling my backpack over my shoulder and limp out of the hotel. There's a diner across the street and I head towards it.

With a cup of coffee in front of me, and a burger with fries ordered, I look at what I can prepare before speaking to Alfonse.

First, I download the Snapchat app to my new phone, then I use the diner's payphone to call Alfonse.

A minute later I'm sitting down and composing a Snapchat message.

At my request, Alfonse has done some of his digital wizardry. This new, disposable cell, has been cloned to be Olly Kingston's. It contains all his contacts, therefore I'm able to request the services of The Mortician under his guise.

As Kingston, I've requested a hit on the man who stormed my house.

The criminal underworld is a small environment, and all the major players will know each other. That means only one thing: word about my visit last night will have travelled.

I get a reply at the same time my burger appears.

The two things are quite contradictory: a staple part of the American diet and a message from an assassin. Strangely, I'm more excited about the message than the food.

I heard you were dead.

This is where I have to box clever. Kingston may have been a gang boss, but he was erudite and well mannered; cultured even.

Rumours of my demise have been greatly exaggerated.

Sometimes you have to be deceitful in public.

Perhaps the Mark Twain quote is a step too far, but to my mind it's the kind of thing Kingston would have said.

Pleased to hear it. Who was it?

My reply is sent without a moment's hesitation. This is what I've been waiting for.

A guy calling himself Brian Johnson. Said he was looking for a job, then went all Rambo. I lost four men. I want them avenged.

It will happen. The usual fee and the usual terms of payment.

My curse draws attention to me and heads turn around the room. I give an apologetic grimace and turn back to the cell phone.

Not only do I not know his payment terms, I don't for one minute think Alfonse and I will be able to scare up the amount needed to pay him.

I have a thought and head to the payphone with a handful of fries stuffed in my mouth.

Alfonse picks up on the third ring and he struggles to understand me as I speak through the fries.

'I said, can you find out Kingston's banking details?'

'What do you need them for?'

'So we can use his banking app to trace the last payment to The Mortician, and pay him this time using Kingston's money.'

'It's a good idea, but it won't work.'

'How?'

Alfonse is familiar with the Scottish use of the word "how" to mean "why?"

'Because you can't use a banking app without a password. That's why. I daresay I could crack that password, but it will take many hours – days even.'

I want to slam the phone's handset into its cradle, but that won't achieve anything. As much as it frustrates me, Alfonse is right.

Another option is for Alfonse to tap directly into The Mortician's bank and pretend to put the money there. Not only is that too much to ask of Alfonse in terms of risk, we would need The Mortician's bank details to fake the transaction.

The burger is two parts cold when I return to my seat and take a bite, but I force myself to eat it anyway. I need the energy and, thanks to Mother's teachings, I hate to see food wasted.

I decide to roll the dice one last time to see if I can engage The Mortician.

Dratted neighbour called the cops. Don't want to move money just yet as they are looking for an excuse to nail me. How does double once Johnson is dead sound?

The Mortician's reply comes as I'm finishing the last few fries.

These terms are acceptable. Do I need to remind you of the consequences of non-payment?

I tell him the payment will be there, as well as where Johnson can be found, and exit the diner.

Chapter 75

I make my way across town to where I've set up it up for The Mortician to execute his hit on me. It's beyond dangerous to hire a hitman to kill you, and be there when he shows up, but that's what I've done. Or at least, something like that.

My plan is a simple one. I am going to observe him as he arrives and wait until he's given up trying to find me. Then I'll follow him.

Once he's in one of New York's many crowds, I'll put a knife in his back and then his heart. As plans go, it's not quite the D-Day landings, but I don't see the point in over-complicating things. The crowds will cover the early part of my escape, and by the time people realise a murder has been committed, I'll be the best part of a hundred yards away.

While it sounds simple, I know that someone who does what The Mortician does for a living will not leave themselves vulnerable. I expect him to run a certain level of surveillance to ensure what I plan to do to him doesn't happen.

I can't decide what to do with my disguise. The scar makes me instantly recognisable, but if I remove it, I'll be showing my real face.

There is a queue of people at the subway but I'm not in any hurry. The location that Alfonse has picked up as The Mortician's home or base, by tracking his cell signal, is a lot further away from the deserted warehouse, which I'm supposed to be holed up in, than I am.

Time is on my side, but I want to get there at least an hour before he does.

The subway is crowded and while I'm used to seeing people from all walks of life, New York is as eclectic as things get. A man dressed in the pinstriped suit of a banker is sitting beside a Goth with dyed black hair and a plethora of studs and rings in her face.

Opposite them is a woman in her early twenties who is wearing a ripped prom dress with torn fishnet stockings and the kind of work boots normally found on a building site. Her face is made up and is pretty, but the further south you look, the more her outfit contrasts with it.

After a couple of stops and one change of line, I exit the bowels of New York and find myself on a street that has seen better days. Nothing looks as if it's been maintained for years, and the better days must have taken place decades ago.

Stores have boarded-up windows and there are gangs of homeless people lining up at a door that hasn't seen fresh paint since Reagan was president.

I feel a vibrating in my pocket and pull out the cell. Only one person can contact me on this number, so it has to be The Mortician.

What I see on the screen makes me launch the cell at the nearest wall with all the force I can muster.

I have made enquiries. Olly Kingston is dead. You are masquerading as him and targeting me. This is a bad idea. You should leave New York in the next hour. Failure to do so will have fatal consequences.

I go back into the subway and think about the ways I can still get to The Mortician. I can only surmise that The Mortician has spoken to one of Kingston's men. If I'm right, he'll have a description of me. At the risk of being conceited, I know that when he is told about what I did last night, I will go up in his estimation. This will make him far more cautious as he goes about his business.

Without the cell he has no way to track me so, despite his threat, I'm safe for the time being. My disguise will have to go, as it's a ready identifier.

I leave the subway and find a store where I buy two more cells. One is a base model, which I plan to use for communicating with Alfonse, the other is more sophisticated and will allow me to access Google, among other things.

As soon as I'm in any situation that could get dangerous, the Alfonse phone will be disposed of.

Never mind the trail of bodies I'm leaving as I cross the Big Apple, I'm tossing cell phones as if they were confetti.

I wander along the street as I bring Alfonse up to speed on the latest development.

He already knows.

To take away my despondency he shares two pieces of news.

Both work for different reasons.

Chapter 76

With the cell phone still pressed to my ear, I hail a cab and tell the driver there's a hundred bucks tip if he does as I say without question.

I sit in the front and repeat the street names and numbers from Alfonse to the cabbie.

The cabbie has the kind of rough leathery face that needs to see a razor every few hours, and there are several years' worth of stories in his eyes.

I guess an experienced New York cabbie has seen pretty much all there is to see about human behaviour.

Alfonse's directions are only coming every five minutes or so, as he has to constantly update the triangulation of The Mortician's cell.

It isn't a problem for me though. I'm just happy that I still have a chance to find and identify him.

The cabbie asks if we're going to Long Island and I just shrug at him. I know the name, but have no idea where it is, other than it's near New York.

When I give the cabbie the next instruction, he tells me he's sure we're going to Long Island.

Pleased that I have someone with knowledge of the local geography with me, I think about the few things I *do* know about Long Island.

To the best of my recollection, it's a place full of holiday homes, retired people, and those rich enough to own a beachfront mansion.

Life on Long Island is taken at a slower pace than that in the centre of New York. This becomes evident as soon as we leave the bustle of the city. There are fewer blaring horns and the drivers are less insistent on going first at all costs.

As the roads widen, there is a sense of space that's absent from the city.

We follow Alfonse's directions until we're at a place the cabbie tells me is called the Hamptons.

My chauffeur seems like a decent guy. He's amiable, and when he tells me about his children and grandchildren I can hear love and pride in his voice. Cameron could learn a lot from him.

After we've taken a road into a suburb, Alfonse tells me that The Mortician has stopped moving. He gives me the general area, so I get the cabbie to drop me a few hundred yards away and walk the rest.

I duck into a small bar and use the bathroom to wash my face and remove all traces of the scars.

Alfonse directs me to the house where The Mortician is holed up.

I give Alfonse the house's number and wait for him to tell me who owns it.

When I hear his answer, I gasp in amazement.

Chapter 77

The name he's given me doesn't mean anything to him, but it rings the wrong kind of bells for me.

Before I can be sure of anything, I need more information. Over the phone I can hear Alfonse's fingers pounding his keyboard.

'Got some pictures coming your way.'

I cut the call, look up and down the street to make sure I'm unobserved, and access the pictures Alfonse has sent me.

It's just as I had thought. Part of me would like to have been mistaken, but the more primeval part of my psyche is glad he's mixed up in this. It means I'll have a chance of following up on my offer to Taylor to recalibrate his sensibilities.

Jason Tagliente, is the drunken lech from the wedding and, according to what Alfonse has told me about him, very much more than that.

A beep from my phone alerts me to more news from Alfonse.

I read the details, with frequent looks up and down the street to check nobody is observing me.

Tagliente is a second cousin of Genaro Chellini, and features on several lists compiled by various law enforcement agencies. While he is not thought to be directly involved in mafia activity, he's known to be a shrewd investor on the stock markets, and has thrice been investigated after accusations of insider trading were made.

None of these were upheld, but I suppose someone with a talent for making money on the stock exchange may well face such finger-pointing as a matter of course.

The picture in my head is clearer than the pope's conscience. Chellini will tip off Tagliente regarding a deal, hit, or some other move he's going to make.

Tagliente will act based on his own predictions as to how the company's share prices will react. He'll buy when the price is low, only to sell at the peak of the market when Chellini's influence has been felt. In other cases, he will know to sell before huge losses are incurred, and then he can swoop in and replace all his sold shares at a fraction of their original value.

For these financial sleights of hand, Tagliente won't just be using his own money, he'll be using the money of whichever corporation Chellini has set up for such purposes.

With this information stored for a better examination at a later time, I take a casual walk up the tree-lined street, with my phone pressed to my ear, and peek through the various gates at the supercars on the drives.

I see plenty of Ferraris and Lamborghinis, and a couple of Rolls Royces before I pass Tagliente's house.

His gates are solid timber, with the same studs you'd see on a medieval castle's door. There are no chinks I can peer through, and the last thing I want is to be caught spying by The Mortician.

As I'm passing the next house along, I hear the muted putter of an engine kicking into life behind me.

I slow my pace and wait to see what kind of vehicle appears.

A small Ford comes out of Tagliente's drive and passes me as it heads to New York. I snatch a glimpse at the driver and see a short man who can barely see over the steering wheel.

His face is unremarkable and has a general meatiness to it that suggests the man has muscle that's turning to fat.

I dismiss the man as a staff member who's just finished work. There's no way he looks dangerous enough to be The Mortician.

I've covered less than a hundred paces when I get a message from Alfonse telling me The Mortician is on his way to New York.

That I've been in close proximity to him doesn't worry me. He doesn't know what I look like, or that I'm tracking him. I dare say if he has tried to track me, the same way Alfonse has tracked him, he'll have figured I ditched the phone after getting his message instructing me to leave town.

Whether I ditched the phone or smashed it in a fit of temper is neither here nor there. It's no longer with me.

His choice of car is interesting. It's by no means a base model, but at the same time it's not a fire-snorting racer that announces its passing with a grumbling exhaust and a paint job a six-year-old could design.

He's gone for something innocuous, yet pacy. The little Ford will be good in the city and will have a decent amount of grunt should he find himself in rural areas. It's the kind of car I'd have given my eyeteeth for when that SUV was chasing me and Cameron.

I'm left with two choices. I can either follow The Mortician back to New York, so I can attack him in his lair, or I can do something intelligent instead.

Intelligence wins out. After my attempt to lure him into a trap, The Mortician will have raised his security levels and general awareness. I'm guessing, but I'm pretty sure that as a professional hitman, his base level of home security is akin to Fort Knox's, lest he be attacked by those seeking to avenge a fallen comrade or family member.

Now I have to choose between asking Tagliente a few questions, and learning more about what I may be facing should I go and knock on Tagliente's door.

Chapter 78

Cameron's head snaps up when he hears a key turning in the lock. He pulls on his shoes and waits to see who comes in.

First through the door is Ivy, and she's followed by six guys – their presence forces him back, onto the bed.

His first thought is that she's organised a beating for him. His second thought is that the beating is coming because Jake has failed.

'Good news, bawbag. The hospital has called John with your results. You're a match.'

'Excellent, I'm so relieved.' Cameron tries to make his voice sound like he means what he's saying.

An arched eyebrow shows her disbelief. 'Of course you are.' She waves a hand at the six guys. 'Some of Jake's friends have come to help you get to the hospital. Isn't that nice?'

Cameron sees the sense in what she's done; he's a definite flight risk and he can't help but admire the way she's thwarted any attempt at escape he may try. Or, he would do, had he not spent the best part of his life working for men who were devious, underhand and downright violent.

Everything about this situation makes him afraid: from the grim, silent faces, to the twitching gait of the six guys with Ivy. Maybe twenty years ago he might have managed to put a couple of them down and have it away on his toes, but there is no chance of that now. He will be going wherever they decide to take him.

Ivy positions herself in front of him and looks him in the eye.

'You look scared, Cameron. Are you afraid these fine gentlemen are here to harm you? That you'll be taken into the wilds and killed?' She gives a little smile. 'Once, I might have wanted you dead, but I've moved on with my life. I've healed from all the pain you caused, and found happiness again. There's no way I'm prepared to spend the rest of my life worrying about going to jail for your murder. You took my happiness once, I won't let you take it again.'

Cameron sees the truth in her eyes, and his fear seeps away.

This might be for the best anyway. Sure, having to hang around and donate to John will delay him getting on with the next phase of his life, but at the same time, the sooner it's done, the sooner he can leave town.

With luck, he'll be long gone by the time Jake returns. Cameron knows his son carries a lot of anger about what happened with the girl, and once he's donated to John he'll no longer be of value to Jake.

He doesn't think Jake would go so far as to kill him, but he does believe his son would use fists, where his ex-wife had used words.

Sometimes, the best defence is not to be on the battlefield.

Chapter 79

My journey back to New York is a train ride that costs about one eighth of what I paid the cabbie to get out here.

Neither time nor money are what's on my mind though. My thoughts are somewhere else altogether.

Jason Tagliente's half-cousin is Genaro Chellini, the notorious mafia head. The wedding I'd met Tagliente at, was that of his brother to one of Taylor's cousins.

Therefore, knowingly or not, my girlfriend's family are connected to the mafia by marriage.

A part of my mind is wondering if there is any way that Tagliente was in contact with The Mortician; whether he'd offered a bonus to the hitman if Taylor were to die as well as Cameron.

While it seems far-fetched on a train in daylight, I know the question will nag at me as darkness falls. I'm aware I may be pointing fingers at everyone I dislike, so I can justify killing them as an act of vengeance, but I do wonder about the possibility. Until I realise there's no way that Tagliente could have known who the girl on the boat was.

I get off the train and make my way across town until I'm back in a familiar area. It's too late for me to make my planned visit so I hole up in a cheap hotel for the night.

Gavriel is opening the pawn shop when I arrive. His expression when he sees me is one of surprise. He goes to speak, and then his mouth closes.

I follow him inside.

Once the door is locked behind me, he takes me to a small office, which has two chairs and a desk that's covered with invoices and bills of sale.

He looks at me with expectancy, and a docile expression. I know he's prompting me to speak and I have no problem with that. I'm here for help – from him and his father. Not practical or physical help; all I want is information.

'I'm here because a situation has developed and there are questions that I need answered. Nothing I'm going to ask will put you or your family in danger, but I would very much appreciate honest and full answers.'

Gavriel stays silent and stares at the wall above my head.

I match his silence and let him have some thinking time. He's smart enough to guess that my questions are about the mafia.

'We have heard some things that we think you may already know something about.' His lips purse as he stifles a yawn. 'I think my father may be a better person to answer your questions.'

He casts me a strange look. It's like he's waiting for me to say something and his manners are preventing him from asking me whatever he wants to know.

I could play games and stay quiet to wait him out. If his name was Alfonse, I most certainly would keep my mouth shut, but you can't be an asshole with people whose help you need.

'What is it, Gavriel? What's going on?'

'You haven't heard?' There's incredulity in his voice.

'Heard—' I stop talking. There's only one thing he can be talking about. Alfonse has released Ms Rosenberg's evidence. 'It's out there?'

He nods. 'It's more than out there, it's everywhere. The police have been rounding up lots of people. Lots of important people. People who think they are either above the law or out of its reach.'

'Sounds perfect. Has the source of the information been identified?'

'No. There are lots of theories floating about, and the most popular is that it's an ex-cop who has spent years compiling the case.'

To my mind, the idea of an ex-cop doesn't just sound plausible, it goes louder and shouts probable.

I start to picture some grey-haired guy, poring over dusty files, but I stop myself. I know who built the case – over a forty-year span. Ms Rosenberg wasn't close enough to me to be called a friend, but I enjoyed her company, and found her to be a decent person who expected the world to share her values and not impede her progress.

'I guess we're going to have a lot to discuss then.'

While I'm pleased that Alfonse has broken Ms Rosenberg's story, I'm worried what effect this new state of play may have on my own mission.

If the guy I'm after is running scared, or incarcerated, I may never get to deliver the justice that Taylor's killer deserves.

The sooner I find out what has happened, and is still happening, the better.

'I will take you to my father, but first you must leave here. I don't know if I'm being watched, but after hearing what you may have done, I can't be seen with you.'

'How will I get to meet your father?'

Gavriel gives me directions to a diner four blocks away. I'm to go there and wait until he passes.

Chapter 80

As instructed, I wait for Gavriel to pass the diner and fall in fifty yards behind him. He's not setting the fast pace of someone who is in a hurry, or is fearful. Rather, he's adopting the gait of someone who has neither purpose nor urgency.

He leads me a few blocks worth of detours until I feel a hand on my shoulder. I glance behind me and see the largest of Halvard's three nephews. For him, the laying of his hand and the squeeze of my shoulder probably has gentle as the intent, but to me, it feels like the jaws of a vice have attached themselves to me and a maniac is winding them tight.

'Come with me, please.' His voice is as deep and melodious as befits his bulk.

I follow him into an alleyway where he leads me to a doorway.

The door opens at his first knock and I see his two brothers.

Two minutes later I'm sitting round a kitchen table that is big enough to seat twelve. Or in this case, just large enough for me, Halvard, Gavriel and the three bruisers.

Halvard's eyes are weary, and belie a lot more than his age, as he tells me about the arrests that have been made and the chaos that has been brought about by so many mafia men being arrested.

I guess I shouldn't be surprised that there have been moves made by most gangs against others, as they use the arrests as an excuse to muscle in on new territory. Halvard hasn't gone so far as to describe a full-on turf war, but I'm sure it isn't far away.

'My Fifi really did a number on him, didn't she?'

I shrug. 'I guess she did.'

I'd say more, but I'm still playing catch-up on the implications and don't want to speak out of turn.

'Gavriel says you want to know more about the mafia connections.' Halvard breaks and glances at his son with fondness. 'I can only tell you about those I know, but what I do know, I'll tell you.'

'Thanks. First off, Genaro Chellini is a big noise and he's not been implicated in this business with Gabbidon's corruption. Does that mean he's clean, or not connected?'

Halvard chuckles. 'He's clean, so far as Gabbidon is concerned. He has many city officials either in his pocket or under his thumb, therefore he has no need to get involved with the mayor as he's already got the other key people on board.'

'Fair enough, what about Jason Tagliente? Is he just a money-man or is he in deeper?'

'He's deep. Chellini has no sons and those in the know, say Tagliente is a definite candidate to succeed him.'

'Interesting. What do you make of that?'

Halvard screws up his face. 'Tagliente will be good for the business side of things, but he won't be as committed as Chellini. He needs to grow up and quit the party life.'

'What connection will he have to The Mortician?'

'Tagliente?'

I nod.

'He'll know him. Perhaps he's even used him.' Halvard's eyes narrow. 'Tell me, Jake, why do you want to know about The Mortician?'

Both Halvard and Gavriel close their eyes in sadness when I tell them about how Taylor died, and my quest to bring justice to her killer.

After I finish speaking, we all sit in silence until one of the cousins speaks. It's not the massive guy, just one of the huge ones.

'Baruch, Yerik, I think we should help out here. If Mr Boulder is going to take on The Mortician, he's going to need all the assistance he can get.'

Massive nods his head and looks to the huge guy who hasn't spoken. 'I'm with Ike. What about you, Yerik?'

'Totally.'

'No. I can't allow it.'

'I'm sorry, Uncle, but you can't stop us.'

Halvard's face drops and his jaw tightens as he looks to me for support.

I keep my face implacable as I work through the idea of having them alongside me.

If there's any kind of fisticuffs, having Halvard's nephews on my side will be enough to guarantee success against any opponents who fail to bring less than a couple of dozen friends to the party.

A counterpoint to this is the glaring fact that the three brothers take up one hell of a lot of space. If bullets start to fly, there's a better than average chance they'll be hit. I'm not by any means a good shot, but I'd be confident of hitting any one of them at twenty paces.

Another point is, being of average height and build, I can use subterfuge and sneak in and out of places. The chances of sneaking these guys in or out of anywhere are zero, unless I find myself storming the elephant enclosure at the zoo.

On the other hand, the extra muscle would be helpful if The Mortician is as deadly as his reputation suggests.

I look at each of the men in turn, assess their resolve, and see only determination. 'What I'm planning is very dangerous. You could end up being killed, having to kill, or being imprisoned if things go wrong.'

It's Baruch who answers for them. 'The Mortician threatened our father and made him sell his business to Chellini. We'll take whatever risks are necessary. You did what you had to do with Kingston, we respect that and want to help you take out The Mortician.'

I give them another good looking at, making sure I hold each of their stares. 'If you're coming with me, you must do as I say, when I say it.'

'Agreed.'

The three deep voices, speaking as one, almost create a sonic boom.

Chapter 81

Dusk is falling as Ike drives us out to Long Island in a silver SUV. I'd have preferred something a little less conspicuous, but at least it has tinted windows to hide the men-mountains we've shoehorned into the back seats.

I'm in the front passenger seat and it's been pulled all the way forward to better accommodate Baruch's bulk. I'm more than a little cramped, but the SUV isn't big enough to accommodate three bodies as large as those belonging to the Weil brothers. Perhaps a stretch limo would be big enough, but it would be a close thing.

The SUV smells of testosterone and sweat, with a hint of lavender coming from the air-freshener. For big, silent guys, they're making a lot of nervous chatter.

I shush them and lay out my plan of attack. They agree with it in the main and their suggestions are a mixture of insightful and downright suicidal.

Yerik seems to be the most hot-headed of the three. He wants to storm Tagliente's house, guns blazing, so we can kill everyone we encounter.

Baruch's voice is full of scorn as he rounds on his brother. 'What about innocents? There may well be servants, or other people there who're nothing to do with the mafia. What do you think will happen if we do as you say? Do you think the police will arrive? Or the guys we're shooting at will start shooting back?'

He gets nothing but a harrumph for an answer.

I leave them to stew for a moment then continue explaining how the attack will take place. I'm more about infiltration than frontal assault and, should things go as planned there will be a lot of guns waved around, but very few, if any, shots fired. Tagliente may well have mafia connections, but it's a fair bet that his neighbours don't. Gunshots may go unreported in certain areas of New York, but it's a racing certainty that out here they would have the locals instructing their servants to call the police at once.

Ike gets us to Tagliente's street without incident, but when he nears his house, I tell him to make sure that he keeps his eyes on the road and his speed consistent. The last thing I want is to raise the suspicions of an observant guard.

He does as I've instructed, while the two in the back crane their necks to look through the blacked-out windows. I get a good look at the house through the open gates as a pizza delivery scooter leaves.

A low whistle emanates from the back seat, followed by Baruch's sonorous voice. 'Man, that's some place he's got there. Did you see them cars?'

If they are the sports cars I saw earlier, there's no point Baruch, or either of his brothers, getting all wistful. It was a struggle to get them in the SUV, there's no way they could squeeze themselves into a sports car.

'Describe the cars, please?'

Baruch replies and I let out a sigh of relief. None of them are a small Ford. Therefore, The Mortician isn't here. It's one thing to lure him into a trap, quite another to walk into his.

As per my instructions, Ike parks a quarter mile along the street, in a cul-de-sac. None of us are carrying anything that identifies us, and if we should fall, we are to be left behind.

We're all wearing ski masks, although I know them by the British term of balaclavas, and there's a generous coating of the rigid collodion on our fingertips.

I roll my balaclava into a hat and walk up the street towards Tagliente's house.

There's nothing underhand or sneaky about my movements: I'm just a guy walking along the sidewalk. I have a pair of earbuds in. They're not connected to anything, but they do make it look as if I'm enjoying a pleasant dusk stroll. My pace is leisurely without being a dawdle. To anyone who's watching, or just sees me as they drive past, I'm not worthy of a second look – at least, that's what I'm hoping they'll think.

When I'm fifty yards from Tagliente's gate, I point across the street and listen for the roar of an engine that my signal should generate.

It comes at once.

I duck against the large hedge of a neighbour and make my way towards Tagliente's medieval gates. As I get closer, I press my back against the privet and look to my left, so I can watch proceedings as I inch closer towards the gates.

As planned, the SUV gets there at the same time I do. There is music emanating from it, but not so loud as to be of nuisance value. Yerik's head pops out of the passenger window and he lifts a pair of shades to better look at the guard who pokes his head round one of the gates. 'Yo, man. Open up and let us in, Jase is expecting us. We got him a real nice present. She's blonde and in possession of the prettiest little ass you ever did see.'

The guard hesitates, looks at Yerik and then back at the little guardhouse.

From the guard's actions, I've learned two things: the first is that people turning up unexpected is nothing unusual to him; the second is that he appears to have company in the guardhouse.

I plant my right foot hard on the ground and get ready to move.

The guard licks his lips, casts another look at the guardhouse, and gives a nod. He steps back so the opening gates don't catch him.

I use the SUV as cover and, just as it passes the guard, I take three rapid steps and throw a hard punch to his temple.

Before an alarm can be raised I continue my run and head for the guardhouse.

A second guard is on his way out of the door and he's raising a gun.

I knock his gun hand skyward with my left hand and bury my right into his gut. He's still doubling over when my knee crashes into his face. It's not enough to knock him unconscious, but it doesn't need to be.

The SUV stops and Yerik gets out.

With his help, I bundle both guards into the guardhouse. I leave them there with Yerik and a roll of duct tape.

Not only will he be able to delay any would-be rescuers for Tagliente, he'll also be able to warn us of any law enforcement that comes our way.

I jog behind the SUV as Ike steers it up to the house.

Tagliente's home is all Georgian uniformity and Grecian pillars. It might not look so bad if it wasn't for the concrete lions flanking the front door.

Either the lions are new, or the gardener has a special trick that prevents them from growing the layer of algae that coats most stone items this close to the ocean.

Baruch and Ike take up station beside a lion's ass and wait for me to open the door. I can't speak for them but my heart is pounding, and I'm feeling a rush of adrenaline as my body prepares itself for what is on the other side of the door.

Whatever it is, we have the element of surprise and all three of us have guns in our hands.

Chapter 82

I twist the doorknob with my left hand and push hard enough to make the door swing back. My eyes are flicking everywhere and the gun in my hand is the briefest of seconds behind them.

There's a hallway containing the usual hallway furniture. It's just this hallway furniture looks more expensive than my entire apartment.

I see a stairway, three doors, and no human beings. Loud music is coming from upstairs, and there's a rhythmic thumping from an overemphasis on the bass levels.

With a wave, I direct Ike left and Baruch right, and I head to the far door. Upstairs can wait – I've already been ambushed with near fatal consequences, and as I'm still pissing blood from that mistake, I don't plan to repeat it.

The two brothers have their brief. Shots are only to be fired if guns are pulled by those we encounter. It's not that I care about the deaths of mafia men, more that I don't want innocents harmed.

There's also the issue of guns being rather noisy things when they're fired indoors. The music upstairs may well be booming but I doubt it's loud enough to cover gunfire.

Ike has an automatic pistol like me and Baruch has a sawn-off shotgun that looks like a child's toy in his huge hand. If he pulls his trigger, all attempts at subterfuge will be over before his shots hit their target.

The three of us stand in front of our respective doors, and I count down from three using my fingers.

When I get to one, I drop my hand and reach for the door handle.

The room I enter is a study – not the man-caves Alfonse and I have, a proper study – with a teak bookcase filled with what looks like first editions, a desk that has been polished to such a level of glossiness it wouldn't go amiss in a Ferrari showroom, and the ubiquitous pair of Chesterfield wingbacks.

A quick scan of the room reveals no human life. Neither does a proper, albeit rapid, search.

So far, so good.

At least it is until I hear a shout, a slap, and the unmistakable thud of a body hitting the ground.

I set off running, wondering which brother needs my help.

A muffled scream comes from the door Baruch had opened so I go that way first. I see him with one of his huge arms wrapped around a girl, and his gun trained on a man sprawled on the floor.

There are groans coming from the guy but very little sign of movement.

I glance at Baruch who shrugs. 'I only slapped him.'

The guy got off lucky. If this is what one of Baruch's slaps does, there's no telling what damage would be caused by a full-blooded punch.

I drag the moaning guy to the middle of the floor and use some duct tape to gag him. I do the same with the girl and, with Baruch's help, bind the two of them together.

Rather than risk them being able to move in unified co-ordination, I put them back to back and head to toe. The guy's arms are taped to the girl's legs and vice versa. For them to be able to move, they'll have to be either Olympic gymnasts or circus freaks. Judging by the girl's muffin top and the guy's spare tyre, it's a fair bet they're neither.

With them secured I check for other doors and find none. This room is a drawing room or lounge. It has more floor space than my whole apartment and the TV fixed above the fireplace is only inches smaller than the bookcase that covers an entire wall of my lounge.

Baruch and I head out of the room and follow Ike's footsteps.

There's a dining room and there's no sign of life. Or death. Just one mahogany table with eight chairs, a dresser, and some fancy paintings on the wall.

There is another door.

A dime gets you a dollar there is a kitchen on the other side of that door.

I push it open and win my dollar.

Ike has his gun trained on two women and a man, who are cowering against the units. Each looks to have Hispanic blood and they all look terrified.

My best guess is that he's startled the help, and there are too many of them for him to have risked tying them up without one of them being able to get away, or, at the very least, letting out a warning shout. Rather than panic, he's shown the guts and gumption to stand his ground and wait for our arrival.

We bind the three of them into a top and tail sandwich, with the guy in the middle, and then we head back towards the stairs.

As we're about to exit the dining room I hear footsteps. The brisk, fast footsteps of someone walking with a purpose.

Chapter 83

The footsteps come our way. Ike and I take one side of the door into the hallway, and Baruch takes the other.

As it opens, Baruch's left hand snakes out and drags a man into his right fist.

The man drops in a heap with a rustle of clothing. He's dressed like a prep school student, which is enough reason for me not to care about the damage Baruch's punch may have done to his face.

I have nothing personal against the prep school type, it's more a general dislike of rich people who have life's opportunities fed to them with a silver spoon. Those who are self-made get my respect, because they've created their own success.

I guess my feelings stem from a lingering resentment of some of the high school jocks I was educated alongside. They had behaved in a way that spoke of entitlement and assumed superiority. I hadn't been liked by them and the feeling was mutual.

Ike and Baruch hog-tie and gag the unconscious man while I take a few tentative steps towards the staircase.

Like everything else in this house its opulence is hard to ignore. The treads look to be marble and the four-foot-wide strips of carpet are plush and thick.

I take slow steps up with my gun in front of me. I'm watching for any sign of movement, listening for any out of place noise, and sniffing, hoping a waft of cologne or perfume will give me warning.

While the carpet's plushness will hide our footsteps, it will also mask those of anyone on the upper floor.

The three of us crest the stairway and find a long corridor. To the right, are four closed doors.

On our left there are three closed doors and an open one.

Through the open door I can see shadows on the far wall of people dancing.

It's logical to assume that's where Tagliente and his guests are, so it's my first target.

Baruch and I pad our way across the corridor and position ourselves by the door. Ike is left behind to cover our rear in case anyone comes out of the rooms on our right.

I hear women's laughter and the jokey tones of horny males, as the music segues from one dance track to another. So far as I'm concerned, Tagliente deserves everything I'm about to do to him for his taste in music alone.

'Freeze. Nobody move!'

Somebody tries reaching for a jacket until Baruch's shotgun, which blasts a hole in the middle of the TV, makes him think that becoming a statue would be an excellent idea.

Baruch takes a swipe at the stereo system, causing it to career halfway across the room.

With the room silent, I waggle my gun at the five women and three men. 'On the floor, everyone.'

'I have money. There's a safe behind the picture. The number is 57-98-43-82. Take everything, but please don't hurt us.'

I kick Tagliente in the ribs and tell him to shut up.

As everyone is congregating in the middle of the floor, I pay attention to the women. They are all beautiful, which, considering Tagliente's money, is a given. They're all wearing slutty clothes, which tells me they're either wisteria girls – who are, by nature, fragrant, decorative and ferocious climbers – or they're hookers.

My money is on hookers because of one simple fact.

None of the women have a full complement of arms and legs.

Each one of them is missing at least one part of a limb, and when the redhead cranes her head to look my way, I see the left side of her face is covered with scar tissue that only a third-degree burn would leave. The eye on that side of her face is a glass one.

Sure, it looks expensive, and the colour is a close, if not exact, match for her right eye, but it's still a glass eye.

Something inside me chills my already arctic blood several more degrees. People living with disabilities should have the same lifestyle choices as anyone else; the fact that Tagliente has found five, beautiful, disfigured women and got them all round to his place, has a deeper meaning.

His actions are not philanthropic or charitable. To me this exposes his desire to feel superior in every way to those he's rutting on top of.

It's all I can do not to put my gun against Tagliente's balls and pull the trigger.

I plant a boot into his groin as a salve to my temper, and bind the other men together as best I can while Baruch covers me.

I guess my anger stems from the fact that all the girls have a disability. Had there been only one of them with a limb missing, I dare say I wouldn't have thought anything of it.

'Hey, Mister. You let us girls go, and we'll give you and your buddies the best night you ever had. Ain't that right, girls?' It's the redhead who speaks and her accent is pure New York.

The other girls echo her sentiments.

'Thanks, ladies, but lovely as you all are, I'm spoken for. If you don't cause us any trouble, no harm will come to you.'

I place a strip of tape over each girl's mouth and smooth it with a gentleness I hope they recognise. A slow wink from the redhead tells me she understands.

With the others bound and safe, I tie Tagliente's hands behind his back and bind his body three times until his arms are taped to his torso. A quick pat down of his pockets locates his cell. I stuff it in my pocket and start believing that my plan will work.

Ike joins us as Baruch grabs one of Tagliente's feet and drags him to the next room.

I police the room, gather up all the cell phones from the folk on the floor, and make sure I have ripped the telephone from its socket. The cells get tossed along the corridor out of harm's way, and I make sure anything that could be used as a weapon, or a tool to cut their bindings, joins the cell phones.

When I join Baruch and Tagliente, I find the latter has been tossed into the middle of a huge bed, which has black, silk sheets and a mattress that is sprung better than an Olympic trampoline.

'Please, please don't hurt me. Whatever you want, I can get you.'

Tagliente looks at Baruch, which is typical of his kind of small man thinking. Baruch may be the largest of us, but it's me who's in charge. In Tagliente's narrow mind, size is in direct proportion to authority. It's the commonly held belief of the small man.

'I only want one thing.' I waggle his cell at him. 'I want you to call The Mortician and get him over here. If you do that for me, you'll be alive when I leave.'

For the first time since we appeared, his eyes show fear. I can tell he was expecting us to be thieves. Now he knows our real purpose, he's scared.

I don't suppose my threatening to kill him will have given him a lot of reassurance.

Tagliente's head shakes back and forth as he babbles a series of denials about knowing The Mortician.

Rather than wasting time making empty threats, I use a knife to slice away his shorts, and retrieve the blowtorch from my backpack.

I press the ignition button and sweep it over his legs. Not quite close enough to burn, yet near enough to singe the hairs on his legs. His yelp is driven more by fear than pain, but I'm cool with that.

Much as I despise him and everything he stands for, I'd rather not have to resort to torture in front of Baruch and Ike.

Tagliente doesn't need to know that though.

I hold the unlit blowtorch above his singed pubes. 'Do you want a moment to think whether or not you know him, or should I jog your memory?'

'I know him, I know him. Please; if you make me call him, he'll kill you and then he'll kill me.'

'It's your choice: either you call him, and gamble what you say isn't true, or, I kill you right now and find another way to get to him.'

'What if he doesn't come?'

I waggle the blowtorch. 'I'll burn as many parts of your body as it takes to make you beg me to put a bullet in your brain.'

Tagliente thrashes on the bed but achieves nothing except a bouncing motion.

I hold up the cell and he nods.

'Good man. Do I need to tell you what will happen to you if you try and warn him?'

He shakes his head.

I lie on the bed beside him, so I can hear both sides of the conversation, and scroll through Tagliente's contacts until I find The Mortician's number.

I press call and hold the cell to Tagliente's head.

Give Tagliente his due, he does a good job of convincing The Mortician that he not only has a job for him, but that he must come over and see him right away.

The Mortician agrees and promises to be here within three hours. I expect him to be here in around two and a half.

Chapter 84

We now have a minimum of two hours to kill; time I intend to put to good use. I instruct Ike to check the prisoners are okay, and dispatch Baruch to check on Yerik at the gate. Their secondary tasks are to secure the house and make sure every door that can be locked, is locked.

As for me, I plan to have a further chat with Tagliente.

I could tell by the way he looked at me that he hadn't recognised my voice as the guy he'd spoken to at his brother's wedding. This doesn't surprise me in the slightest. People like Tagliente don't pay attention to the little people like me. Unless we can provide them with a service, we're of no interest to them.

I'm pleased he hasn't identified me as I haven't yet decided whether he deserves to live or die.

I pull a padded chair to the side of the bed and look at him. A part of me is enjoying the terror in his eyes, while another part feels revulsion at what I've become.

'We need to talk.'

The old favourite break-up line makes his eyes widen, and there's a tremble to his voice as he begs me not to use the blowtorch.

It's good that he's afraid I'll use it to make him talk; it means I don't have to stoop to that level again. I'm fully prepared to use the blowtorch on him, but only if I have to. Every step I walk along the road to vengeance is costing me a piece of my identity.

Last week I was a doorman who broke up fights – sure, I have taken a man's life on two previous occasions, but only as a matter of self-defence.

Since Taylor's death, I have set out to kill. I have planned murders and have executed my plans – and anyone else I felt may have impeded my path to Taylor's killer. A line has been crossed and, while I know I can never undo the implications of my crossing it, I don't want to travel so far over to the dark side that I lose sight of the line.

'I want to know all about The Mortician. Who he is, where he's from, where his loyalties lie, and his background.'

Tagliente's head thrashes against the silk sheets as he shakes it. 'I can't help you. I don't know any of that stuff.'

I pick up the blowtorch. 'What do you know about him?'

'Just what he does. And that he's very good at it.' He yawns but I ignore it. It's almost midnight, I'm threatening him with a blowtorch, and a paid assassin is coming to his house. I'm confident he's tired rather than bored. 'The tales I've heard about him are the stuff of legend. He kills his targets and never leaves a trace.'

'Why do they call him The Mortician?'

Tagliente gives a sigh of relief; this is the kind of question he's happy to answer. 'It's because, after meeting him you'll be needing a mortician.'

'Where do his loyalties lie?'

'You mean whose side is he on?' I nod. 'He works for the Italian families as far as I know. He is freelance and has a rule that he won't take out a target who works for any of his regular employers.'

'How much does he charge?'

Tagliente is a money man. He will know the answer to this question.

'It starts at fifty thousand and goes up from there depending on the difficulty of the job.'

'What is his background?'

He shakes his head.

A press of the blowtorch's ignition doesn't make him talk, but as soon as I lean forward with it aimed at his pecker, he starts chattering.

'It … it's only rumours, but I heard he used to be Special Forces; that he's done tours in both Afghanistan and Iraq.'

What he's saying makes sense. A former Navy SEAL or Army Ranger would make for a good hitman. They are trained killers who've been taught to use guns, knives, and their bare hands. I'm no expert, but I'd expect them to have a working knowledge of explosives as well.

None of this information is comforting, but I've no plans to take on The Mortician in either a shooting match or a one on one fight. Instead, he'll be ambushed, told the reason he is going to die, and executed.

'Is he right or left handed?'

'I don't know.'

It's a shame he can't answer this question as the answer may prove useful. I don't push him though. It's too easy for him to lie and I'd rather not find out the hard way that he's spun me a line.

I'm about to leave him be when I hear the creak of a floorboard.

I turn, expecting to see Baruch or Ike, but the person creeping my way is a stranger. He has a baseball bat in his hands and fury in his eyes.

As I turn my body towards him, he dashes forward and swings the bat at my head.

I have enough time to duck beneath its tip and shoulder charge him against the wall before he can halt the vicious swing.

I'm inside his arms, throwing punches at his kidneys and ribs, and he's banging the bat against my back and shoulders.

When he catches the back of my head with his bat, I disengage myself and put some distance between us.

'You chickenshit pussy. Come and fight like a man.'

He's misunderstood my reasons for finding space. He thinks I'm running away.

As he advances, I pull out the carving knives and wait for him to reconsider his options.

He smiles at me. 'They ain't gonna help you none.' He strokes his bat with one hand. 'This here, has got way more reach than your knives.'

'You're right, it has.' The knife in my left hand flies towards him.

He swings the bat at it, but he's too slow and the handle of my knife bounces off his thigh.

Before the first one has fallen to the floor, the second is arcing its way towards his stomach. This one needs to be accurate and successful, otherwise I'll be fighting him with my bare hands.

The knife digs into his skin and its handle flops downwards as gravity takes hold.

As he's dropping the bat and reaching for the knife, I'm on the move.

I get to him as his fingers grasp the knife's handle.

Instead of wrestling for control of it, I deliver a hard palm-strike to the top of the handle, driving it further into his gut.

He yelps, giving me a strong whiff of stale barbecued meat.

My next blow strikes his hands, driving the knife in his gut sideways. I grab his wrists and shake them until he loosens his grip.

The knife is slick with blood as I grasp it and open his stomach.

Entrails slither from the wound as he crumples to the floor.

I put him out of his misery with a stab to the heart and turn away from him. He's dying, and I don't want to watch the light in his eyes diminish.

Who he is doesn't matter. He's not The Mortician; that much I do know. This guy is tall and thin, whereas the glimpse I got of The Mortician confirmed that he's short and stocky.

I check there are no more unexpected assailants, and leave Baruch standing guard over Tagliente and the people in his upstairs lounge.

With that dealt with, I find a quiet space and call Alfonse. We talk for a few minutes and hearing his voice makes me feel normal again, but I don't learn much beyond the fact that he changed his plan for the release of Ms Rosenberg's information, and sent it out under the cloak of the Anonymous Hackers Group.

It's the thing he excels at and I don't need to ask him if he's protected himself from detection.

The most important thing he tells me is that Cameron's donation has gone ahead, and John has received the necessary treatment.

I cut the call and offer up a silent prayer that it works.

Chapter 85

While searching the house Ike found the intercom, which connects the house with the guardhouse where Yerik is stationed.

When its buzzer goes off, Baruch, Ike and I tense. My hand reaches its telephone first and I put it to my ear.

'What is it, Yerik?'

'There's someone here. I don't think it's him because he's driving an SUV, not a Ford.'

I relax a little and tell him to get rid of whoever it is.

Baruch and Ike join me at an unlit window and together we watch as Yerik leaves the guardhouse and walks to the gate.

The garden's lights cast a mixture of shadows and glare and it's not easy to see much more than a silhouette, but Yerik is more than big enough to stand out.

For some reason I start to get an uneasy feeling. It doesn't just tell me things aren't right, it tells me they are very wrong.

Before I can verbalise my concern, I see the driver's arm snake from the SUV's window.

There's a gun at the end of the arm and, as Yerik halts and returns to cover, it flashes.

Yerik drops to the ground and doesn't move.

Beside me I hear an outburst of Yiddish from Baruch and anguished wails from Ike. There's some scuffling and more Yiddish, but neither man leaves the room.

I leave them to manage their grief and keep watching. The car's door opens and a short, stocky man steps towards the gate. He slips through the opening, puts his gun against Yerik's head and pulls the trigger before dragging him behind the wall. As with his first shot, there's no sound. His pistol must have a silencer.

A minute later he's opened both gates and is driving the SUV in.

He turns the vehicle so it's facing the gate and climbs out.

I watch as he reaches into the back seat and pulls out what looks like a machine pistol.

There's no doubt in my mind that this man is The Mortician, despite being way ahead of his stated ETA.

This, along with the way he dispatched Yerik, tells me a few things. First, he is not here answering Tagliente's call. Instead, he's got his own reasons for being here, and the way he killed Yerik suggests they're not friendly in nature.

Second, he straight away murdered an unknown, and then prepared his SUV for a swift exit which tells me he's got his own agenda.

Third, you don't pack a machine pistol when you're making a social call, even if it's dressed up as a summons. Therefore he either knows we're here, or his agenda has something to do with Tagliente.

I whirl to face Baruch and Ike. We have seconds to make a plan that will see three amateurs face a trained assassin.

We have two automatic pistols and a sawn-off shotgun, while he has a machine pistol, plus the silenced pistol he used to kill Yerik. That's before we even mention his superior training and the fact that he does this for a living.

All we have going for us is the element of surprise as he'll be expecting no defence from Tagliente.

As he's coming through the front door, Baruch and Ike move an antique dresser so it will provide cover for us should we need it.

I pull out my gun and check the safety is off – and that the spare clip is easily accessible from my jacket pocket. I'd gotten more ammunition courtesy of Baruch, and I wasn't dumb enough to ask questions about where it had come from.

With the barricade established, I make my way to the far end of the landing.

The Mortician has been here before, therefore he'll know the layout of the house and will probably head for the upstairs lounge and Tagliente's master bedroom when he breaches the top of the stairs.

I plan to creep up behind him and put a bullet in his back. It may not be gallant, but that's tough; he killed my girlfriend. So far as I'm concerned, the normal rules of engagement don't apply.

There's no sound of footsteps but I hear the racking of a gun's slide an instant before a deafening clatter erupts.

Chapter 86

I don't see The Mortician, but he must be firing both ways as I'm forced to duck back into the bedroom of the doorway I'm hiding in. All I can hope is that neither Ike nor Baruch have been hit.

To limit the possibility of detection, I lie prone on the floor with my gun in front of me.

The Mortician's voice rings out. 'I know you're there. I've seen you've tied up some folks downstairs. Where's Jason Tagliente?'

'I'm here. There's two of—'

A heavy slap silences Tagliente.

It's too little too late. The Mortician now knows there's at least two opponents and that at least one of them is with Tagliente. Our only hope is that The Mortician thinks Tagliente was giving him a total head count, rather than the full locational information I'm sure he was about to give.

I should have either gagged or killed him when I had the chance.

It feels strange that I regret not doing the latter more.

I crane my neck so my line of sight increases and I can see more of the upstairs corridor. Where the bedroom door blocks my vision I can see the outline of a man's arm.

I'm about to crane further when the arm whirls round and I see a gun pointing down the corridor towards where I am hidden.

I hold my breath, afraid to move lest it attracts him.

The arm turns round, so I crane an extra couple of inches until I can see The Mortician's back.

He whirls again after a second step.

Like the trained professional he is, he's keeping a good watch on his rear. My plan wasn't much, but it's useless in the face of his superior firepower and techniques. Unless we get lucky, or take near suicidal risks, he'll pick us off one by one.

I hear the double boom of Baruch's shotgun and see large amounts of plaster blast from the corridor's rear wall.

The Mortician fires off a couple of bursts and I hear a pained yelp, followed by the considerable thud of Baruch falling to the ground. He's moaning, which means he's still alive, but it doesn't mean he will be for long.

Ike bursts from the lounge where he's been hiding. His gun is blazing but he's shooting in anger without any amount of thought for his aim.

I'd join in with his fusillade were I not more fearful of us hitting each other than The Mortician. I'm maybe twenty feet away, and I know that's further than I can aim with any level of accuracy.

The Mortician's first bullet hits the shoulder of Ike's gun arm, the second and third blast into his kneecaps. He falls with a scream and does his best to press his hands on his wounds.

I watch as The Mortician approaches the stricken Ike and kicks his fallen gun away. 'Oh dear, has baby got a boo-boo?'

The Mortician drags Ike into the master bedroom and props him next to his brother. 'It's time for you to tell me a bedtime story before you go to sleep. First, you can tell me who you are and why you're here, then you can tell me who sent you.'

Ignoring the fact that he's killed one new friend and crippled two others, I'm pretty sure I'd hate The Mortician based on the way he speaks to his victims.

I rise and take slow, tentative steps towards him as he pulls a combat knife from a sheath on his leg.

'Who wants to tell me a story?'

Chapter 87

I'm twenty feet away and closing when Baruch roars with pain as The Mortician buries three inches of steel into his leg. Beside him, Ike is fighting to stay conscious, his face slick with sweat and twisted in agony. The wound in my leg aches in sympathy with Baruch's injury.

The Mortician gives his knife a twist, but Baruch's elephantine head just shakes. His jaw is set and he's not letting another sound escape his lips. His hands are clasped against his stomach and blood is oozing out between his fingers.

Eighteen feet. Every step is taken with caution as there's nowhere for me to hide should The Mortician become aware of me sneaking up behind him.

The knife is removed from Baruch's right leg and plunged into his left. His face judders, but he maintains his silence.

Fifteen feet.

The knife is removed and wiped clean on Baruch's pants.

The Mortician uses a gloved hand to remove Ike and Baruch's ski masks.

'Your buddy looks awful like you. I'm guessing he's your brother, or a cousin. If you're not going to talk for your sake, perhaps you'll talk for his.'

The Mortician moves his knife until it's within an inch of Ike's left eye.

Twelve feet. If I can get within ten feet, or less, I'm confident that I can put a bullet in The Mortician's body without missing, or hitting Ike or Baruch.

My knuckles are white as I grip the pistol. My entire concentration is on what I can see over the gun's sights.

Ike turns his head, so his eye is moved away from the knife, and his left eye is now looking my way. He sees me.

Eleven feet.

'Screw you.'

As he speaks, Ike throws his head forward, driving his right eye onto the knife, and twists, so the knife is wrenched from The Mortician's hand. He screams as he reaches up with his good hand and plucks the knife, complete with his eyeball, from where it has lodged.

I see all of this from the corner of my eye as I pump two bullets into The Mortician's back.

Ike slams the knife into The Morticians leg then collapses to the floor and howls in agony.

I keep my eyes on The Mortician as I dash forward. My gun is trained on his back and as much as I'd like to kill him outright, now that he's down and wounded, I need to tell him why he's going to die. I want to see the fear in his eyes fade to nothing.

I'm two feet away when I realise what I'm seeing, but not seeing.

There's no blood on the Mortician's back; I've shot him twice yet there's no sign of any blood.

I realise why there's no blood at the same time The Mortician flips over and fires his silenced pistol my way.

The only reason his shots miss is because my lizard brain must have arrived at this conclusion before the rest of me, and therefore instigated the necessary dive for safety.

The two bullets I put in his back had enough force to knock him flat, but not so much that they were able to penetrate the bulletproof vest he must be wearing.

Chapter 88

I roll to my feet and dive into the lounge where the hookers and Tagliente's buddies are. My gun is in my hand as I look for cover and an escape route. There are French doors leading to a balcony, but to get the doors open I'll have to turn my back to the entrance. The idea of doing that doesn't seem appealing.

There's a sturdy occasional table in the middle of the room. It looks thick enough to stop a bullet, so I tip it over. If nothing else, it will protect me enough to give me a chance.

I hear The Mortician's voice – he's singing a lullaby; there's a cough, followed by a loud scream.

The screaming must have come from Tagliente, as the pitch is way too high to be either Ike or Baruch.

As much as I want to go to their rescue, I know The Mortician is trying to draw me out, rather than come hunting for me. He's aware I have a gun and, while I know a little about him, he knows nothing about me.

He'll be wondering if he's facing someone as good as he is, or a rank amateur. In his position, I'd assume I was facing a pro and take the necessary precautions. So far as I can tell, that's pretty much what he is doing.

I risk a peek over the upturned table. There's nothing to see, other than an empty door showing me the corridor. I'm about to make a run for the French doors, when I notice the light in the doorway changing.

The machine pistol comes around the door frame and starts barking as it spits out bullets.

I duck behind the table and watch as The Mortician stitches bullets one way then the other.

The table holds firm when a bullet hits it, but the glass of the French doors shatters, as do ornaments and various other fripperies that decorate the room.

When the machine pistol clicks empty, I bob up and train my gun at the door in case The Mortician has entered the room.

He hasn't.

Instead, I see him whirl across the doorway with his silenced pistol looking for a target. I fire a couple of shots his way, but I don't hear the slap of a bullet hitting flesh.

The fact he's wearing a bulletproof vest makes things even more difficult for me. It means I have to aim for either his head or his legs. Both of these targets are far smaller than the torso, and both are liable to be in constant motion.

That Ike has wounded one of The Mortician's legs gives me something of an advantage; yet my own leg is stiff, and it aches whenever I move with anything approaching urgency.

I put another shot through the doorway and turn to run through the starred glass of the French doors.

My shoulder charge sends square marbles of safety glass cascading across the balcony.

As soon as I reach the railing, I vault onto the sloping roof and slide towards the gutter.

Not knowing what I may land on, I flip on my stomach and use my toes as brakes. They don't work too well, and I bounce over the gutter when I reach it, but the action has at least slowed me enough for me to grab it with both hands.

I hang on to the gutter until I have seen how far I have to drop, and what I'm going to land on.

My feet slam down on the pathway and I throw myself into a roll to break the impact. It was only ten feet or so, but the paving blocks are hard and unforgiving.

I swap the used magazine in my gun for the full one in my pocket. I now have ten shots again, plus a spare five should I need them.

I hope to God I don't.

Chapter 89

Cameron eases his feet to the floor and levers himself upright. He'd seen no point in staying in hospital, but had gone along with it for one simple reason: when he's in here, he's not under Ivy's watch.

He retrieves his clothes from the cabinet beside his bed and tiptoes to the bathroom.

It takes him longer than usual to dress himself, as he feels weak and unsteady, but he doesn't worry too much about time. The nurse did her hourly check a few minutes ago and he's content in the knowledge that he'll be gone before she returns.

Taking an extra two minutes to dress won't matter either way; once he's out of hospital, he's answerable to nobody.

He peeks through the door's porthole and sees the nurse's station is devoid of life.

Ivy is sitting on a chair in the corridor, outside his door, but her head is on her chest and he can hear her gentle snores.

He makes his way past her with his shoes in his hand.

Cameron chooses the stairs over the lift – it's only one floor and there'll be no beeps or floor announcements to wake a sleeping dragon.

The news broadcasts he'd watched on the hospital TV had brought him the best of news. Somehow, Jake had prevailed and had managed to take out Olly Kingston.

This means the price on Cameron's head will be lifted; that he won't have to spend the rest of his life looking over both shoulders at once.

He sits on the third from bottom step, pulls on his shoes and ties the laces.

While today is the first day of the rest of his life, the last day of his old one had turned out well enough.

He'd saved the life of one son, while another had eliminated his enemies. On the whole, Cameron figures it has worked out even.

He doesn't know which way he'll go, or where he'll end up, but that's fine by him.

Life is an adventure, and he plans to live it to the full.

Cameron whistles as he walks out of the hospital and looks for a taxi.

Behind him, unseen, a woman places her hand flat against a first-floor window and tries to suppress the tears pricking her eyes.

Chapter 90

I get back into the house via a door that leads into the kitchen. The people we'd left tied up now have bullet holes in their heads.

All my senses are on full alert as I try to not only locate The Mortician, but get the jump on him too. I'm positive he'll be doing the same as me, and although I'm feeling a massive amount of guilt at leaving Ike and Baruch at his mercy, I'd be less use to them dead.

I hear a rustle and whirl towards it with my gun extended, ready to fire, but it's only the breeze blowing a drape. The last thing I want to do is pull my trigger and alert The Mortician to my location.

I grab a vase with my left hand and launch it from my vantage point at the base of the hall. It arcs through the air, bounces off a wall, and lands on the thick stair carpet.

The crash of breaking glass I'd been hoping for doesn't happen, but there is a dull thud.

I wait for a reaction.

Gunshots at the vase would be ideal.

The sound of running footsteps would do.

I hear neither.

What I see is something I don't want to.

There are wisps of smoke coming from the door to Tagliente's study.

As I'm becoming aware of the smoke, I see the door to the downstairs lounge teasing its way open.

I sight my gun, but The Mortician sees me and whips up his machine pistol as I pull my trigger.

There's no way I could have hit him – I was ducking away as my finger tightened on the trigger. The bullet will have been wild and, so far as I'm concerned, it's a waste of a precious round.

I retreat to the kitchen and wait for him to come to me.

The position I've taken up gives me cover behind a central workstation and I can see the doorway clearly. As soon as he steps through it, I'll have him.

I hear footsteps and there's a sudden crash as he charges through the door. He's less than a step inside when he pulls the triggers on Baruch's sawn-off shotgun. I get a shot off, but there's no way of knowing if it's hit him.

The top of the workstation erupts in splinters by my head and I feel a thousand pinpricks in my scalp. While it hurts like hell, I don't think there's any real damage done.

I hear his machine pistol chatter, and as soon as it clicks on empty I whirl to the opposite side and fire three shots of my own.

We're now on either side of the workstation.

Both of us have to guess which way the other will go.

To go the wrong way will bring us face to face. To go the right way, but too slowly, will expose our backs.

I pull a pan from a cubbyhole and toss it to one side.

He shoots at it and there is the clang of metal as his aim is accurate.

I dive to the other side and aim two shots at the booted feet protruding from the safety of the workstation.

One of my shots produces a puff of red from his ankle and a pained yelp.

First blood to me.

In a fight like this it doesn't matter who draws first blood, only who is left standing.

At least my bullet will have further affected his mobility.

Above anything else, I now have the advantage as I'm able to move more freely.

'Hey there, Mr Mortician. How does it feel to be shot?'

My taunt is enough to make him fire a couple of shots my way, but he recovers his composure far quicker than I'd hoped.

'It stings a little, but don't worry, you'll find out soon enough.'

He fires three shots my way and there's a clicking sound.

I throw myself towards him with my gun firing, until it too clicks on empty.

Chapter 91

The Mortician is unscathed by my bullets but he's on his ass, while I'm on my feet, so I aim a kick at his head.

He ducks under my boot and one of his hands snakes out and grabs my ankle. He yanks, and I fall.

I land face down and he clambers up my back.

His fists batter at my kidneys and ribs until he's in a position where he can land his blows on my head. Due to his wounded ankle he's lying on top of me, instead of properly straddling me, and getting plenty of purchase behind his punches.

Rather than squirm round to offer him my face, I lever both of us from the floor and whip my hands on the one he's trying to snake round my throat. We fall together, but now one of his hands is beneath me and that means he's off balance.

I push up with one hand while holding on to his wrist with the other.

I tip him off me and whip myself away from him, delivering a kick to his ankle as I go.

He yelps and suggests I'm of a similar nature to Oedipus.

I pull myself to my feet and kick him in his gut as he tries rising to his knees.

He grunts, but the bulletproof vest must have taken most of the venom from the blow.

I'm about to deliver another kick when his hand grasps at his jacket and produces a knife.

Ike's blood still taints it, and I'm not fool enough to go near him while he's holding it.

The Mortician uses my reticence to clamber up to his good leg.

I use the time to pull out my own knives.

He's better than me with a knife, I have no doubt about that.

His eyes flick to my knives, and an understanding brightens his face when he sees they are ordinary domestic knives, rather than the hunting knife he holds.

He now knows I'm an amateur, that I don't have any great amount of training, and that every piece of hurt I've inflicted on him so far has been achieved by dumb luck.

'If you walk away now, there's very little I can do to stop you.'

'You shot my girlfriend. I'm only going to walk away when you're dead.'

He pauses.

'The girl on the boat?'

I nod affirmation as he slashes his knife towards my throat.

Instinct makes my hands go up to deflect his blow and I feel his knife slice through my jacket, opening deep cuts on my forearms.

One of the knives slips from my hand as the pain causes my fingers to uncurl.

Adrenaline takes a stance and my empty hand grasps the handle of a large frying pan.

It's longer than his knife and, with the right amount of force behind it, is heavy enough to break a bone.

I take a few half-assed swings with the frying pan. I'm not trying to hit him: I'm judging his range and the speed of his reactions.

He's quick and there's a certain mobility to him despite the fact he's only putting any real weight on one leg.

I swing the pan again, taking care not to put so much power into a missing swing that the momentum carries me to a point where I'm vulnerable.

His face shows he's assessing me as much as I'm assessing him.

A spark in his eye warns me of a counter lunge, and I deflect his attempted stab with the frying pan.

With his arm knocked out wide, I swing the frying pan upwards towards his balls. It gets trapped between his legs, but he's off balance. A yank on the frying pan forces him to put weight on his smashed ankle and he yelps as I bury my knife into his bicep.

His knife goes into my shoulder and I feel it scrape my collarbone as we fall to the floor.

We both roar in pain as we fight for control of the knives.

I use both my hands to twist his wrist to breaking point. He drops the knife and I give his wrist a sudden rotation that makes the bones crack.

I'm not done there though. I lever myself off him and do the same to his other arm.

He's now only got one limb that doesn't have broken bones.

I pull my knife from his arm and lay the blade against his throat.

There's fear and pain in his eyes, but also acceptance. I guess with his kind of profession you expect that one day it may well be you who dies.

'This is for Taylor.'

I slide the knife across his throat and leave him gushing arterial blood onto terracotta tiles.

Chapter 92

When I open the door from the kitchen to the dining room, I see the room is already filling with smoke.

I double over, and half limp, half trot, to the door that leads to the hall. It's warm to the touch, but there's not a lot I can do about that.

I duck lower to avoid the billowing flames that come in when I open the door. Once the initial gust has passed, I dash through the burning hallway to the stairs as fast as my wounded leg allows.

My thoughts are on those who're left upstairs: Baruch and Ike; Tagliente and his buddies; the five hookers.

The heat is intense, and the smoke has me coughing and choking by the time I reach the foot of the stairs.

I reach the upstairs corridor on hands and knees to keep the worst of the smoke from being sucked into my lungs. While the heat hasn't yet reached here, the smoke is thick and noxious. It pervades the whole building and shields the ceiling from view.

The pain in my shoulder is riotous to say the least, but I ignore the agony as I scurry, still on my hands and knees, to where Baruch and Ike are.

Ike is unconscious, but I see a spark of life in Baruch. I go to lift him and fail.

He shakes his head. 'That ain't gonna happen. I'm done for, and so is Ike. Ain't no way you're gonna be able to carry us out of here before the fire gets all three of us. Even if you do, I can't see us making it.'

'Don't talk nonsense.' I try to be sincere and determined, but he looks at me knowingly.

'You got a gun? Burning and screaming in agony ain't the way I want to go.'

I pull out the gun I retrieved from the kitchen floor, and insert the clip containing five bullets.

Baruch lifts his good arm, with his hand open, and I lay the gun in his palm. The pistol looks tiny in his great paw.

I look at his face and see nothing but calmness.

'No regrets, Jake.' He swallows and coughs. Bright arterial blood seeps from the corner of his mouth. 'Now, get yourself out of here.'

I give him a nod of thanks and sneak a look at Tagliente before I leave.

He's still laid out on the bed, but now he has a bullet wound in his left side. I stand and take a better look. There's a huge, ugly exit wound on his other side, but his chest is still rising and falling.

I'm hit with a sudden new level of comprehension. The Mortician was here ahead of schedule because he was coming here anyway. His purpose was murder. Whatever had gone on between him and Tagliente had angered someone to the extent that Tagliente's death had become a priority.

Perhaps he'd pissed off The Mortician, but my guess is that he'd tried to hire him to take out Chellini, and whoever else was in the running to take over Chellini's organisation.

The length of time The Mortician had been away was enough for him to have been able to get to New York, speak with Chellini, and return.

The damage that The Mortician's bullet will have wrought to Tagliente's intestines is unimaginable and, while I'm the first to acknowledge I'm not a doctor, I really don't fancy his chances of surviving a rescue attempt.

With the fire blazing away downstairs, the only way left for us to escape is over the balcony I'd used earlier.

I take the gun from Baruch, put its muzzle against Tagliente's forehead, and pull the trigger. It's a mercy killing and, while I'm not sure he deserves my mercy, I feel released from murderous instincts and the desire to inflict serious pain now that both The Mortician and Tagliente are dead.

Baruch takes the gun from me and looks to his brother. As I leave the room, he's lifting the gun towards Ike's head.

He shoots once as I cross the hallway, and again when I reach the lounge door.

Their deaths, along with those of Taylor and Yerik, are something I know will eat at my conscience, but that's a matter for another time.

Chapter 93

I enter the lounge and slam the door shut. It won't stop either the fire or the smoke, but it will slow them. The open French doors that were smashed by The Mortician's bullets, and my mad dash, are drawing the fire upwards, so everything I can do to limit the free movement of air will buy us time.

There are seven bodies lying on the floor but only six of them are trying to look my way.

The redhead with the scarred face is motionless and there's a crimson stain on her white dress. One of The Mortician's bullets must have caught her when he was raking the room trying to kill me.

I check for her pulse without success.

I pull the knife from my boot and free the other six. Twelve eyes show fear as they stretch their limbs and massage tender areas to stimulate blood flow.

Tagliente's two buddies look reasonably buff. Whether their muscle comes from the gym or hard work, they'll be able to help the girls.

'Right, you lot. Listen up. This is the plan. We're going to go over the balcony, slide down the roof, and drop to the ground.' I point to Tagliente's buddies. 'You two go first, and I'll lower the girls as far as I can so you can catch them. Don't worry, ladies, it's only a few feet from the edge of the roof to the ground.'

One of the guys says something about being afraid of heights, so I drop him to his knees with a gut punch.

'Listen up, douchebag. I killed The Mortician tonight. You'll do as you're told, or you'll be next. Do you understand me?'

He nods as he clambers to his feet.

I lead everyone to the balcony and take the two guys to where I'd made my escape earlier.

'Guys. There's a drop of roughly ten feet once you go over the gutter. Don't try and stay on your feet; roll like you've done a parachute jump. I'll do my best to make sure the girls come down as slowly as possible, but you'll have to catch them. Can I trust you to do that, or do I have to make threats?'

The guy I hadn't punched shoots me a look of disgust. 'Shit, man. You came back for us and the girls. You coulda left us to burn, but you didn't. We'll help them all we can.'

I nod, and point to the edge of the balcony.

He climbs over the rail and slides down the roof.

When I hear him shout a confirmation that he's down, I help his once-punched buddy over the balcony. He's shaking like a plate of jello being driven over a mountain track, but he doesn't hesitate for more than a heartbeat.

The girls are jostling for position, but I halt them with a raised hand and clamber over the end of the balcony myself.

With one hand wrapped around the balcony rail's corner post, I help the first girl over the rail and hold her arm as she slides down. My arms burn at the strain, but that's nothing compared to the agony of where The Mortician's knife dug into my shoulder.

When I can extend myself no further, I let go of the girl's arm and release her. She slides down the roof and disappears over the edge.

A moment later I see the two guys laying her on the manicured lawn behind the house.

The second and third girls follow without incident, but the fourth is a different proposition.

She has most of one leg and all of one arm missing. That's a problem, but not an insurmountable one.

The real issue is her state of mind. She's gone beyond fear, passed terror, and totally ignored petrified. The girl is having a full-blown panic attack and is wailing and thrashing herself around.

I gently take hold of her and try to use a soothing tone without letting too much urgency creep into my voice.

'You killed Ruby; you and that other man. You're going to kill me now, aren't you?' She swings her arm at me.

Her hand bounces off my head as an explosion fills the air. The lounge door crashes to the floor and a huge fireball billows towards us.

I throw myself on top of the girl and use my body to shield hers from the fireball's volcanic breath.

She squirms beneath me until I realise there's no way I can calm her down before we either get incinerated, or die from smoke inhalation.

From inside the house there's the sound of collapse, so I make a fist and hit the girl just hard enough to make her groggy.

It's wrong on many levels, but I force my aching leg to carry me back into the lounge. Somehow, I can remember the code Tagliente gave us for his safe when he thought we were burglars. The dial spins beneath my fingers and I get the safe door open in less than a minute.

There's a stash of money and what looks to be a variety of drugs. The money goes into my backpack and I toss the drugs onto the floor by the door so they're sure to burn.

I don't like stealing and I don't consider myself to be a thief. The only reason I've taken this money is to repay Alfonse what he's loaned me, and so I can afford to finish this affair in a way that's right for all concerned.

With the money stashed, I head back to the balcony and lift the final girl's inert body over the rail.

Now when I put my hands on the slates, they're hot from the fire below. Not twenty feet from us a section of the roof falls in and sends a shower of amber sparks billowing upwards.

I lay the girl on the slates and lower her to the extent of my reach before letting her fall.

Beneath me the roof creaks and shifts downwards a little.

As soon as I see the guys are out of the way, I release my grip on the corner post and slide down the roof.

There's no attempt at braking this time, and I don't even try to grab the gutter. Instead, I'm preparing myself for a hard landing.

I thump to the ground, roll twice, and come to a halt in a row of rose bushes.

The pain from their jagging, scratching thorns is welcome: it tells me I'm alive; that I've survived this ordeal.

I drag myself to my feet and thrust a hand into my backpack. I grab a bundle of money and toss it towards the girls. 'That's from Tagliente.'

Next, I lurch round to the front of the house.

Ike's car is still there.

For the first time tonight I have a spot of good luck: the keys are in the ignition. So are the keys to The Mortician's SUV.

I back The Morticians car up to the guardhouse and haul Yerik's body into the driver's seat.

After opening the fuel cap, I plant Yerik's foot on the gas pedal, release the parking brake, and send the SUV tearing off toward Tagliente's burning front door.

The fire ignites the SUV's gas tank as I'm climbing into Ike's car.

Whether the fire will burn hot enough to destroy the bodies of my three new friends is anybody's guess, but I've done as much as I can to make sure there's no trail leading back to Halvard and Gavriel.

Chapter 94

I dump Yerik's car in an alleyway and clamber out. There were several moments on the drive back to New York from the Hamptons when I thought the sirens arrowing towards Tagliente's house were about to turn and pursue me.

None of them had, and because I was afraid of being spotted I took back roads wherever possible.

I'm at the point of exhaustion when I totter through the door of Halvard's pawn shop and approach the counter.

Gavriel sees me coming and lifts a flap in the counter with one hand, waving me through with the other.

Halvard is sitting in the office chair, and the way he looks over my shoulder before examining my face tells me everything I need to know.

'They fell?'

'They did.'

I'd say more, but there are times when words are useless.

What could I tell him? Would it help, knowing that one nephew had been murdered by a ruthless killer? That his other two nephews were so badly injured they couldn't escape the fire he'd lit?

His eyes are rheumy and there are occasional tears running down his cheeks.

He looks at my dishevelled state and goes back to staring into space. I wonder if he's remembering them – as children, attending their bar mitzvahs and watching them grow from children into the huge men they'd become.

'Did they die in vain?'

'No, they didn't. The Mortician's dead and they died heroes.' I lick my lips and ponder on how much to tell him. He won't want to know about individual suffering, or how Baruch had killed his brother out of mercy before turning the gun on himself. I decide Ike's bravery, in spearing his eye on The Mortician's knife, is worthy of telling, even if the details are best left unsaid. 'All three of them were heroes, but especially Ike. His courage knew no limits.'

Halvard gives the faintest of smiles. 'Ike always was fearless. There was nothing that boy wouldn't try to climb.'

We sit in silence for a while and then I rise to leave. I still have one task left before I catch a plane back to Casperton.

Chapter 95

Alfonse picks me up at the airport. His face is full of concern and there's no mistaking the fact that he's had very little sleep since I returned to New York.

As I walk towards him I see his eyes watching my every movement. He'll be noticing that I can barely lift my feet, that one arm is tied up in a rudimentary sling, and that my face and scalp are covered with minor contusions.

'Is there any part of you that isn't beat up?'

I shake my head.

'This isn't you, Jake.' He pulls a face. 'You may have seen yourself as an instrument of vengeance, but that's not what you are. You know it and so do I. I'm not saying the people you have killed didn't deserve to die, I'm saying it's not your place to decide who lives or dies, and it's not your job to deliver that kind of justice.'

I'd hang my head in shame if I was still a kid. 'I know. I knew it before I went after them, but haven't you ever been so angry?'

I let the question tail out; there's no rationalising what I've done, not to him, not to anyone else, not even to myself.

Alfonse turns out of the airport parking lot and heads towards town. 'Have you any idea how often Chief Watson has been in touch, demanding I tell him where you are?'

'I guess it's a lot.'

I want to apologise to Alfonse for everything he's been through on my account, to thank him for his support, but the words won't come out. All he's doing is putting a voice to the thoughts that have plagued me since I climbed in Yerik's SUV and drove away from the disaster zone that was Tagliente's house.

Nothing he can say to me will be as harsh as what I've been thinking myself. Every criticism he voices is nothing more than a faint echo of what I've been whispering into my own ear.

'What now?'

'I better go see Chief Watson.' I hesitate and sneak a sideways look at him. 'And Taylor's parents.'

'I'm sorry, man.' Alfonse lays a gentle hand on my arm. 'Taylor's father has been in touch with me. He doesn't want you going there, offering your condolences. He's even said that if you try and go to Taylor's funeral, he'll have you arrested.'

I close my eyes and accept the bitter pill of rejection. Taylor died when she was with me, and nothing I can do or say will ever change that. Only Alfonse and Mother know the truth about her death. Everyone else has been told that she and I had fought and parted company.

'How's John?'

'He's doing well.' Alfonse pauses. 'There's something else you should know though.'

I look at his face. It's serious, but not grave.

'Don't tell me. Cameron has shot the crow.'

'Huh?'

The Scottish term for running off has confused him. I explain what I mean, and he tells me I'm right. Well, correct. Alfonse and I never tell the other when they're right, only when they're wrong.

Cameron being gone doesn't matter. We've got what we needed from him and there's nothing to be gained from him staying around.

The news from New York is good too. Gabbidon has been arrested and is under investigation for events that span several decades. Even if he is acquitted on all counts, there's enough mud sticking to his name to ensure he never becomes mayor.

Chapter 96

Three nights after arriving back in Casperton, I leave my apartment, throw a couple of backpacks into the trunk of my Mustang and put the key in the ignition.

Since getting back, my time has been spent answering questions from Chief Watson and some FBI suits who flew in to interrogate me.

I played dumb and stuck to my story, and they couldn't break me. The lies I concocted pained me to say, but the alternative was admitting my part in a killing spree, to people who could imprison me for life.

My first stop tonight is Alfonse's place.

I put the keys to my apartment in his mailbox, along with a letter explaining that I need to leave town for a while.

With everything that's happened running through my mind, and my newfound dislike for myself growing every day, I need to find some space to try to re-find the Jake Boulder I was a week ago.

Another reason for me to get out of town is the way people have been dying when they're in my company. After losing Taylor, I'm left with Alfonse, Mother and my sister, Sharon. I can't bear the idea of another person suffering because of me, so it's best for them if I'm not around to attract trouble.

With the keys and letter secreted in Alfonse's mailbox, I take a slow drive to the edge of town.

Casperton cemetery is well kept and lies on the town's western fringes. It takes me a while to locate the right grave in the dark, but I use my cell's torch to read the inscriptions attached to the fresh flowers on the most recent graves.

My heart catches when I read Taylor's name.

I clench my jaw and think only of her smile as I bend down and roll back a slice of turf.

My hand shakes as I pull the ring box from my pocket and place it on Taylor's grave. 'I love you, Taylor, and I want you to have this ring. I would have preferred to have put it on your finger, to hear you say yes when I proposed, but I never got the chance. I love you.'

To my ears, my voice contains nothing but the truth. It's there in every crackle, in the pauses I make as I fight for composure, and in the quiet, heartfelt whisper I use to say the words I'd never expected to say.

I'm halfway back to the Mustang before I'm confident that the tears blurring my eyes aren't going to fall.

The End

Acknowledgements

I would like to take this opportunity to say extend my grateful thanks to all at Bloodhound Books for their professionalism and hard work in bring this book out. Fred, Betsy, Sarah, Alexina and Sumaira have helped my writing soar, yet it's Jo whose keen editing eye has kept me grounded, and improved my writing with every comment or suggested change.

Thanks also go to those who've supported me in my writing, my good friend and mentor, Matt Hilton, Col Bury who brainstorms ideas with me late at night over the odd glass of something hangover-making, the Crime and Punishment gang, all my writing and non-writing friends and of course my family.

I'd also like to say a huge thank you to all the bloggers who've taken the time out of their busy lives to support me. They are the unsung heroes of the book world and their support really has made the difference.

Last but by no means least, my readers. Without your support, kind reviews and enthusiasm for my writing, I'd be nothing more than a stenographer for the voices in my head.

Lightning Source UK Ltd.
Milton Keynes UK
UKHW01f2311170918
329072UK00001B/203/P